PROOF OF LIFE

PROOF OF LIFE

A NOVEL BY
DAVID ROBBINS

BASED ON THE SCREENPLAY
BY TONY GILROY

AN ONYX BOOK

ONYX
Published by New American Library, a division of
Penguin Putnam Inc., 375 Hudson Street,
New York, New York 10014, U.S.A.
Penguin Books Ltd, 27 Wrights Lane,
London W8 5TZ, England
Penguin Books Australia Ltd, Ringwood,
Victoria, Australia
Penguin Books Canada Ltd, 10 Alcorn Avenue,
Toronto, Ontario, Canada M4V 3B2
Penguin Books (N.Z.) Ltd, 182–190 Wairau Road,
Auckland 10, New Zealand

Penguin Books Ltd, Registered Offices:
Harmondsworth, Middlesex, England

First published by Onyx, an imprint of New American Library,
a division of Penguin Putnam Inc.

First Printing, December 2000
10 9 8 7 6 5 4 3 2

PUBLISHER'S NOTE
Proof of Life is a work of fiction. Names, characters, places, and incidents
either are the product of the author's imagination or are used
fictitiously, and any resemblance to actual persons, living or dead, business
establishments, events, or locales is entirely coincidental.

The motion picture and novelization of *Proof of Life* were inspired by the
Vanity Fair article "Adventures in the Ransom Trade" by William
Prochnau and by the book *Long March to Freedom* by Thomas R. Hargrove.

From William Prochnau's
"Adventures in the Ransom Trade"
(*Vanity Fair*, May 1998)

The huge number of multinational businessmen being abducted abroad (hundreds a year at ransoms reaching $30 million) has made organized kidnapping a big business. It has also spawned a counter industry—getting them back—and a secret drama involving former spies and revolutionaries. AK-47s and armored cars, helicopter drops and hideaways in the Andes.

In the go-go global life of the 90s, in which billionaires have become common and multinational companies have G.N.P.s heftier than those of most countries, the kidnap business is booming. Over the past 20 years, multinationals have quietly paid out at least a billion dollars in ransom for kidnapped executives. As for the vulnerable superrich and famous, so much secrecy shrouds the business that you can't even get an estimate—except that perhaps one in three kidnappings goes unreported, and that the payoffs are almost always understated. In some countries ransoms of $5 million are not uncommon. Kidnappers recently got $30 million for the return of a Mexican banker.

The cost of protection—armored Mercedeses, "nuke-spooner" and radiation alarms which can be hidden inside briefcases, multimillion-dollar kidnap-and-ransom insurance, $4,000-a-day professional kidnap-negotiation services—totals far more than the ransoms. A fully equipped, bullet-proofed Lincoln Town Car sells for well into six figures. It can take fire from any modern combat rifle, comes with flip-down gun portholes, and has a device that discharges an oil slick to foil followers in a chase. Some high rollers even implant homing devices in their bodies, although the pros say the devices aren't worth the effort and leave a telltale bruise.

Americans alone now spend more on personal security than the budgets of the F.B.I. and all U.S. police agencies combined. The security industry employs nearly two million men and women—more than served in the U.S. Army at the height of the Cold War. These numbers come from Brian Jenkins, a former Vietnam Green Beret and Rand Corporation analyst who gained celebrity as *Nightline*'s resident talking head on terrorism. Jenkins now consults for Kroll-O'Gara Company, a large New York corporate-security company that has branched out into kidnap negotiations.

International kidnapping has become an emblem for the 90s. Gone with the Cold War are the romanticized days when ransoms mixed with leftist philosophy and often provided the "war tax" for Marxist political movements. Now, like everything in this overheated age, it's just about money.

Today professional kidnap squads are more likely to be exiles from that world—men who learned their trade under red banners but now work only for profit. The typical hit is exquisitely and professionally planned, often pulled off in broad daylight on public streets, with such overwhelming speed and force that lifelong body-guards quickly drop their weapons—or drop dead.

The so-called K&R industry, which provides kidnap and ransom insurance and hardball negotiators for high-priced kidnap cases, is a world in which Cold War exiles—a roguish business of small companies and locked doors and names such as Control Risks—will send ex-spooks, special forces, or Scotland Yard men anywhere on earth, on a moment's notice, to bail you out when the kidnappers are demanding millions.

A year ago, a friend of mine who sells kidnap insurance in London suggested that I might be welcomed into the heart of the bizarre K&R business. I began weeks, then months, of negotiations with K&R operatives, one of whom repeatedly answered his phone (as I sat in his code-locked office), "Yes, Yuri, $2 million," followed minutes later by "No, Yuri, $2 million."

The grand tour eventually took me from Washington to London, Paris, Panama City, Miami, and, finally, the epidemic's ground zero, Colombia. I wandered through a shadowy gallery of former spies and F.B.I. agents, old British Special Air Service operatives who spoke in a special slang half salvaged from the bureaucratic worlds they had all hated, half gleaned from the streets. Each kidnap negotiation was a deployment, each ransom a settlement. Between deployments and settlements, the K&R men lived in a world of door kickers and "bent" cops, and used euphemisms such as "de facto death penalty" and "vaccination." They pitted themselves against an array of professional bad guys with cop-novel nicknames. Grabbers. Movers. Keepers. Talkers. Drop men.

My prime target was London's Control Risks Group Ltd., the oldest and most regal of the K&R firms, with a client list that includes 91 Fortune 100 companies, 9 of the top 10 Forbes multinationals, and a top secret list of rich and famous people. Situated just blocks from New Scotland Yard and a short walk from Parliament, Control Risks quietly makes its home in an old redbrick building so innocuous that it could house insurance-company clerks or an MI5 secret unit. But when a phone rings at 83 Victoria Street, the response is guaranteed: you will, within 15 minutes, get a call back from a seasoned negotiator; you will have him at your side, anywhere in the world, within 24 hours. He will spend the next two years of his life with you, if that's what it takes—and sometimes it does.

I doubled back to Miami, where the most respected K&R operative, Mike Ackerman, runs his company from an island in Biscayne Bay. Ackerman has all the brassy American bravado of a C.I.A. street man, which he once was. "I hire guys," he growls, "who use the back door and can flash a wad of cash." He has dropped $275,000 out of a helicopter hovering over armed guerrillas in the Guatemalan jungle, and surreptitiously microfilmed a $6 million ransom payment while Argentinean kidnappers held a gun to the head of his billionaire client's son. *Forbes* has described Ackerman as the man American companies call "when the hostile takeover turns lethal."

I also met with David Lattin, a former U.S. Navy spy who spent most of his government career in Eastern Europe, doubling Soviet-bloc agents—persuading them to spy for the West while remaining in their old jobs. Lattin, who looks more like an insurance agent, is the American operations director for Control Risks. He has made more than 50 "deployments" and tells war stories like a trooper. One of his favorites involves a local flight he took in the Far East. He found himself seated next to the peasant-hero chieftain whose men had just kidnapped his client. Lattin calmly asked for and received the chieftain's autograph.

But cooperation with a journalist during a live kidnapping, Lattin finally told me pleasantly, is unheard of. "We're cross-cultural, you and I," he said. After months of trying, I seemed dead in the water. In reality, however, I had already been drawn into a strange and morally ambiguous netherworld where up often meant down, in often meant out, and men would tell me that death threats were a good sign.

In the United States, Lattin says, the crime is played out against generally efficient and honest police departments; 95 percent of all American kidnappers are caught. The penalties are severe and consistent, and therefore discourage the development of an experienced criminal workforce. So poor is the reputation of the North American kidnappers that *The Miami Herald,* which covers both locals and internationals, once dismissed a kidnapping as "a garden-variety American job, badly thought out, risky, potentially murderous because of the captors' incompetence." In fact, you are more likely to be killed by American kidnappers, who are inclined to eliminate witnesses. "In the United States, only loonies do [kidnappings]," says Peter Dobbs, a former British special-forces man and Control Risks negotiator who now sells kidnap insurance for Asset Security Managers Ltd.

But go elsewhere—Colombia, Mexico, Guatemala, Brazil, Russia, the Philippines, Taiwan, even China—and everything turns on its head. In Colombia, where thousands of people and scores of multinational executives are snatched every year, 99 percent of all kidnappers are never convicted. In Manila, one expert says that up to 80 percent of the police force is on the take, and human heists are so routine that kidnappers take personal checks.

In these places, I found disenchanted Cuban ideologues and the spent forces of a dozen Latin revolutions who'd grown into an unlikely capitalistic middle age—like American hippies driving Suburbans. But the kidnappers aren't just retired revolutionaries. In many countries, kidnappings are organized by cops and ex-soldiers. In Nicaragua, retired contras have taken up the trade. And out-of-work soldiers, cops, and guerrillas have kept the kidnap trade booming in Guatemala.

So the same gangs negotiate, over and over, with the same kidnap negotiators. They get to know one another's voices and M.O.s. Codes of conduct are established, such as the Preserve the Porcelain Rule: Keep the victim alive. "If you are running a china shop," Dobbs said, "you do not break the china." A few hard-nosed kidnappers have tried to ransom dead bodies. But the discount is large. The object of both sides is to get 'em back alive.

An overseas company has more than one way to deal with a kidnapping. Most multinationals go with the K&Rs because they bring hostages back alive and minimize problems with the host government. Some Japanese firms, for example, have a cultural tendency to pay fast and in full for humanitarian reasons. Others, mostly churches, missionary groups, and altruistic organizations, either don't have the money for insurance and ransoms or take a God-is-on-our-side approach. They just won't pay.

But one of the peculiarities of the K&R industry is that it provides little of substance in the way of prevention. Corporate customers get tidbits of advice: dress down, forget the Jaguar, and don't flash your corporate logo overseas, lest you draw the attention of logo hunters, who occupy the bottom level of the kidnapper food chain. The K&R industry is there to step in *afterward* and give its customers the best chance of coming out alive—with as little derring-do as possible. "Our customers expect to pay a ransom," says Ackerman.

Kidnap insurance may be the ultimate defensive device. The survival rate for all insured victims is about 85 percent. A policy buys more than ransom money. It pays lost wages to a corporate victim and even covers a family vacation and psychiatric help afterward. Most important, it buys an Ackerman, Lattin, or Dobbs to deal directly with the kidnappers. They do not come cheap. Ackerman charges $2,000 a day, and if two men are needed (as they almost always are in complex negotiations), he throws in the second for $1,350. Expenses run high. The negotiators like the best hotels and good food. After the kidnapping of an Occidental Petroleum executive, Ackerman charged $400,000 to negotiate the ransom down to less than $2 million.

Nor is the insurance cheap. Those feeling particularly kidnap-prone can buy insurance from both sides. You can buy the conventional plan at annual premiums ranging anywhere from $10,000 to more than $150,000 per person. One South American billionaire has insured 90 members of his family; many insure their mistresses. Or you can buy a *vacuna,* or vaccination, directly from the kidnappers. In Bogota, a $60,000 *vacuna* will protect you from a half-million-dollar kidnapping. This saves both sides wear and tear.

Most corporations, as well as billionaires, Hollywood stars, and athletes, stick with the conventional policy, often insuring all of their overseas employees. But getting someone to admit it is another story. Some policies call for cancellation if the customer talks. Boris Becker was not happy when, at the height of his career, a newspaper outed him as having kidnap insurance. Becker was insured for $10 million, with a top-of-the-line annual premium of $160,000.

But for every high-profile celebrity who is never kidnapped, there's an anonymous executive who is. I asked Dobbs to help me find a kidnapper, perhaps in a South American jail.

"Not many of those," he replied. "No death penalty in most of those countries, you know. But few survive the drive to jail. We call it the de facto death penalty."

Chapter 1

It was hell being responsible for the lives of others.

Terry Thorne should know. He tried not to dwell on the fact that if he didn't hustle, if he didn't make the rendezvous in time, a man would die. An innocent man whose only mistake in life had been to be in the wrong place at the wrong time. A man with an adoring wife and three adorable kids anxiously waiting for their devoted husband and father to come back to them safe and sound.

Whether that happened depended entirely on him.

Sometimes Terry wished he'd never become involved in the high risk Kidnap and Ransom business, or K&R, as it was known in the trade. He told himself he shouldn't become emotionally involved. He reminded himself that personal feelings weren't to enter into the equation. But it did no good. That was all a crock, just like the old Mafia adage about never letting business become personal. *Everything* in life was personal. Anyone who claimed otherwise was a damned liar.

Terry raised his camera and focused the lens on the rows of Swiss currency spread out over a pair of Russian ammo boxes. Fifty hundred-franc notes were arranged so the denominations and serial numbers were visible. He pressed the shutter release and the camera flashed brightly.

Initially, the kidnappers had demanded a ransom of three million dollars, but Terry had been able to talk them down to seven hundred and fifty thousand. True to form, they'd huffed and puffed and repeatedly threatened to kill their golden goose. It was all a bluff, of course, all part of the game. After handling over four dozen ransom negotiations, he had the routine down pat. He was generally regarded as one of the best in the business, and he took great pride in the fact that he had never lost a client.

As Terry shifted to take another photo, he caught a glimpse of himself in a shattered mirror on the wall. He was dressed in combat fatigues to better blend in with the locals. The fatigues brought to mind his days with British Special Forces, where he had received much of the training that helped make him an effective K&R negotiator. He needed a shave and his face had a rugged look that seemed to show the wear-and-tear of every day of his thirty-plus years.

A chilly gust of wind reminded Terry where he was: in the old ruins of a mosque deep in Chechnya, in an upstairs room with ancient, splayed floorboards, busted windows, and cracked walls. It was bitterly cold, with the wind howling against the sheets of plastic he had spread over the windows so the money wouldn't be blown all over creation.

Terry glanced down at his feet, where a duffel bag crammed with the rest of the money sat. A check of his watch showed he was almost out of time. Quickly, he set to work photographing the last of the bills.

His superiors at Luthan Risk International would be immensely pleased the final total was within six percent of their original target figure and consistent with recent ransom payments in the West Asian, post-Soviet republics. But all Terry could think about was Marcel Lenoir, who was going to die a particularly awful, violent death if he didn't deliver the suitcase on time. He finished snapping the photos, put the camera in its carrying case, and bent over the ammo boxes to perform one last but extremely essential task.

Terry was almost ready. Moving to a crack in the wall, he peered out. A stand of barren trees was to the left of the old mosque. To the right the frozen ground was dotted with shell holes and the shattered remains of a crippled tank. Directly in front waited the Russian soldiers who were to take delivery of the ransom and deliver it to the kidnappers. Terry counted two dozen troops and half a dozen vehicles. They were lean, hard, wolfish men in threadbare uniforms, some stamping their feet against the freezing cold, others with their hands shoved inside their jackets. Only the colonel in charge wore a parka. At that moment, he was standing on a BTR-50 P armored personnel carrier, his arms folded across his barrel chest, impatiently tapping a gloved hand.

"If you think I trust you, Colonel Yakov, you miserable son of a bitch," Terry said to himself, "you have another think coming."

Leaving the duffel there, Terry gripped one of the ammo boxes and dragged it down the warped stairs to the chapel. Two Russian soldiers were waiting. They helped him haul the box out into the harsh glare of bright sunlight. It was heavier than it should be, but Terry doubted they would catch on until it was too late.

The colonel and many of the soldiers smiled. Hungry, greedy smiles. Proof Terry had guessed correctly.

Colonel Yakov said something to the driver of the personnel carrier, the only man among them who spoke English. The driver rose partway out of his seat to say, "You have taken your photographs, Aussie?"

"All done." Terry didn't much like how the man never called him by name, as if he were a simpleton beneath their contempt. They figured they had the better of him, but they were about to learn differently. The trick was for him to do what he had to do to get out of there before they caught on. These were ruthless, violent men. They would shoot him to ribbons if they knew what Terry had planned.

"All the money is there, Aussie?"

Terry had to shout to be heard over another shriek of wind. "It's there! Tell your colonel he's responsible now, right? Tell him if he fucks about, I'll be the least of his problems! You got that, mate?"

The driver translated and Colonel Yakov grinned and nodded as if he had every intention of doing his part. At his command, the two soldiers hoisted the ammunition box to their shoulders, carried it around to the rear of the vehicle, and stowed it in the storage compartment. His mouth curling in an oily smile, the officer smugly handed a large lock to Terry.

"He wants you to do the honors, Aussie," the driver said.

Terry yearned to pull the leering bastard off the vehicle and pound him silly, but instead he played along. He accepted the lock and secured the compartment. "There you go. Better hurry now. If you're late, my client will be killed."

"Do not worry, Aussie," the driver relayed a comment by the colonel. "We know just what to do."

My ass, Terry thought, stepping back. He smiled and waved as the personnel carrier and the troop transports growled to life and wheeled in a tight U-turn on the dusty rural road.

Three soldiers had been left behind to guard the position. Or at least that was the official line. Terry knew they were there to ensure that he stayed where he was. The colonel didn't want Terry meddling, didn't want him to suspect the colonel was going to keep the money and let the client die.

Sliding a bottle of vodka from his fatigue jacket, Terry uncapped it and took a swig. The three soldiers were all attentive, licking their cold, cracked lips and regarding the bottle as if it were liquid gold.

Terry grinned and held the bottle out to them, acting friendly, good-natured. "Would you poor frozen stooges care for some gut warmer?" he asked even though they couldn't understand a syllable. When one tentatively extended an arm, he placed the bottle in the man's hand. "Help yourselves."

The convoy was out of sight beyond the trees. Terry sidled toward the mosque, tensed to spring if the three soldiers tried to stop him. But all they were interested in was the vodka. Slipping inside, he raced to the duffel, slung it over a shoulder, and then sped on through the battered building and out the rear door. His jeep and a nervous local driver were waiting fifty yards away, hidden behind a stone wall.

Terry tossed the duffel into the back and hopped in. "Get me to the farm as fast as you can, Grigori."

"Yes. Yes. Will do. Will do," the man said in thickly accented English.

Terry held on as Grigori whipped the jeep in a circle and sped northward. He scanned the unending sea of frozen farmland and spied the personnel carrier and the transports well to the east, heading for the primary extraction site. But Terry knew that well before the convoy was to rendezvous with the kidnappers, Colonel Yakov would veer off toward the distant mountains to the northwest. There, the colonel and his men would divide up the ransom and head for parts unknown. Terry only hoped they waited until they reached the mountains to open the strongbox. They were in for a rude shock when they discovered that he had filled it with books.

The threat assessment by LRI's crack team of specialists had been right on target. The region was a hotbed of deceit and treachery. No one in authority could be trusted. Which was why LRI had advised Terry to minimize the involvement of the Russian military. Accordingly, he'd told his Russian liaison that he didn't want the army involved, but Colonel Yakov had insisted on being present during the long negotiations and had then demanded to come along when the money was delivered.

Earlier, when Terry mentioned that he needed to photograph the ransom before turning it over, for a minute he'd thought the wily colonel would refuse. But Yakov had to play along. Stealing the money was one thing; killing Terry would embarrass the government and land Yakov in a tempest of political trouble.

Terry pulled the collar of his jacket up against the cold and concentrated on the rutted track of a dirt road. He allowed himself the indulgence of a grin at how cleverly he had outwitted Yakov. The officer had been unaware that a back channel of communication had been established with Marcel Lenoir's kidnappers and that the extraction site had been changed. "Faster, Grigori," he coaxed. "We don't want to be late."

"I go fast, I go fast."

Terry's grin widened a bit. Grigori always repeated himself. Maybe because the man was unsure of his linguistic skills, such as they were. Terry had hired him because Grigori was one of the few locals who possessed a smattering of English and because he needed someone he could trust. For a few paltry hundred dollars—the equivalent of a year's income in that poverty-stricken region—Grigori had agreed to drive to the mosque well ahead of the convoy and wait there for him.

They took a narrow turn doing over fifty miles an hour. The jeep fishtailed, and Grigori spun the wheel like mad to compensate.

Terry gripped the dash as they sloughed wildly, straightened out, and sped on amid a roiling cloud of dust. "Stay calm, my friend," he said.

"I calm, I calm," Grigori responded, his bearded face mirroring stark panic.

It took half an hour to reach the site. By then the wind had died down, and the sun shone brightly.

The rebels had chosen a spot in the middle of a vast, open plain to prevent either party from springing a nasty surprise on the other. Or so their negotiator had told Terry. But now, as the jeep roared toward the small band of Chechin insurrectionists, Terry spied a low rise to the east, a convenient cover that might hide more rebels. It could well be they had no intention of honoring the agreement. Like Colonel Yakov, they might intend to take the money and run—without handing over Lenoir.

"Stop," Terry commanded, and Grigori brought the jeep to a lurching halt a hundred yards out. Snatching a pair of binoculars from the backseat, Terry pressed the eyecups to his face, and adjusted the focusing control. There were twenty-eight Chechens: ragtag soldiers armed with a mix of AK-47s and older weapons, including a few Tokarev rifles. Most of the rebels were clustered on and around a flatbed truck. A few were beside a pair of badly dented jeeps.

"We go on? We go on?" Grigori asked, not sounding happy at the prospect.

"We stay put," Terry said, consulting his watch. Their timing was near perfect. "When I start toward them, I want you to turn around and get the hell out of here. Don't linger. You hear me? If things go sour, I don't want you anywhere around."

"I leave. I leave," Grigori promised.

A tall Chechen was waving a gloved hand, beckoning them nearer, but Terry wasn't budging until his transport arrived. Instead, he reached around for his walkie-talkie and switched it on. The tall Chechen must be his contact, Petenka, the man he had been negotiating with for Lenoir's release. Static crackled and he tweaked the gain.

"Look! Look!" Grigori called out, pointing at the sky.

A tiny speck had appeared far to the south, a speck that swiftly grew in size, assuming the silhouette of a helicopter. Some of the rebels spotted it, but no one raised a weapon. Extraction by chopper was part of the agreement.

Terry pressed the transmit button. "Petenka? Do you copy? You there?"

The tall Chechen produced a walkie-talkie of his own. "Yes. We are all set. Bring the money."

"In a moment. Where's my client?"

Petenka nodded toward the flatbed and said something to the soldiers on it. They parted to reveal a man on his knees, blindfolded, and bound at the wrists. "The package is here as promised."

The helicopter was flying low to avoid Russian radar. The pilot set down off to the left, a hundred yards from Terry and the rebels. Again, it was all part of the agreement. Terry wasn't to go near the copter until he had handed over the money.

Grigori was admiring the chopper. "She is big one, yes?" he said, not repeating himself for once.

Too big, Terry thought. Too big and too bulky and too slow. He would rather have a sleek modern model, but the best he could do was arrange for an old mil Mi-4, a warhorse well past its prime that had been converted to civilian use—worse, a warhorse stripped of armaments. Only Russian military copters were allowed to be armed. Civilian choppers fitted with hardware were automatically assumed to belong to the rebels and summarily shot down.

The pilot stared through the cockpit window at Terry and grimly nodded.

"Time for the swap," Terry said into the walkie-talkie, then tossed it onto the seat. He slung the duffel over his left shoulder and headed for the Chechens. He was totally exposed, completely vulnerable. If they saw fit to eliminate him, all it would take was a sniper shot to the head or the heart. He steeled himself against a growing feeling of dread, his eyes darting right and left, alert for any hints of treachery.

Petenka had moved to the flatbed. Several rebels were none-too-gently lowering Lenoir to the ground.

Amateurs were always unnecessarily rough, Terry reflected. Rough and brutal. He'd rather deal with a pro any day.

"So we meet face-to-face at last!" Petenka cordially greeted him, studying Terry's features. "You look as tough as you sounded."

Terry only had eyes for his client. Marcel Lenoir was doubled over in exhaustion. Bandages brown with caked blood covered half of Lenoir's head, as well as his left hand. His ear had been chopped off. So had three fingers. Tokens sent as proof of life. Lenoir's suit was grimy, torn, and barely adequate to keep him from freezing to death in the mountainous terrain of Chechnya.

Bending, Terry hooked a hand under the poor man's arm. "Mr. Lenoir? Terry Thorne. We're leaving now. Do you understand? You're going home."

Lenoir's head twitched, and he uttered a pitiful groan.

Terry glared at Petenka. "You call this keeping him in good condition?"

"He is alive, isn't he?" the Chechen leader glibly replied and snapped his fingers. "The bag, if you please."

Terry flung the duffel to the ground. As he carefully helped Lenoir stand, the rebels pounced on it like jackals on a carcass. They greedily tore at the clasp, shoving one another out of the way in their eagerness to see the money.

Petenka had to push a few of his soldiers aside and speak sternly before order was restored. He opened the duffel himself and out spilled their ill-gotten gains. Again they crowded around, laughing and whooping and sorting through the bills in gleeful abandon.

Supporting his client, Terry made for the helicopter. Lenoir was little help. Pathetically weak from loss of blood and lack of nourishment, he could do no more than slowly shuffle his feet. Terry tried to quicken their pace, but Lenoir simply wasn't up to it. And Terry never knew if or when the Chechens might decide to kill them anyway. Disposing of witnesses was another amateur trademark.

It was going to be a long hundred yards.

Terry had only gone a short way when he was startled to see his jeep right where he had left it. Grigori hadn't driven off. The simpleton was sitting there, enthralled by the drama unfolding before him.

The helicopter pilot was fidgeting in his seat. Terry had paid a lot of money for the retrieval, but there was no guarantee the man wouldn't suddenly take it into his head that the situation was too dangerous and bail.

Terry covered twenty yards. Forty. The rebels were paying no attention to him whatsoever, which he construed as a good sign. But then his gaze drifted beyond them to the low rise, and his breath caught in his throat.

Vehicles were spilling over it, foremost among them Colonel Yakov's personnel carrier. The colonel had become aware of Terry's ruse, and now he and his entire unit were about to wreak their vengeance. They had brought along two other BTR-50s as well as half a dozen transports and a monstrous tank.

Terry wrapped both arms around Lenoir and propelled his client toward the copter. Yakov's personnel carriers were bad enough; in addition to 7.62-mm machine guns, both had been retrofitted with SAGGER antitank missile launchers. Compared to the tank, though, they were lightweights. It was a T-72 battle tank with a 125-mm main gun, a 7.62-mm machine gun, and a 12.7-mm antiaircraft gun. In short, it was a metal behemoth capable of dispensing violent death on a massive scale.

One of the Chechens shouted. The rebels were awakening to their peril. Petenka began shoving money back into the duffel while bawling at his men, most of whom were scrambling for their vehicles. A few foolishly opened fire on the approaching Russians, even though Colonel Yakov's unit was well out of range of an AK-47 or a rifle.

Marcel Lenoir mumbled a few words.

"Mr. Lenoir?" Terry said, breaking into a lumbering run, virtually carrying the man now. "Can you hear me? We're in great danger. If you can help out, I'd appreciate it."

Rebels were piling onto the flatbed in terror. They were guerillas, hit-and-run specialists. The last thing they wanted was a pitched battle in open terrain, and they were desperate to depart before the battle tank came within range.

There was only one problem.

It already was.

Terry heard the shriek of an incoming shell and dived flat, pulling Lenoir down with him. He covered Lenoir's body with his own as a tremendous blast rent the chill air. The earth under them shook and a heartbeat later they were pelted by a deluge of dirt, rocks, and dust. Flinching against the stinging pain, Terry surged upright before the blast had faded and sprinted toward the copter.

The pilot was scared witless. At any moment he might take off. He ducked low when a second shell struck, although neither had hit anywhere near the aircraft.

Nor, for that matter, had the Russians struck anything else. Terry remembered hearing that the automatic loading and targeting systems on the T-72 left a lot to be desired and that their accuracy rate was something like sixty percent. Gaping holes on either side of the flatbed seemed to support the intel.

Terry was halfway to the chopper. Another fifty yards, and they could fly south toward safety.

Colonel Yakov entered the fray in full force. A plume of smoke spewed from his personnel carrier.

A clear sign a SAGGER antitank missile had been launched. It streaked true, and one of the Chechen jeeps was enveloped in a roaring fireball just as it started to speed off. Flames shot high into the air and scorched bits of metal blistered nearby rebels, ripping through them like so much molten shrapnel.

With forty yards to go, Terry's muscles protested the severe strain. He was bearing Lenoir's full weight, zigzagging as he ran, breathing shallowly against a spreading cloud of smoke that threatened to limit visibility. "Don't leave!" he shouted at the pilot, but he doubted the man could hear him over the bedlam.

The rebels were firing nonstop and being fired on in turn by Russian troops spilling from the transports and the carriers. Petenka's band was doomed. Petenka himself was running after the flatbed, which had growled into motion. He had the duffel clasped to his chest and wouldn't let go, even though the added weight ensured that he would never overtake the truck.

Terry saw it all. A round from the tank screeched out of the ether and obliterated the rear half of the flatbed in an eruption of volcanic proportions. He saw Petenka hurled backward like a rag doll caught in a hurricane, saw Petenka roll and tumble only to rise again, blubbering and clawing toward the duffel. It had been knocked loose and bills were fluttering every which way. Petenka grabbed at them, wailing whenever one eluded him.

A cry snapped Terry's gaze toward his jeep. Grigori was trying to escape, but in his fright he was grinding gears, gaining speed as slowly as a tortoise. Go! Terry mentally screamed. Go! Go! Go!

Grigori wrenched the gearshift, his gritted teeth showing through his beard as he brought the jeep up to speed. He looped westward, the vehicle bouncing over a rut. Swiveling, he looked back toward Terry and in a split second his head and shoulders dissolved under a burst of machine gun fire. Tracers and slugs tore through him like red-hot knives through wax, reducing him to a riddled heap. The jeep coasted another twenty or thirty feet and came to a halt.

Terry's gut churned. Indirectly he was to blame for Grigori's death. He had hired him, had talked Grigori into leaving his family to serve as guide and driver for a few days.

Twenty-five yards remained. Suddenly, the pilot motioned he was about to take off.

"Don't you dare!" Terry yelled, expending the last of his strength and energy in a herculean effort to reach the chopper before it was too late.

The Chechens were returning fire in earnest, but too few of them were left to do more than temporarily slow the advancing line of Russian troops. The tank and the personnel carriers were rumbling along at full speed, Colonel Yakov gesturing and bellowing to his men to continue the assault.

Out of the corner of his eye, Terry glimpsed Petenka. Oblivious to the mayhem rampant on all sides of him, the man clutched loose bills to his chest in a paroxysm of glee. His glee was short-lived. Heavy-caliber rounds stitched the insurgent's torso, turning him into the equivalent of a human sieve. Petenka died holding the money that had meant more to him than his own life.

Ten yards to go, and Terry was about done in. His legs were wobbly and his breath came in great, labored gasps.

The helicopter started to rise.

"No, damn you!" Terry roared and threw himself

at the bay door. He pumped his arms, heaving Lenoir inside, and gripped the doorframe to pull himself in. An explosion dangerously close to the Mi-4 slammed him against the door. He felt a moist sensation on his forehead and started to lose his hold on the rescued hostage. Lenoir, incredibly, had rallied and reached out to help him.

"Wait for me!" Terry bellowed at the cockpit, but the pilot was too scared to heed. The helicopter continued to rise, Terry hung on by the tips of his fingers. Suddenly it banked sharply away. Terry lost his grip and fell. For a bloodcurdling moment he thought he was done for, but he fell into the chopper's bay, not toward the ground, and crashed against its side.

Outside, something whisked toward the copter in a blur. A rocket missed the undercarriage by a whisker, then was gone. The pilot tried to level off, but overcompensated and the chopper spiraled downward. Cursing furiously in Slovak, he regained control, rapidly gained altitude, and shot like an arrow to the south.

Terry pulled himself up into a seat. He was battered, bruised, and bloody thanks to a deep cut over his eye. Blinking hard, he focused on the bleak terrain, on the burning Chechen vehicles and blistered rebel bodies, on the Russian armor and Russian troops, all rapidly growing smaller.

Weary to the bone, Terry closed his eyes. Another job well done. Another kidnap victim spared. If only Grigori had lived, it all would have gone perfectly.

A groan from Marcel Lenoir roused him. Terry moved to tend the man as best he could. He saw the pilot turn, flash a grin, and give the thumbs-up sign.

"If you only knew," Terry said softly.

Chapter 2

"You can take a man out of Texas, but you can never take Texas out of the man." Peter Bowman's grandfather had been fond of that saying, and now, forty-odd years later, Peter had to agree that his grandfather had been right. He'd left Texas decades ago, but he still spoke with a bit of a nasal twang, still favored cowboy boots, and had retained that Texan air of ruggedness and independence about him.

Seated in a corporate helicopter climbing toward the summit of a river gorge deep in the South American jungle, Peter frowned and said into his cell phone, "No, you wait, Keith. Excuse me, but that's pure Oklahoma horseshit." He barely glanced at the steep, vegetation-choked walls or the rapids far below.

Peter was boiling mad, but he contained his temper. "I've got sixty people sitting up here with nothing to do! We've been twiddling our thumbs for weeks now, and I'm tired of it."

The copter came in for a pinpoint landing on a makeshift helipad. When the door was flung open, Peter strode out ahead of the dozen hard hats with whom he had shared the flight. He moved toward a collection of Quonset huts, mobile homes, and warehouses that served as the headquarters for the construction site he oversaw. "I'm almost a month behind schedule. Unless you send the equipment you've promised, it will get worse." Peter paused. "What equipment? Blasting canopies, blades, gantry assemblies, we need it all—"

Peter abruptly clammed up. Waiting to greet the copter were five clean-shaven men in crisp suits. Engineers sent by the front office, he had been told, to inspect the site and report back on his progress. They were hanging on his every word. For privacy's sake, he moved toward the jungle and lowered his voice. "Hell, Keith. We're supposed to be building a dam here, and I don't even have a working dragline!"

The voice at the other end belonged to Keith Harness, a friend, a colleague, and Peter's liaison at QUAD-CARBON, the company they both worked for. "There's been a high rate of turnover at the top recently, as you well know," Keith replied. "Securing approval on any project is just about impossible. I suggest you be patient awhile longer."

"Hell!" Peter spat in disgust. "Here's *my* suggestion. Go find whoever's in charge up there this week and remind them that this little water project was the key to their whole pipeline contract. Plain and simple—no dam, no pipeline."

"I'm doing the best I can," Keith said.

Peter stopped short. A work gang was seated in shade under the trees, twenty swarthy workers waiting for word to go to work, their dark eyes fixed on him in curiosity. Sighing, Peter angled toward the gorge rim. "Keith, I'm just trying to get this dam done. Each day I'm down here trying to make you guys look good, and at least once a week I have to call and beg for equipment that's been budgeted and approved, but never shows up."

"I'll make another call as soon as you hang up."

"Fine. You do that," Peter said, his thumb stroking the OFF button. So frustrated that he could hardly stand it, he clenched his fists and seriously considered taking out his anger on a nearby bush. Someone discreetly coughed behind him, and he spun to find his Tecalan assistant, Alfredo. "What is it?" he asked harshly, regretting it when faithful Alfredo flinched as if he had been struck.

"So sorry, señor. But those men, the bigwigs, they are ready to leave." Alfredo was portly and balding and had the perpetually sad eyes of a cocker spaniel.

"I know. I saw them," Peter said, shoving the cell phone into a pocket. "Did you show them around? Let them see our records like they wanted?"

"Sí, Señor Bowman. I did as you instructed." Alfredo pinched his lips together, a sign that he wanted to say more, but was hesitant to do so.

"What is it?" Peter prompted.

"I do not like them, señor."

"Suits always make people nervous," Peter said. The five men in suits were about to enter the helicopter. He thought it strange that they hadn't bothered to bid him good-bye or at least comment on the result of their inspection.

"They are hawks, señor," Alfredo said. "They look everywhere and miss nothing. And they spent more time going over your books than they did going through the camp."

"They did?" Uneasiness filled Peter, but he quelled it by reminding himself that he was one of the best construction engineers in the business, and QUAD-

CARBON wasn't about to dismiss him when the project had barely begun.

"Sí," Alfredo said. "They wanted to know how much it cost to clear the jungle and build this camp, how much the helipad cost, how much this and that cost."

Peter took a step toward the copter, but changed his mind. It wouldn't do to make a nuisance of himself. The home office wouldn't appreciate having their inspection team badgered. Shrugging, he acted casual. "It's no big deal. Tell the men I'm expecting the equipment any day now, and we'll resume work as soon as it arrives."

"The men are upset, Señor Bowman. They do not like coming up here day after day expecting to earn money, as you promised, and being told day after day that there is no work and no money."

"I know, I know." Peter rubbed his temples. Sometimes he felt as if he had the weight of the world on his shoulders. He needed some time off, needed to recharge his inner batteries. But until the dam was completed, extended R&R was a pipe dream. The best he could hope for were a few hours entertainment that evening at the annual Tecalan Country Club Charity Ball. "Things will improve," he told Alfredo. "Wait and see."

Alice Bowman turned heads wherever she went. Her lean but full body, her deep tan, and her subtle yet sensual elegance were like a magnet to every male within sight. It was an effect she'd always had, an effect she had trained herself to ignore, to treat as if it were as commonplace as the sun and the stars.

Dressed in a light shift that clung to her like a second skin, Alice wended through the open air market in the heart of Tecala City. Over one arm hung a Parisian mesh bag filled with produce.

Beside her strode Maria, her housekeeper, a motherly matron who always adopted a protective air when they were in public. "For your own good," Maria had said once when Alice teased her about it. "Many bad people in Tecala now. Not like when I was small. Then, everyone was happy. Now, everyone mostly scared."

They stopped at a pepper stall. Maria saw some goathorn peppers and spent the next five minutes wrangling with the man selling them. "This one is a thief," she said to Alice at one point. "He calls himself King of Chilis. But he is King of Robbers, I think. He wants much money."

"Pay him," Alice said. She had better things to do with her day than bicker with a simpleton.

But to her friend it was a matter of honor. Maria never let herself be swindled. "Make this liar happy? I rather eat dirt."

Laughing, Alice scanned the aisle ahead and caught sight of something new to the market, something she had never seen before.

Maria was too busy wrangling with the pepper vendor to notice.

Alice moved toward a colorful open-air tent that had been erected amid the food stalls. A hand-painted sign over it announced ADIVINA in bold letters. The center of attention was a girl who couldn't be much older than seven or eight. Alice had to watch awhile before she caught on to the fact that the child was a psychic or a fortune-teller of some kind.

The girl's face was incredibly serene, and her extraordinary hazel eyes, rare for a Tecalan, had an almost hypnotical lure. Two older women flanked her, her mother and grandmother, Alice guessed. Seated in front of them were a sad Indian couple so poor their clothes were in tatters. Alice imagined their problem must be exceptionally grave to justify spending precious money on a seer.

The little girl fascinated her. Alice edged closer. She thought of how much she'd always wanted a girl of her own, and how hard she and Peter had tried.

Suddenly the girl lifted her head and scanned the crowd of onlookers. Her riveting gaze fell on Alice, who stopped dead. The girl stared, boring into Alice with those piercing eyes. Both the mother and the grandmother tried to get the girl to devote herself to the Indian couple, but she kept staring at Alice.

Alice wanted to leave and couldn't. Her legs wouldn't move. She saw the girl whisper to the mother, who called out to her in Spanish. *"Dice que te ve todas las semanas. Mas cerca cada semana. Cuando le vas a hablar? La nina tiene mucho contarte. Cuando te vas a acercar?"*

Alice had no idea what it meant. Thankfully, Maria arrived, carrying a bag of goathorn peppers. "What is the woman saying?" Alice asked.

"Nothing. These people make things up. They go around taking money from the gullible."

A peculiar compulsion to know spurred Alice into saying, "Please. Translate for me. Is it my fortune?"

"No. It is your past." Maria listened a moment. "It makes no sense. Something about Africa. Egypt, I think."

Alice reacted as if a thousand volts of electricity had coursed through her. She didn't stay to hear more. Uttering a low sob, she whirled and fled the market as fast as her feet would carry her. She didn't care what anyone thought. She had to escape the little girl, had to get away from those terrible penetrating eyes.

But there was no running from the memory of the darkest day of her life.

The Tecalan Country Club radiated prestige and luxury like the sun radiated light and warmth. It was where all the rich and powerful came to play golf and tennis, conduct business, or frolic late into the night. Built almost eighty years ago and situated on a hill overlooking the sprawling city, it was a Tecalan landmark, as famous as the Cathedral of St. Tecala or the imposing stone statue of the city's founder out by Tecala Bay.

Peter Bowman stood at the top of the marble steps leading to the ballroom and gazed out over the sea of twinkling lights. Ironic, he thought, that just below was the poorest quarter of the capital, where decrepit hovels were stacked together like cardboard boxes, where people lived on the perpetual verge of starvation, scarcely eking out a living.

Poverty always upset Peter. When he was younger, he had never understood why governments didn't do more to eliminate it, why they didn't divert some of the billions they spent on arms and political pork barreling to help those who never knew from one day to the next where their meal was coming from.

Peter liked to think that in his own small way he was helping the poor people of the world. The projects he worked on always resulted in new jobs and new opportunities for those who otherwise would live in squalor and filth. The new dam alone promised to help revitalize the Tecalan economy, yet another reason he was so determined to see the project through.

Peter entered the ornate building. The black-tie fiesta to benefit flood victims was in full swing. The bar area, just off the main ballroom, was emptying out as revelers migrated toward their tables for the fancy dinner.

Peter spotted his wife at the bar. Beside her were two of their neighbors, a middle-aged couple, Norma and Eliodoro, the three of them sipping cocktails and merrily chatting away. Remembering he hadn't quite finished dressing in his rush to arrive on time, Peter began fixing himself up as he hurried toward them. He buttoned his waistcoat and adjusted the French cuffs on his dress shirt. When he looked up, his lovely wife was gazing tenderly at him. "Hey, baby. Sorry it took me so long."

"You made it, and that's what counts," Alice said, tilting her face to return his quick kiss. "Although I was getting a little worried. You've left me in the lurch before, you know."

Peter didn't care to be reminded. To change the subject, he nodded at their neighbors. "Norma, *buenos noches.* Elio."

"I told her you would make it," Eliodoro said. "No one who is anyone misses the great ball."

So much for changing the subject, Peter mused, and tried another tack. Turning to his wife, he asked, "How do I look?"

Alice pursed her rose-red lips. "You're a little out of whack here and there. Hang on." She tugged at his cummerbund, then fiddled with his white bow tie. "I swear. If it weren't for us women, you men would be content to go around looking like something the cat dragged in."

"I was in a hurry," Peter said, attempting to justify his lapse. "I rushed down from the site and had to deal with heavy traffic all the way here. I changed in the car. And get this." He winced when her nail accidentally scraped his neck as she adjusted his tie, "I'm out there changing my pants, and I look up and there's something like sixteen armed guards watching me. They thought it was comical."

"You are comical, my darling," Alice said, "in your quaint boyish way."

"Was that a dig?" Peter didn't mean to be so defensive, but she had been on his case a lot of late, with not-so-subtle comments about his long absences and how much she wished they could spend more time together. He was doing the best he could, and it peeved him that she couldn't see things from his point of view.

"No, dearest," Alice said. "I'm sure it was thrilling for the guards, too." She gripped his collar. "Here. Turn around. Let me do this right." Alice winked at Norma. "My husband the engineer. He can build million-dollar dams, but he couldn't dress himself if his life depended on it."

"Men," Norma said in a tone that suggested she had just explained everything that was wrong with the world.

Grinning, Alice smoothed the collar and patted Peter on the shoulder. "Okay. Turn back around. James Bond, eat your heart out."

Peter couldn't help grinning. "I admit it. I'm forgetful. I don't know how I'd get by without you."

"You wouldn't," Alice said honestly.

Eliodoro chuckled and gripped his wife's elbow. "I think we're going to find our table. See you inside, my young friends."

"See you inside," Alice said.

Peter gave his wife an appraising stare and said with a little extra Texas twang thrown in for effect, "Well, damn, Missus Bowman, but you're lookin' mighty sweet tonight." She'd always liked his accent. It was one of the things that attracted her to him.

Alice played along. "I'm lookin' mighty sweet all the time, sugar. You might oughta come around more often."

"I mean it. Look at you. Wow."

"My Tecalan debut as a corporate wife."

"Whatever it is, it's working." Peter stroked her hair as a bevy of men in tuxes and women in opulent dresses flowed past. "They sure know how to do it up down here."

"Well, it's for charity, right? Might as well go for broke."

Peter bent to kiss her again, with passion, when suddenly he realized he hadn't spotted anyone else from QUAD-CARBON. It surprised him so much he stiffened and looked around. "Is everybody else already here?"

"I haven't seen them, no," Alice said, the corners of her mouth quirking downward.

"Strange. They're probably all inside. We should go in, too."

"Don't you want a drink?" Alice asked, placing her warm fingers on his.

"I'll get one inside." Peter started to rise when it dawned on him that she wanted to stay. "What?"

"I haven't seen you in three days. Can't we have five minutes to ourselves?"

"Not now. The others are expecting us." Peter motioned. "Come on. Next week will be better. I promise we'll have more time together." He pulled, and Alice let herself be drawn into his arms. The sadness in her eyes hurt him, and he impulsively clasped her waist and spun into a slow dance in time to the music wafting from the ballroom. She smiled, her sadness evaporating as he swirled her through the great doors and onto the ballroom floor, blending into the flow of people moving toward their respective seats.

Over two hundred guests were on hand, grouped around large banquet tables adorned with white silk tablecloths, sterling silverware, and crystal goblets. Most of those present were Tecala's business elite. A few were notorious drug lords masquerading as legitimate business magnates. Then there were high-ranking members of the Tecalan military, their uniforms glittering with medals, as well as top-level policemen in formal greens. Politicians were plentiful, pumping the hands that fed their campaign chests. Peter also saw a number of expatriated Americans, Europeans, and a few Japanese.

Buffet tables bordered the room, heaped high with food and decorated with lush flowers and elaborate ice sculptures. Waiters in immaculate uniforms were on hand to assist those who deemed it below their station to wait on themselves.

Holding Alice's hand, Peter ambled toward the center of the vast room, toward a prominent spot near the dance floor. QUAD-CARBON traditionally had one of the "tables of honor," as they were known, commensurate with the conglomerate's status.

Peter nodded at the mayor, smiled at a leading businessman, waved at a few other people he knew. He was almost at the table when the crowd thinned enough for him to see it, and he halted in midstride in bewilderment.

The table was empty. The centerpiece read QUAD-CARBON in bright gold letters, but none of the twelve gilded chairs were occupied

Shocked, Peter let go of his wife. "What's going on here? How can this be?"

"There has to be an explanation," Alice responded. She pulled out a chair for him. "You'd better take a load off, husband mine. You look as if you're about to have a cow."

Still too dazed to think straight, Peter slowly sank down. He didn't find it the least bit amusing. Not with all that had been going on. The turmoil at the head office. Their failure to send the equipment he needed. The five-man team sent to inspect the site. He wasn't a fool. He knew it all spelled trouble. And now this. "What do we do?"

Alice seated herself. "We eat, we drink, we giggle a lot. What else?"

"How can you even think of food?" Peter shook his head in annoyance. "Where can they be?" He slumped forward, his forearms on the tablecloth. He heard Alice say she was going to get some food, but he didn't reply. He was too upset, too overwhelmed by the latest development. She didn't realize what was at stake, what they stood to lose. Worry spiked through him, numbing him to his surroundings. He tried to reason out what he should do, whom he should contact. His friend Keith might be home and he might have some answers. But he had left his cell phone in the car.

Plates plunked down, three of them piled with selections from the buffet: beef slices sauteed with zucchini, steak with guacamole, squares of beef heart on skewers, pork sausage, fish, chicken, and more.

"Help yourself," Alice said, sitting. "I've brought a little bit of everything." She selected a small tamale, took a bite, and smacked her lips. "Hey, you should try one of these. They're delicious."

"I'm not hungry." Peter felt like the whole world

was crashing down around them, and all his wife could think of was feeding her face.

Alice gave him a concerned look. "Do you want to go home?"

"I want to know what the hell is going on," Peter said testily and gnawed on his lower lip. "Nobody phoned?"

"Not that I know of, no."

"You were home all day?"

"I was there all day. Well, except for an hour or so when Maria and I went to the market. But her helper, Cinta, said we didn't get one call."

Peter's anxiety mounted by leaps and bounds. He almost missed hearing their names called. Coming toward them was Ivy Winsted, the wife of another QUAD-CARBON employee. A bottle-blonde Alabaman, she must have once been beautiful, but her fondness for food had taken its toll.

"Hey, you all! Sorry we're late."

"Where is everyone?" Alice asked.

"Nobody called you?" Ivy was juggling a plate of food high enough to qualify as a skyscraper. Carefully setting it down, she looked at each of them in turn. "Are you shitting me? Unreal. Fellner, Buddy, their whole group had to go to Houston this morning. Some kind of big powwow." Ivy plopped into a chair and turned to Alice. "Peggy said if her man was going, she was going, and then I guess all the girls jumped on that. So I guess it's just the four of us."

Peter perked up. "Is Jerry here?" he inquired, asking about her husband.

"He was right behind me a second ago." Ivy shifted. "He's probably off doing a comparative cleavage survey." Tittering, she lowered her voice to a whisper. "I mean, do these women get into it, or what?"

"What kind of powwow?" Peter asked, trying to keep her focused.

"How the hell should I know, handsome? No one ever tells me a damn thing." Ivy picked up a chunk of beef heart and bit into it with relish.

Peter was about to quiz her anyway when he spied Jerry angling toward them, a couple of drinks in one hand and a plate in the other. "Jerry!" Flooded with relief, Peter held out a chair for him.

"Hey, hey, hey, folks!" Jerry was pushing fifty, but still on the lower end of the corporate totem pole. A decent, hardworking man, he lacked the shark instinct needed by those who rose to higher ranks. He gave the plate and a drink to Ivy, then sank down with a tired sigh. "It's great to get a load off. Alice, you look stunning tonight."

"She always does," Ivy said, her mouth crammed with cow heart.

Jerry rotated toward Peter. "So. Did Ivy tell you?"

"About Houston?"

"A call came in early this morning. Before we knew it, Fellner had chartered a plane and everyone flew off." Jerry sipped his Dewar's and sighed again in contentment.

"So what's in Houston? What was the call about?"

"New money," Jerry said.

"That doesn't sound good."

"Only if we all lose our jobs."

The band was in full swing, and the bandleader was making an announcement, but Peter shut the sounds out and asked, "How did it get so bad so fast?"

"Where the hell have you been, buddy?" Jerry responded.

"I've been trying to build a dam."

"Hell, you should pick your head up every now and

then and look around you. This deal's been cratering for months."

"How's that possible?" Peter was still trying to make sense of it all. How would a buyout affect his position?

"Come on, man. QUAD-CARBON came down here hoping for a lucky break and got nailed. This whole damn country is up for grabs. Narcos have the money, guerrillas have the mountains, the army has the weapons. Everybody's trying to trade up and QUAD-CARBON couldn't handle it. Our billion-dollar pipeline hasn't spit out a gallon yet. Oil prices are in the toilet." Jerry paused in his litany of problems. "Hell, they've leveraged this thing so many times they don't even know how much debt they're in. When the market closed today, QUAD-CARBON stock was down ten and falling. The vultures were circling."

Peter's dreams were shattering before his eyes. "So who's winning?"

Jerry hesitated. "Octonal. It looks like Octonal will buy QUAD-CARBON out."

Dear God, Peter thought. The company he had devoted everything to, the company his future was riding on, was about to be swallowed alive by the worst barracuda in the business. How could things possibly get any worse? he wondered. Just then Ivy tapped him on the shoulder and pointed, and he looked up to see his wife dancing with another man.

Chapter 3

There were times, Alice Bowman thought, when her husband was less than lovable. Such as when he became so absorbed in his work they didn't see each other for days or even weeks on end. Or when he ignored her to talk shop when they were supposed to be out for a night on the town.

Over the years, Alice had been as supportive as she knew how. She'd been willing to accept his long absences and only made an issue of it when he neglected her to the point where she no longer felt as if she were married. She'd let him drag her all over the globe, and she lived under conditions most women wouldn't tolerate. She'd accepted hardly ever seeing her family and friends in the States. She had bent over backward for him, and she was growing tired of it.

Alice didn't ask for a lot. A roof over her head, food on the table, a few decent things to wear. Nothing fancy or expensive. But she needed some quality time now and then, needed to know her husband still loved her, needed a breath of intimacy in the sterile wasteland their lives had become. For weeks she had looked forward to the big ball, to a night when she was guaranteed to have him to herself. She had imagined them dancing and laughing and behaving as if they were newlyweds again.

Now it had all gone to hell.

Alice placed a hand on Peter's shoulder, hoping to distract him from his conversation with Jerry so they could take a spin on the dance floor, but Peter merely patted her and kept on talking. She doubted he was even aware of what he had done. Stung, she sat back and heard the bandleader's voice boom from the speakers.

"My friends, we have some famous dancers here with us tonight. Maybe if everyone will join me we can get the couple to dance for us."

Many of those present clapped and called out for the dancers to perform. Alice gathered that the couple must be immensely popular. She saw a fiftyish man and woman rise from a table farther back and move toward the open floor. They feigned reluctance, but it was an act. As they passed, Alice observed that the man dyed his hair and the woman hovered between voluptuous and overweight.

But Lord, they could dance.

The pair swirled into an exotic number with an up-beat tempo, the man whirling the woman in dizzying spins and supporting her when she arched her back and thrust her legs toward the ceiling, their two bodies flowing as one, smoothly, elegantly, with breathtaking precision and consummate skill.

Alice envied them. Envied their abandon, their closeness, their passion. What she wouldn't give to have the same with Peter! Other couples were moving onto the floor, and with high hopes of joining them she glanced at her husband, but he was too engrossed in QUAD-CARBON business to ask her.

The bandleader hopped down from the stage and

sashayed over to the first couple. He tapped the man on the shoulder and the man smiled and relinquished the woman. For a few moments the man watched them, then he pivoted and scanned the onlookers as if seeking another partner.

His gaze fell on Alice. She knew he wouldn't ask her, not with her being a foreigner and there being so many beautiful Tecalan women anxious for the honor. But to her amazement his mouth curled in a dazzling smile, and he walked directly toward the QUAD-CARBON table. She glanced right and left to see if some other woman was standing nearby, but no, he was definitely coming toward her.

The man said nothing. He simply extended an arm for her to take and lifted his thin eyebrows in invitation.

For a moment Alice balked, but only for a moment. Peter was still ignoring her. Any qualms she had vanished as she took the man's elbow, and he grandly ushered her toward the dance floor. She was embarrassed at first because she was so out of practice, but as he swept her along she began to loosen up.

Alice glimpsed Peter watching them and hoped he would be jealous enough to cut in, but he went back to talking to Jerry. So be it, she thought. If he insisted on behaving like a horse's hind end, she would make the best of the situation and have a little harmless fun.

Melting into the rhythm, Alice let herself go. She was enjoying herself, really enjoying herself, and it felt great. Vaguely, she realized Ivy had snuck over and snapped a photo of the two of them with a small camera Ivy always kept in her purse.

Alice contemplated having it framed and hanging it on the bedroom wall just to tick Peter off.

It would serve him right.

* * *

Their driver's name was Sandro. A beefy local, he had grown up in Tecala City and had every highway and byway memorized. As he braked the QUAD-CARBON jeep in their driveway, he looked back and asked, *"Mañana?"*

Peter had been staring off into the night, his thoughts a jumbled confusion of uncertainty and resentment. Odds were Octonal's bid to buy out QUAD-CARBON would succeed, in which case he might find himself out of a job. Until he knew for sure he couldn't go around spending money the company might not have. "No. Take the day off. Call me on Sunday."

"Sí, Señor Bowman."

Peter climbed out and held the door for Alice, who had been unusually quiet on the ride home.

"Night, Sandro," Alice said.

They entered the Scorpion House, as Peter had dubbed it. Large, modern, and well-built, it had been one of the nicest rentals on the market when they were searching for a place to live. It was well out in the suburbs and afforded some much needed privacy. The grounds boasted a well-tended garden dominated by a gurgling fountain. The house itself was unique in that the man who had built it had been obsessed with scorpions and used them as the main motif. They were everywhere: etched into the glass, painted on the tile, carved into drawers, spread over entire walls. Scorpions everywhere.

Peter stared at a particularly nasty black one on the foyer wall as he moved down the hall to their spacious kitchen. He glanced at the answering machine and saw the red light wasn't blinking.

"Any messages?" Alice teasingly asked.

34

"Zip it," Peter said. He stiffened when she walked by and playfully ran a hand down his back. Pulling away, he sarcastically commented, "Nothing like dancing with a drug lord to get a girl revved up, is there?"

Alice opened a cupboard. "Ivy told me he's a lawyer. Some friend of a friend of a friend knew the guy, or something."

"Right," Peter said, leaning against the counter and rubbing his pounding temples.

"He's a lawyer, I tell you." Alice rooted in the cupboard and suddenly a saucer fell to the floor with a crash.

"What are you doing?" Peter demanded. He wasn't in any shape to tolerate one of her moods at the moment.

"Trying to find Maria's cigarettes."

"That's all you can think of at a time like this?" Peter moved to the table and claimed a chair. "I don't know. Maybe you missed it. But this happens to be a very big deal for me."

Alice was on the tips of her toes, searching the highest shelf. "I think I know that. Give me some credit, why don't you?"

"You sure don't act like you do," Peter said. When he needed her the most she was too wrapped up in her own little world to notice.

"By wanting a cigarette?" Alice turned, her expression making it plain she was mildly confused by his attitude.

"Forget it."

Alice did no such thing. "How should I act, then? Tell me? How do you want me to act?"

"Oh, I don't know. Maybe behave as if you understood what's at stake." Peter was growing madder by the second.

"Act like you, you mean? So we both can be freaking out?" Alice came to the table, her eyes ablaze. "Spell it out for me."

Peter looked at her, trying to summon patience. "If this thing falls apart, if my dam project goes down the tubes, then what was the point?"

Again Alice was confused. "The point of what?"

"Of what?" Peter practically shouted. He was trying so hard not to lose control, but it was difficult. Taking a deep breath, he said, "How about everything? How about Africa? How about Egypt? How about Thailand? How about eight years of shit postings? Eight years of working for assholes? Eight years of building someone else's bad ideas."

"That's what you think of our last eight years? It's all just shit now?"

"Is that what I said?"

"I thought we were living our lives."

"Don't twist my words, damn it." Peter ran his hands through his hair, haunted by a feeling of impending failure. "This dam isn't just a job. It's everything I've prepared my whole life for. It's huge for me, and you know it." She started to speak, but he anticipated her next question. "So what if it's Octonal? you ask. Well, if Jerry's right and they take over, I am royally *fucked.*" He was so worked up he couldn't stop. "You want me to just flush the whole thing? When this project is the payoff for all those years of lousy assignments and just getting by? This is my baby, Alice! My design! My people! My project from the get-go! If I complete it I go home a winner. If not . . ."

Alice bowed her head a while, exhaled loudly, then stepped to a different counter and commenced pouring herself a tall glass of wine.

Peter wasn't done. "I mean, Christ. That's why we came here, isn't it? To fulfill our dream?"

"I don't know anymore," Alice said quietly.

"That's great. Very supportive."

Alice gestured with the wineglass. "Who knows?" she said sympathetically. "Maybe Octonal wants a dam of their own. Maybe things will work out after all."

Peter resumed rubbing his temples. "Octonal doesn't build dams, sweetheart. Octonal kicks ass. If their people come in, they will close the project down so fast you won't believe it. They'd rather have a civil war than a water project."

"You wanted to work for an oil company," Alice brought up.

"That's not what this is about. I'm building a dam that will save thousands of lives."

"You're building a dam so an oil company can get a pipeline through."

Peter clenched his teeth. "Who the hell cares who pays for it?"

"Apparently no one." Alice raised her glass in a toast and cracked a wry grin. "Here's to flushing Africa, then. And all those other shit postings."

"You're drunk."

"Magnificently intoxicated, maybe, but never drunk," Alice bantered. She swallowed some wine. "Maybe it's a sign. Maybe it's time to go home."

"That's great, Alice," Peter said in mild disgust. Their world had come apart at the seams, and she took it as a fortunate omen.

"I mean, if it's all gone to hell—"

"Your timing is impeccable." Peter closed his eyes and considered going up to bed. Sometimes talking to her was like talking to an adobe wall. It got them nowhere.

"Be honest. You don't like this place either."

"I like the project."

"How nice. But I don't have a project."

Peter faced her. Somehow he had struck a nerve. She was so angry her whole body quaked with suppressed emotion. It made him madder to think that she blamed him. "And that's my fault? Five months we've been here. Five whole months! You could be involved in any number of things. You've hit the ground running everywhere we've been sent except here."

"I'm sorry I'm not bouncing back faster."

"Five months, and you haven't even started learning the language." Peter had, though, and could get by fairly well by now.

"I'm not getting pregnant again in the Third World," Alice said. "If you want to have a family, we're going home. And that's final."

Peter blinked. Had he heard correctly? "Who said anything about you getting pregnant?" He vigorously shook his head. "No, you don't. Absolutely not. You are not going to bring that into this."

Alice grew chalky white. *"That?"*

"When the hell are you going to move on? It's over. It happened. It wasn't meant to be. Get over it."

For the first time Alice raised her voice. "I don't want to move on, damn you!"

"Well, I have. And I've got to tell you, I'm right here, right now, tonight. My whole life is falling apart, but instead of discussing that, we're back to this agenda."

"I am not an agenda," Alice said flatly.

Peter studied her intently, trying to determine what

she really wanted, what she was really saying. She always accused him of not listening; of not appreciating her side of things. Now he was going to prove her wrong. "You know what? Go home."

"What?"

"I'm serious. That's what you want, isn't it? Take a break. Even if the project is dead and my career is in a shambles, you go home. It'll take a while to close the project down, anyway. Why hang around?"

Alice appeared dazed. "Wow."

"You're going then?"

"I never said that's what I wanted."

"Then I guess it's me." More irritated than ever, Peter rose and stalked from the room. He had tried, he had honestly tried. He had given in, and she had backpedaled and thrown it in his face. Fine. Let her think it over. Maybe then she would realize he only had their mutual best interests at heart.

Maybe then she would realize just how much he loved her.

Terry Thorne was a new man. Rested and fed and dressed in a smart new suit, a bandage over his eye, he stood at the head of a long conference table beside a large presentation chart, summing up his report on the Chechen K&R.

Eighteen international kidnap cases were listed on the chart, but his had been crossed off. After the name of each client was the date of their abduction, the first demand, the target figure, the last proof of life, and the country in which the kidnapping had occurred. Currently, the countries were Mexico, Guatemala, Pakistan, Colombia, and the Philippines.

Terry paused to moisten his throat, then continued.

"Mr. Lenoir was examined by mobile medical and transported to Athens for surgical treatment."

Ten men and two women were seated at the table. On the wall to their right hung the company logo: LUTHAN RISK INTERNATIONAL. On the other side of the room a wide window afforded a panoramic vista of central London.

"At the moment, we have contracts with all three insurance underwriters holding K and R policies in the West Asian, post-Soviet republics," Terry mentioned. "The area is in a critical state of transition and demands the most vigorous security precautions."

Harry Luthan stirred. The company's director, he sat at the head of the table. As slick as they came, he was a savvy Brit who had built LRI from the ground up.

Beside Luthan sat his human shadow, Ian Havery, pushing sixty, but still lean and energetic, their Kidnap and Ransom Division's chief of operations.

When neither interrupted, Terry wrapped up his account. "All three insurance carriers need to increase awareness among their policyholders. Underwriters need to be made aware of increased costs and liability. Extractions in the future may prove increasingly difficult." He stepped toward his chair, stopping when Luthan posed a question.

"What did they bill last year? Out there, I mean. The three of them."

"Total premiums?" Ian Havery clarified.

When Luthan nodded, all eyes were fixed on Yasmine Vema. A Sri Lankan, her official title was assistant director, but her job responsibilities were those of a glorified secretary. Given her six-figure salary, she didn't seem to mind. Consulting a ledger, she reported, "Total premiums were thirty-eight million dollars."

"And what was the ransom total?" Luthan inquired.

"Covered on policies?" Yasmine flipped to another page. "Twenty-six million."

"Bloody hell," Luthan said. "Doesn't leave much of a profit margin, does it?" He wagged a finger at Havery. "Set up some premium meetings. Wave the red flag. Tell them their people have got to start keeping a lower profile and taking more precautions or pretty soon they'll be in the red." Almost as an afterthought, he swiveled toward Terry. "Excellent job, Mr. Thorne. As always, outstanding. Thank you."

Terry went to acknowledge the compliment, but Luthan had already turned away.

"All right, where are we? Let's have the Pakistan update next. Maybe we can squeeze in Colombia, too, before we break."

Terry eased into his chair and rested his chin in his hands. Sometimes he wondered why he bothered. If it weren't for the satisfaction that saving innocent lives gave him, he'd quit the business in a minute. He honestly would. People like Marcel Lenoir, who had gratefully pumped his hand until his arm nearly fell off, were the only reason he stayed in. The money was nice, but money wasn't everything. Terry needed meaning in his life, needed to believe he was making a difference.

If only there weren't people like Luthan and Havery to deal with.

A stray shaft of sunlight warming her face awakened Alice Bowman. She sat bolt upright in bed and immediately wished she hadn't as torment spiked her head. "Oh God!" she said aloud. "How much did I have to drink last night, anyway?"

Squinting against the harsh glare, Alice glanced to

her left. Peter's side of the bed was empty. "What in the—?" she blurted, trying to remember if he had been with her when she turned in. She remembered the country club fiasco, the tense ride home. Dimly, she recalled their heated argument in the kitchen. Not the details, though. Peter had been right. She had been drunk.

"Damn me," Alice said, sliding out from under the blanket. She had on her panties, and nothing else. Donning a light robe, she padded to the kitchen. It was early yet, not even seven, and Maria hadn't arrived for the day. Coffee was on, though, and a small handwritten note had been propped against the coffeemaker. She picked it up. It was from Peter. " 'I'm sorry,' " she read aloud.

Sorry for what? Alice asked herself. As best she could recollect, the argument had been as much her fault as it had been his. One of the many minor misunderstandings every marriage suffered from time to time.

Yawning, Alice poured a cup and walked to the calendar to check her schedule for the day. She had a workout with the tennis pro at nine. Other than that, the day was hers to do with as she pleased.

Alice moved to the glass doors and gazed out over the city. The details slowly came back to her. She remembered Peter telling her she should go back to the States ahead of him, and it jolted her to the core. In fourteen years, they had never been separated. Not once. Where he went, she went. Every rotten posting there was, she was always by his side, willing to endure the hardships and dangers.

That was what marriage was about, wasn't it? Alice reflected. Or maybe she'd been deluding herself all those years. After all, it was Peter who routinely neglected her, not the other way around. She had gone with him all over the world, and he was always so absorbed in his work he was often gone for long periods, leaving her to fend for herself. Leaving her alone.

Alice hated being alone. Loneliness was the bane of existence, a vile emptiness that ate at a person like termites ate at wood, sucking all the fun out of life, destroying all the happiness. Yet she had put up with it. She had endured countless spells of suffocating loneliness in the name of love, and now the one she loved had told her she should go off to endure more.

"Damn him," Alice said, her cheeks pinching in indignation. How dared he push her away! How dared he treat her as if her feelings didn't matter. She reached for the phone to give him a tongue-lashing but it dawned on her she had no idea where he had gone. He was supposed to get weekends off, but he rarely did. The workaholic in him compelled him to go in almost every Saturday and sometimes on Sunday, to boot. She decided to wait another hour and then call up to the construction site. He had apologized so she should do the same. And tell him they needed to talk over the separation business.

If he was serious, what should she do? That was the big question Alice wasn't prepared to answer. It could be a sign their marriage was in much worse shape than she had imagined. It could be his way of saying he didn't want to be with her anymore, and he was using their spat as an excuse to get rid of her.

Alice went to the kitchen table and sat down, too depressed to finish her coffee. She had always thought marriage would be different. Happier. More fun. *Better*. She'd always wanted kids, wanted a family and the joys and hardships that came with it. But all the postings, all that bouncing around, had convinced them it was wiser to wait until their lives had stabilized.

That, and the other thing, the awful thing, the one thing Alice never talked about or let herself even think about, the thing that had devastated her. Her mother said she shouldn't have let it get to her as deeply as it did, that it happened to women all the time, but she would never forget. She would take that terrible morning with her to her grave.

Shuddering, Alice lowered her head to her hands. God, what had she done? Half her life was over and what did she have to show for it? No children, no family, no home of her own, and a husband who thought more of his career than he did of her.

Alice caught herself. Was that true? Was she being fair to Peter? He worked so hard for them both, not just for himself. He always tried to make their future brighter. That was the whole point of it all. It was why they had gone without. Why they had endured so much hardship.

But now Alice wondered if they had been misguided. In their quest for the golden ring, as it were, they had lost years they could never relive. They had denied themselves so much; denied themselves things now lost to them forever.

Alice's eyes moistened, and she stifled a sob. How had they let it happen? Once they had cherished such glorious plans! Once their future looked rosy and bright. But now their life was in a shambles, and she didn't quite know what to do to set it back on course. Or if it was even possible to do so anymore.

Oh Peter! Alice mentally cried. What had they been thinking all those years? She was tired of going without. She was tired of living as an outsider in foreign lands. Most of all, she was tired of being denied his companionship.

Alone, yet married. Now there was a contradiction in terms if ever Alice had heard one. She craved more intimacy. Needed to feel loved. Longed to be touched and held and told how much he cared. Call it silly. Call it childish. But Peter had once been that way, before he took the engineering job with QUAD-CARBON. Before his career became everything to him.

"I need you so much, and you're never here for me," Alice said aloud. If only he would come to his senses. If only he would realize what he had done and make amends before it was too late. Because as much as she loved him—and she truly still did—there were limits to how much neglect and loneliness she would tolerate.

Alice didn't want to go back to the States by herself, but she would if he insisted. If it turned out to be the literal straw that broke the camel's back, then the blame was on Peter's shoulders, not on hers. He had driven the wedge between them, not her.

Alice raised her head, blinking back tears. God, what would it take to save their marriage? What would it take to bring the two of them closer together again?

The answer was as obvious as it was frightening.

It would take a miracle.

Chapter 4

Peter Bowman hadn't slept a wink all night. He'd
tried, but all he had done was toss and turn. He was
too upset at Alice and at himself. Several times he'd
rolled over and stared at her, drinking in her incredi-
ble loveliness. She was as beautiful as the day they
had met. Watching her filled him with a searing ache
deep inside. He wanted to reach out, to touch her, to
stroke her—but he didn't. She might wake up and
renew their argument.

So Peter had rolled onto his back, propped his head
in his hands, and stared at the ceiling as the bedside
clock ticked the seconds and minutes and hours away.
He was almost glad when the curtain brightened
faintly, a harbinger of the impending dawn. Rising, he
quietly gathered some clothes, went into the bathroom, and closed the door.

Peter had intended to spend the day with Alice, but
after their row he figured a little time apart was best
for both of them. He opted to go into work. After
splashing some cold water on his face, he brushed his
teeth and dressed. He wasn't hungry, but he stopped
in the kitchen to put a new pot of coffee on and to

write a short note of apology. It wasn't much, but it would show Alice there were no hard feelings.

Peter stepped outdoors. The sun had not yet risen, but the eastern horizon was ablaze with vivid hues of orange, yellow, and pink. About to climb into his red Volkswagen, he paused and glanced at the Scorpion House. He had a strange urge to rush back in and scoop his wife into his arms and tell her how much he cherished her. But it could wait. He had a lot to do, and a lot to think over, first.

Sliding in, Peter inserted the key into the ignition and cranked the engine over. He drove down the deserted street, turned right, and held to the speed limit. Instead of going up to the dam site he headed in the other direction, into Tecala. He had to find out if the takeover was a fait accompli. There might be a few early birds who would know at the QUAD-CARBON office building in the heart of the city.

Suddenly Peter recalled his talk with Jerry the night before and a phone number Jerry had given him shortly before he'd left the ball. He slipped his wallet out, sorted through the money, credit cards, and I.D., and finally found the slip he had written it on. Picking up the car phone, he stabbed the number. The voice that came over the car speakers was crisp and commanding, befitting Ted Fellner's position as one of QUAD-CARBON's upper echelon.

"This is Ted."

"Ted, this is Peter. Peter Bowman."

A long silence occurred before Fellner responded with a noticeable lack of enthusiasm, "Oh. Hi, Pete. How are you doing?"

Peter's mouth went dry. "I've heard about the buyout bid. I'm surprised you didn't let me know before you flew off to Houston."

"Sorry, Pete. But I had to leave on such short notice there wasn't time to contact everyone I should have."

"So what's the latest?" Peter asked, dreading the reply.

"It's a done deal. As of ten o'clock last night Octonal bought out QUAD-CARBON. I'm now an Octonal employee, if you can believe that." Fellner laughed with no real mirth. "All of us are."

Peter woodenly negotiated a turn. Traffic was increasing and pedestrians flocked on both sides of the road. Peter got right to the point. "What about the dam, Ted? What about my project?"

"Pete, the takeover just took place. You've got to give Octonal time to assess their options and priorities."

"Don't bullshit me, Ted. You must have heard *something*. You must know whether they intend to continue or fold."

Fellner sighed. "I wish you had waited to have this talk until we could do it face-to-face. Yes, I've heard something. Octonal received a preliminary report from the team they sent down to assess the project, and they weren't particularly impressed."

Peter thought of the five-man team who had been at the site the past few days. "Those were Octonal people? Why wasn't I informed?"

"Because you'd only get bent out of shape, just as you're doing now," Fellner said. "Hell, Pete, sometimes you treat that dam as if it's your only child."

"In a way, it is," Peter said quietly. Then anger kicked in, and he growled, "Give it to me straight. Are they or aren't they going to go through with the project?"

"No."

There it was. Peter clenched the steering wheel with

all his might, wishing it were the throat of every Octonal executive who had voted to kill his dream. His life.

Fellner was speaking again. "I don't know what to tell you, Peter. QUAD-CARBON needed financial help. This was the only way of bailing out. Sure, Octonal has their way of doing things—"

"I won't let them close it down," Peter declared.

"Excuse me?"

"You heard me. And there are others. It's not just me, Ted. I'm not the only one going to fight for this. You'd better tell Octonal how much local support we've got down here."

Fellner's tone became flinty. "If that's a threat, Peter . . ." He stopped. "I'm not sure what that is, but you're way out of line."

A church plaza appeared, and Peter downshifted. The high-rise buildings of downtown Tecala were silhouetted against the rising sun. "I've got people down here who burned their bridges to come and work with us."

Static crackled from the speakers. Amid the interference Fellner could be heard saying, "—can barely hear you—"

Peter whipped out of the plaza onto a winding road. "What the hell am I supposed to tell my people?" he angrily demanded.

"Tell them to get their resumes out."

Another burst of static filled the Volkswagen. "Ted? Ted?" Peter shouted. "I'm heading for the office. I'll call you back on a landline. Can you hear me?"

A dial tone was Peter's answer. Beside himself, he pounded the steering wheel a few times. Almost too late he saw a religious procession crossing the street up head. Traffic was blocked off in both directions. Slamming on the brakes, Peter snapped, "I have no

time for this!" He had to get to the office quickly, had
to get Fellner back on the phone. A junction was the
answer to his prayers. He wheeled right, intending to
circle around the procession and on into Tecala.

The new road, though, didn't loop in the direction
Peter needed. It led him way from the city, not toward
it. Extremely agitated, he looked for another turnoff,
but there was none. He traveled for three-quarters of
a mile before seeing that the road ahead was also
blocked. This time an accident was to blame. A tanker
truck was on its side. Flares had been set out and a
uniformed policeman was on the scene.

"Screw this," Peter said, braking. He was going to
make a U-turn and go back, but when he looked behind him he discovered a bus right on his bumper.
The driver leaned on the horn, which caused the cop
to look around.

Swearing, Peter pulled past the policeman and on
around the upended tanker. Suddenly he braked
again. "Oh, shit!"

Two hundred yards farther a roadblock had been
set up. A checkpoint, with a lot of green uniforms and
a police car with its lights flashing. Over twenty vehicles had been stopped and other cops were going from
car to car checking identification papers.

Stay calm, Peter told himself. Traffic checks were
routine. The authorities were always on the hunt for
rebels and bandits. But he didn't like it, being
hemmed in at gunpoint. To his left was a slope over-
grown with chaparral, to the right a short embankment
and a river. The Volkswagen might be able to squeeze
through, but the police would take a dim view if he
tried to abruptly cut out of there.

The green uniforms came closer. Peter saw some
drivers standing spread-eagle against their vehicles

and a knot of thirty or forty people who had been herded to one side. There were lots of drawn guns, and a lot of tension. It wouldn't take much to trigger violence.

Almost on cue, two teenaged youths doubled up on a motorcycle broke from the line as a cop neared them. The kid at the handlebars spun the bike around onto the embankment and raced back toward the up-ended tanker. Cops were yelling at them to halt, but they weren't stopping for the law or anyone else.

The cycle was almost abreast of the Volkswagen, and Peter thought they were going to make it when, out of nowhere, the staccato retort of automatic fire rang out, punctuated by the impact of multiple heavy slugs. The two youths were torn from the bike and smashed to the dirt, their bodies thrashing and convulsing, oozing blood.

Stupefied, Peter gawked. A cop hastened past him, his smoking submachine gun leveled. It was the same cop stationed beside the upended tanker. Other policemen were converging. So were men who had materialized out of the chaparral, men in ski masks and camouflage fatigues, ten, fifteen, twenty in all, armed to the gills.

"Oh, God," Peter breathed.

One of the men in the ski masks wore a red bandanna. He began shouting furiously at the policeman who had gunned down the teenagers, heaping abuse and gesturing as if he intended to shoot the cop.

No, he's not a cop, Peter thought. None of them were. He knew what was happening, knew what he had blundered into. He had to get out of there before they found him. Sliding onto the floor, he tried to punch up the cell phone, but his hands were shaking uncontrollably. His heart hammered in his chest, and his blood was racing a mile a second. "Please," he said. "Please, please, please."

A ski mask filled the window. The snout of a machine gun was thrust in at him and the bolt was violently jerked back. *"Venga! Venga! Rapido!"*

Peter dropped the phone and elevated his hands to show he wouldn't resist. The eyes in the ski mask were those of a wild animal primed to kill, and a forefinger was crooked around the trigger. One twitch and he would be shot to ribbons.

"Don't shoot!" Peter said, sitting up. The door was yanked wide, and he was grabbed by the shirt and hauled out. More ski masks ringed him. His wallet was taken and given to the leader, the man with the red bandanna, who sorted through it, then cried out and held aloft one of Peter's cards.

"Listen—" Peter pleaded, but they weren't listening. Six of them surrounded him and pushed him toward the checkpoint. To fight back would be futile. Peter passed other drivers, many as scared as he was, a few bestowing sympathetic looks. Beyond the checkpoint was a bridge and on the other side of it sat a pickup. More guerrillas in ski masks were there, and the bed was packed with other hostages.

Peter dug in his heels. "Just hang on, okay? *Lento, por favor! Una momen—*" A jarring blow to the spine knocked him forward onto his knees. One of the guerrillas had slammed a gun butt into his back. The world spun chaotically. Too dazed to fight back, Peter felt himself grabbed under either arm by a pair of swarthy huskies.

The man in the red bandanna bawled orders. All the guerrillas and most of the phony cops were on the move, leaving before real cops showed up. Two of the false cops in green planted themselves and fired into the stolen police car, cackling as they shot the hell out of it, shooting until their magazines went empty.

Peter was thrown onto the pickup truck. Several masked guerrillas jumped on and another ran to the cab. Peter sat up as the truck hopped forward. A gun muzzle was shoved into his face, and Peter shoved it aside. Looking back, he saw the police car in flames, and the drivers and passengers who hadn't been taken milling about in confusion.

Reality sank in. Over and over in Peter's mind the same phrase repeated itself: *I've been kidnapped. I've been kidnapped. I've been kidnapped.*

The tennis courts at the Tecala Country Club were the best in the city. They were always fully booked, which was why Alice had her weekly rounds with the tennis pro scheduled well in advance.

The club was extra busy today. Alice recognized a number of people who had been at the gala ball. A few courts over, much to her surprise, were the couple the bandleader had invited onto the floor as well as the man she had danced with. Alice was tempted to go over and say hello once her session was over. She hadn't gotten to say a single word to him during their dance, and she wanted to thank him.

The pro zinged a forehand toward her. Alice moved to meet it and swung smoothly, forcefully returning the ball.

"You are on your game, Señora Bowman!" he called out.

"Ain't I, though?" Alice said and laughed. Little did he know she was taking out her frustrations on the ball. Every time she made contact, she was really hitting Peter, repaying him for the years of neglect, for the loneliness, for pushing her away when he should have been holding her close.

The ball cleared the net in a streak and Alice side-stepped, her racket connecting solidly. "Take that, you ingrate," she said, chuckling.

A commotion intruded on Alice's concentration. She glanced toward it and was taken aback by the sight of Ivy Winsted rushing toward her straight across the courts, not caring how many matches she interrupted. What in the world? Alice thought and let a return volley go by.

"Alice! Oh, Alice!"

Ivy's tone was urgent, troubled. Alice motioned for the pro to wait and moved toward the edge of the court. "What has you all flustered?" Alice asked as the other woman came right up to her and gripped her by the shoulders.

"God, this is hard."

"What's hard?" Alice said, trying to shrug loose of Ivy's grip.

"Jerry just called. He's at the office and took the call from the police. It's Peter . . ."

Alice stopped trying to pull away. "Peter?" she said aghast, fearful he had been in a car wreck or there had been a mishap at the dam site. "What about him?"

Icy sucked in a breath and spat it out. "Honey, he's been kidnapped."

"Kidnapped?" Alice tried to digest the news, but it was unpalatable. Peter had gone to work, not deep into the mountains where the rebels were based. True, there had been news reports of people being kidnapped close to the city in recent months, but she couldn't see it happening to her husband.

"About an hour ago," Ivy said. "Guerrillas set up

a fake roadblock and suckered in a bunch of drivers. Peter was one of them."

"A roadblock?"

"That's how it's done, dearie. They get the cars to stop, then haul people out and whisk them away before the law shows up." Ivy gave Alice a tender squeeze. "I'm so sorry for you. So, so sorry."

Alice felt faint. Her fingers went limp, the racket clattering to the court, and she raised a hand to her brow. "Guerrillas."

"Jerry said you need to get in touch with him right away. He has a number for you to call. We've got to get the ball rolling."

Galvanizing to life, Alice snatched Ivy's wrists. "What do I do? Who do I contact?"

"Jerry will fill you in. He's making calls himself, to the head office, to Ted Fellner, to anyone and everyone he can think of." Ivy steered Alice toward the club. "We have to get you home, pronto."

Terry had just sat down in his office when Yasmine popped her head in and announced, "Ian has been looking for you."

"Any idea what about?"

"He didn't say." Yasmine glanced down the hall, then sidled inside. "I was thinking. Maybe you'd like to come over to my flat tomorrow evening? Supper on me."

"What happened to your city banker?"

Yasmine's smile was delightfully disarming. "I'm bored." Winking, she stepped back out. "Think it over and let me know."

The musky scent of her perfume lingered long after she was gone. Terry found it hard to concentrate. He thought about his ex-wife and the many happy times they had shared until his job got to be too much, and she couldn't take it anymore. The long hours away, never knowing when he would be called off on yet another emergency. Terry didn't blame her for divorcing him. She was happily remarried several times over and rearing their son, who he saw twice a month if he was lucky.

A knock on the door ended Terry's reverie. "Come in," he said, already guessing who it would be.

Ian Havery held a file. The K&R chief gingerly slid into a chair as if he were sitting down on tacks, mustering a wan smile. "So you're all right, then? From what I understand it was just a few nicks and scrapes."

Terry touched the bandage over his left eye. "If five stitches constitute a scrape, then yes, I'm fine."

"Right." Havery nervously switched the manila file from one hand to the other. "In any event, you made it out alive, and that's what counts."

"I couldn't agree more," Terry said dryly.

"Just so you know, we had Ronny in Frankfurt standing by at the airport ready to back you up."

"What do you want, Ian?" Terry bluntly demanded. Havery had a habit of small-talking him to death before getting to the point.

"Am I that transparent?" Havery asked.

"No. You always want something."

Havery coughed and laid the file on the edge of Terry's desk. "We've received a call from Tecala."

Terry straightened. "You're not asking me to go down there?"

"I think if you'll hear me out—" Havery started suavely.

"I just got off the bloody plane from Russia yesterday!" Terry growled, rankled by the man's gall.

Nodding, Havery leaped right in. "Listen to me. I

understand. I truly do. But you saw the board. I needn't tell you how busy we are at the moment. Our field agents are stretched incredibly thin." He paused. "You've heard about Jenkins and Clyde?"

Terry shook his head. He refused to be mollified or persuaded. He was due some desk time to recuperate, and he damn well intended to take it.

"They've left us to go to work at Vanguard," Havery disclosed.

"Didn't you poach Jenkins *from* Vanguard last year?"

Havery squirmed. "Yes, well, that's hardly the issue. The issue is that a client of ours has had one of their own kidnapped, purportedly by leftist guerrillas, but we really don't know for sure yet. You know how volatile the situation is down there. It's a madhouse and—"

"Look, I'm just not good to go right now," Terry cut him off.

"You're tired. It's the jet lag talking."

"It's bloody *me* talking." Terry shook his head in disbelief. He shouldn't waste his breath. Havery didn't know the meaning of the word *no*.

"Terry, the firm needs you down there. I need you down there. The poor SOB who was kidnapped needs you down there." Havery grinned slyly. "I want you to consider this your first management assignment. The first of many, I might add."

"Ian."

"May I confide in you? Mr. Luthan and I have been quite impressed by your performance. You've pulled off extractions we didn't think were remotely possible."

"Ian." Terry was boiling inside, a pot about to explode, but the next words out of the K&R chief's mouth threw an icy wave on his rising fury.

"The wife is taking it hard, we hear. She'll need counseling. The usual. Tell her we'll do the best we can. Assure her we'll get her husband back alive. That sort of thing."

"The client has a wife? What about children?"

"None that I know of." Havery tapped the folder. "It's all here in the preliminary report. The husband's down there to build a dam, of all things. Why in hell the rebels took him, if indeed they did, I'll never know. He's there to help their country, not exploit it."

"Ian?" Terry said again and this time Havery looked at him.

"What?"

"You're a bastard."

"Is that the best you can do?"

"A vile, manipulative, coldhearted bastard who would send his own mother into the heart of darkness if it saved the company a few dollars."

Havery nodded. "I'd call that a pretty fair assessment. I make no bones of the fact it's business before all else. QUAD-CARBON has been a customer in good standing for years. They deserve swift action. They deserve the best man we've got. And that means you."

"Flattery will get you nowhere," Terry groused, reaching for the folder and slowly pulling it toward him. Only two sheets were inside: a transcript of a phone call from a Jerry Winsted at the QUAD-CARBON corporate offices in Tecala City, and a sheet listing the next flights out to South America. "I take that back. You're worse than a bastard. You counted on me going before you walked in here."

"I had high hopes, yes," Havery admitted.

"I should tell you to fuck off."

"But you won't. And do you know why?" Havery

was at ease now, confident of victory. "You're not in the business for the money. You're in it to help people. That's your trigger. That's what motivates you to take the risks you do, to put your life on the line time and again for people you don't even know."

"You make that sound like a bad thing."

"Bad, no. Stupid, yes." Havery made a tepee of his thin hands on his knees. "Look at me. I'm twenty years your senior. I know what I'm talking about. You can't let personal feelings influence you in our line of work."

"Bullshit." Terry refused to become a calculating shrew like Havery or Luthan or the rest. It wasn't in his nature.

"Listen to yourself. Defending lunacy." Havery clucked like a mother hen. "One of these days your attitude will get you killed. You can't treat these people as if they're your own family, for Christ's sake. You have to treat them as what they are. Disposable commodities. Profit or loss figures on a balance sheet."

"Damn, you're a cold fish."

"I'm a *live* fish. I was in the trenches for decades. I've seen it all, done it all. And I'm here today because I learned the important lessons early on. Never let an assignment get to you. Never take risks you don't absolutely need to take." Havery plucked a piece of lint from his suit. "The secret is not to care. Flat out condition yourself not to give one good damn about the clients or their families. Not only wear a poker face, but have a poker heart, as well. Do that, and you'll live to a ripe old age, just like me."

"You make it sound like an accomplishment to be proud of," Terry commented.

"Insult me all you like," Havery said, not offended

whatsoever, "but I'm right and you know it. You're just too stubborn to admit it."

"Go away."

Havery rose and opened the door. "Which flight should Yasmine book you on? The early one or the late one?"

"The early one," Terry said, resigned to the inevitable.

"That's my boy," Ian Havery crowed and was gone.

Chapter 5

They had only been on the road a few hours, but they were in a whole different world.

Lush jungle hemmed the winding road, the shadowy, gloomy tangle of vegetation as alien in its way as an otherworldly landscape. From out of its depths came occasional cries and screams, eerie, bestial sounds that almost made Peter Bowman glad he was in the speeding pickup.

Ahead loomed cloud-shrouded mountains. Judging by the sun, the rebels had been traveling generally northwest from Tecala City. The pickup was part of a convoy. Two cars were in front, two trucks were behind.

Peter's initial fear had subsided and been replaced by boiling outrage. Every time the pickup slowed to go around a sharp curve he considered jumping out and making a break for it, but common sense held him in place. He wouldn't get ten yards before they gunned him down, just like those youths on the motorcycle.

The guerrillas in the ski masks hadn't uttered a word except to tell a woman hostage to stop blubbering and an older man to stop praying.

At one point Peter tried to engage them in conversation by asking where they were taking him. He was rudely told to shut up or he would lose some of his teeth.

Suddenly there was a shout from the lead car. A village made from a ramshackle assortment of huts and tin shacks hove out of the greenery. One building was made of cinder blocks. On it a crudely painted sign had been hung identifying it as the village school.

The kidnappers yanked off their ski masks and began to smile and laugh. They had reached their destination.

Peter was struck by how young they were. Kids, really, most in their late teens, a few in their mid-twenties. The oldest was the guy with the red bandanna. Within moments, the convoy halted and everyone spilled from the vehicles.

Villagers stopped whatever they were doing to watch. Most were dirt-poor, their shabby clothes and scarecrow bodies mute testimony to the soul-grinding conditions under which they lived.

The hostages were herded over to the schoolhouse and lined up against the outer wall, Peter among them. For over five minutes he waited in anxious anticipation. Presently the man in the red bandanna approached, his hands clasped behind his back, his dark, active eyes scrutinizing them intently as he roved down the line. He stopped when he came to Peter.

"Habla usted español?"

"Sí, hablo español," Peter answered. To a degree, at any rate. Provided they didn't speak too fast.

"Your name?" the man asked in Spanish.

Peter told him and added, "You're making a mistake. I'm not rich or anything. I work on the dam—"

The man held up a hand. "I don't care what you

do, gringo. What happens to you next is not up to me. You will go first."

"Go where?" Peter nervously inquired. He'd heard tales of hostages being taken so deep into the mountains no one could ever find them.

"There," the man said, pointing at the doorway. "Go in there. Now."

The other rebels were lounging about, at ease, smoking and joking. But they still held their weapons, and Peter entertained no illusions about what they would do if he resisted. Girding himself, he warily entered.

Most of the desks had been pushed to one side. At the head of the room, three desks were arranged in a semicircle facing the door. A tribunal of older rebels occupied them. All were in their thirties, one possibly his early forties.

On another desk nearby lay Peter's wide-open briefcase. Beside it were his passport, his keys, even his cell phone and photographs, among them one of Alice of which he was especially fond.

Peter started toward it, but stopped when three armed guards detached themselves from a corner and spread out, covering him.

"Come close, American," the oldest man said in English, beckoning. After Peter complied, he said, "*Ejercito de Liberacion de Tecala.* You know what is E.L.T? What it means?"

"The Tecalano Army of Liberation," Peter answered. Now he knew who had him, and his blood froze in his veins. Of the various rebel factions, E.L.T. was notorious for being particularly vicious.

"You are a prisoner," the man said in a dull tone, "in our glorious armed struggle to rebirth Tecala."

"Okay, so can I—" Peter looked at each of them

"—can I talk now? Because this is wrong. I'm a humanitarian worker. I'm here to help the Tecalan people. I'm here to build a dam. *La represa, a la Rio Chimaya.*"

One of the other leaders held up Peter's I.D. card, the words "QUAD-CARBON" emblazoned in large red letters. "*Sí, por el pozo petrolero,*" he said with contempt.

"No!" Peter said, pleading his case to the man who spoke English. "That's what I'm trying to tell you. I don't work on the pipeline. *No trabajo por la pozo petrolero.* I'm building a dam in Chimaya. *La represa de Chimaya.* To stop the flooding there." He had to make them understand. "*La represa de Chimaya!*"

"For the pipeline," the first man said.

"No, no, no! How many times must I tell you?" Peter was losing his temper. "I don't work on the pipeline. I'm here to help your people!"

The third honcho spoke now, past Peter at the guards. "He goes with Tajo tonight," he said in Spanish.

"Wait," Peter begged. "*Por favor.* Didn't you hear me? I just told you—"

"*Basta!*" the first man commanded. "Silence! You are a prisoner! *De la guerra.* Do as we tell you."

Peter bit his lip. The guards had trained their guns on him and looked all too eager to use them. He began to turn, then made bold to point at the desk where his belongings were piled. The first man glanced over and nodded.

Peter picked up the photograph of Alice on his way out.

So many photos, Alice thought. Almost two decades together and all they had to show for it were hundreds of silly pictures. She had just lifted a large cardboard box from the top shelf in the closet and upended it on the bed. Scattered inches deep over the comforter were all the snapshots she had collected over the years.

Alice pulled one out. It showed Peter and her on a motorcycle, a stark mountain in the background. "That's Mount Kilimanjaro," she said. "We toured parts of Africa by bike. It was great fun." Her voice broke, and she fought back tears. Choosing another, she held it up. Peter and she were on a tennis court holding a mixed-doubles trophy aloft. In the far background was a pyramid. "This one is from Egypt."

"Please," Norma said, not wanting Alice to make herself crazy with grief.

Alice smiled. They were alone in the bedroom. From downstairs came muted voices and the drone of a radio. "I'm all right. Really I am."

Norma's eyes accused her of lying. "There is no need for this."

Alice selected another photograph. "I forget where this one was." Peter and she were in outlandish costumes, linked arm in arm, stupidly drunk and grinning like idiots. "What if he never makes it back? Will I forget it all?" She leaned on the box, racked by remorse.

"Enough." Norma gently took the photo and dropped it into the box. "You must stop this, Alice. I will take the box down and help you go through them. The police only need one good picture of his face."

"I'm sorry," Alice sniffed. She kept trying to be strong and kept failing miserably, alternating between bouts of optimism and severe depression.

"No. There is no reason for you to be." Norma squeezed her shoulder. "I am the one who is sorry. I don't understand my country anymore." She gave Alice a light push. "Go. I will gather these up and bring them down."

Folding her arms across her chest, Alice bleakly nodded. She descended the stairs in a haze. Maria and the young helper, Cinta, were in the kitchen, preparing food. Sandro, their driver, and several of his trusted buddies were there, huddled at the table.

Alice drifted past them into the living room. A couple of men from the dam, Peter's assistants, were talking in whispers. Off in the study, Eliodoro was hunched over a telephone, taking notes on a pad. She hoped he had some news. Not knowing anything made the ordeal ten times worse.

A breath of fresh air was in order. Alice went out the side door and around to the pool, morosely gazing at the stars. She didn't realize anyone else was outside until she heard Jerry Winsted's voice. He was pacing back and forth, a cell phone to his ear.

"—no, it was completely random. He was out, I guess, near the barrio. They have these roadblocks. They steal cars, money, whatever." Jerry paused. "No. No, we really don't know a damn thing at this point. The police have been no help whatsoever. He could be anywhere—there's nothing definite at all." He turned and saw her. "Um, look, let me call you back, okay?" He punched off.

"Who was that? Fellner?" Alice didn't wait for a reply. "You're telling him we don't know what happened?"

"Alice, at this point we're—"

"For crying out loud, Peter has been kidnapped!" Alice was exasperated by his idiocy.

Jerry came toward her. "Look, until we have definite contact—"

Alice was mad enough to slug him. "Contact? We

don't need *contact* to know what happened! He was taken by the E.L.T. at gunpoint. Twenty-five people saw him driven away in a pickup truck. They said the men who took him were all wearing ski masks, a trademark of the E.L.T." Alice lowered her arms. "I don't know—maybe it's me—but it sounds pretty fucking definitive!"

"To a degree." Jerry stopped and looked past her.

Ivy had come out of the house. She was holding another phone. "Your sister-in-law again, sugar," she said.

Snatching the phone, Alice moved out of earshot. "Janis? Did you get the flight you wanted?" She saw Jerry and Ivy exchange a look at her expense, as if to say, "The poor dear is losing control." Turning her back on them, she said, "Of course I'll be there to meet your plane." She was glad her sister-in-law was coming down. At least Janis wouldn't treat her like a mental case.

The Tecalan International Airport hadn't changed much since Terry's last visit. It was still the smallest international airport in the world. Armed soldiers still hovered everywhere, ogling female passengers. The immigration officers were still polite, if condescending. When Terry's turn came, he handed his passport to a burly immigration officer.

"Is this your first visit to—" the man began as he flipped open the passport. Both pages were completely covered with stamps. The officer blinked, taken aback, then flipped to the next page, and found more of the same. Edge-to-edge embarkation imprints. "You have been to our country before, señor."

"And everywhere else," Terry said.

"Are you here on business or pleasure?"

"Business. Always business."

The man pounded a stamp on the passport and gave the passport back. "Enjoy your stay, señor. Remember Tecala's motto. 'As friendly as we can be.'"

"I've seen the advertisements," Terry said, retrieving his briefcase and carry-on. "Do you think anyone has told the E.L.T. or the T.L.F. or the T.T.R.?"

The immigration officer took it seriously. "Who can tell rebels anything, señor? It is the rest of our people who count."

Not for Peter Bowman, Terry thought. He hailed a cab and directed the driver to take him to the Intercon Hotel, one of Tecala's best.

"Bienvenidos, Señor Thorne," the elderly desk clerk greeted him.

"Algo ha venido para mi esta tarde?" Terry asked.

"Sí." The clerk reached under the counter and handed him a big envelope. "Do you want the same suite as last time?"

"If it's available, Ramon." Terry palmed a pen to sign in. "My luggage is out in the cab. If you could have someone bring it up?"

"Certainly, Señor Thorne." Ramon snapped his fingers and a gangly bellhop materialized.

"I could also use a bite to eat," Terry mentioned. "Eggs, perhaps? Bacon and toast." It didn't really matter. Eating was like everything else in his life of late. Something he did out of habit, mechanically, with no real zest. Except for the times when he was on assignment, his life had a monotonous blandness.

"As you wish, Señor Thorne," Ramon said. "I will have it sent up."

Terry's first order of business when he reached his room was to set up the Nokia Sat-fax. The latest model, it was uplinked to a satellite and could receive messages and images anywhere on the globe. He was expecting an update from Ian Havery anytime now.

Slipping out of his jacket, Terry went into the bathroom to wash up. He soaked a washcloth under the hot tap, then bent and applied the cloth to his face. The sensation was soothing. He held it there awhile. When he stood, he felt something brush his eyebrow.

"Bloody hell." The bandage had come loose and pried off the scab with it. He was bleeding again. "Will this damn thing never stop?"

Terry had more bandages in his travel kit. As he stepped into the bedroom the fax machine beeped and a sheet started to slide out onto the floor. Three more followed. He waited until the transmission ended before settling onto the bed to examine them.

Havery had relayed Bowman's dossier. A photograph had been included. Peter Bowman was handsome in a typically boyish American way. The rest of the fax was biographical information along with the latest intel. The police believed the E.L.T. were to blame. They had no other leads, not one clue to speak of. Nor had they tried hard to obtain any, Terry mused. According to knowledgeable sources, eighty percent of the police force was on the take, and at least half that many were secretly allied with different rebel groups.

The same assessment applied to the government. Politicians everywhere were routinely corrupt, but those in Tecala had refined it to an art their peers in other countries would envy. Under-the-table payoffs were the standard way of doing business. No money, no cooperation.

Peter Bowman's only ray of hope for being released quickly was if QUAD-CARBON became involved.

The corporate giant wielded tremendous clout. Politicians would bend over backward to help if QUAD-CARBON prodded hard enough.

Tossing the pages onto the bed, Terry flopped onto his back and closed his eyes. It was almost four in the morning. He needed sleep before he paid the wife a visit. Another few hours shouldn't make much of a difference.

Alice slept only three hours all night. Maria woke her up at seven, and then she showered and dressed for the ride to the airport. Sandro told Alice that he and his buddies were asking around, trying to learn something, anything, but so far it had been fruitless.

Customs was crowded with passengers just off the plane, and other people on hand to meet them. Alice stood to one side of the throng, her eyelids leaden, her stomach empty, her spirit drained. She perked up when she spied Janis Bowman giving an immigration officer a hard time. Janis was five years older than Peter and had the same smooth-faced Bowman look, the same sandy hair, and the same irascible temper.

Alice moved nearer. She had never exactly hit it off with Janis, but they didn't despise each other, either, as some in-laws were wont to do. Janis was happily married to a lawyer, and they had three precocious kids.

"I'm telling you, it's not business *or* pleasure, you simpleton," Janis tongue-lashed the customs man. "My brother has been kidnapped, and I'm down here to help out!"

"Sí, señora," the man said. "But I need to check a box on my form—"

"Shove your form where the sun doesn't shine, buster," Janis said. "I'm out of here." She marched on through, saw Alice, and advanced with her arms outspread. "Oh, my poor baby. Are you okay? Are you?"

Alice was enfolded in a bear hug and clapped on the back. "I'm fine. I'm okay."

Janis gripped her by the shoulders. "We're going to get through this. I'm here now, and I'll take good care of you. All we have to do is be strong."

"That's the plan." Alice had forgotten how pushy her sister-in-law could be. "Overbearing" was how Peter liked to describe it. "Let's get you to the house. You must need to rest."

"At a time like this? You must be joking." Janis linked their arms. "Have your hired help, here, bring my bags." She nodded at Sandro. "You and I have a lot to discuss. Start at the very beginning and tell me everything there is to know."

A strange car was in the driveway when they arrived at the Scorpion House, and as soon as Alice had stepped inside, she knew something was up. Maria came hustling toward her, all flustered. Over at the patio doors, Eliodoro and Norma were peeking outside.

"He is here maybe, I don't know, twenty minutes after you go," Maria said, waving a card in the air.

"Who?" Alice said.

"A big man. He says he is here about Señor Bowman. He gave me this." Maria shoved the business card into Alice's hand.

"'Luthan Risk International,'" Alice read. The name meant nothing to her. "You say he's here about Peter?"

Janis snatched the card from Alice's palm. "What in the world is Luthan Risk? It sounds like an insurance firm."

Eliodoro turned. "He says he is a negotiator."

"What's he negotiate?" Janis said, and barged toward the patio door. "Let's find out, shall we?"

Alice trailed along. She was accustomed to her sister-in-law taking charge. At family outings it was always Janis who arranged everything, Janis who told people where to sit, Janis who always had to get the last word in.

The man who rose to greet them was indeed big, and extremely good-looking. Alice mentally chided herself for finding him so attractive. Her husband had barely been missing over a day and here she was admiring this stranger. Or was it just that she was so tired she couldn't think straight?

"Hi. I'm Janis Bowman," Janis introduced herself. "Can we help you?"

"Terrence Thorne. Call me Terry. How do you do?" Terry offered his hand.

"Under the circumstances I guess we're doing all right." Janis shook. "And this here is Alice."

Now it was Alice's turn. She averted her gaze out of guilt.

"How do you do? I'm with Luthan Risk International." Terry pulled another business card from a pocket. "We're an international consultancy—"

"We have one," Janis said, waving it.

"Right." Terry slid the second card back into his jacket. "Anyway, I'm with LRI. We're based in London. I'm with our security and crisis response unit, and I'm sorry to just appear like this, but—"

Janis broke in. "Listen, you're not selling anything, are you? Because you could hardly pick a worse time if you tried."

Alice was mortified. "Janis! Please. Let the man finish. He's traveled all the way here from England. The least we can do is hear him out."

"I didn't do anything wrong," Janis said defensively.

Terry Thorne was smiling. "Please. No. It's all right." He paused. "Let's try this again. My company, we're the designated K and R consultants for QUAD-CARBON. It's all covered under their insurance policy."

"Hold it," Janis said. "One thing at a time. What's K and R?"

"Sorry. Kidnap and Ransom."

"You mean there's insurance for things like this?" Janis said. "For kidnapping?"

"There certainly is."

Janis kicked into high gear. "Covering what, might I ask?"

Terry was formally polite. "Pretty much all of it. Everything from our services straight through to the ransom payment."

"You're kidding." Janis was astounded. "I never knew. You can understand why I'd be confused."

"Please. Don't even think about it."

Alice liked his way with people, his knack for making them feel at ease. It was obvious that he was extremely good at his job. "So you just flew in?"

"Late last night, yes."

"Have you spoken with QUAD-CARBON?" Alice had repeatedly tried to get through and had been given the runaround. "All they ever do is put me on hold. I'm about ready to go over there and strangle someone."

"London may have. I don't know." Terry nodded at a folder on the patio table. "All I have at the moment is this useless employment dossier. What I'd like to do is get a proper file going. I have questions, lots of questions. And I'm sure you do, as well. I'll try to explain as much as I can to the best of your satisfaction."

"You're very kind," Alice said.

Janis was nodding. "Good. We need some explaining. Maybe somebody can tell us why nobody from the police has even bothered to come by. Why no one has taken a statement. Are they even bothering to question witnesses from the roadblock?" She snorted. "I mean, really. This is what I've been hearing, and I can't believe it."

"Right," Terry said. "No surprises there."

"What the hell does that mean, Mr. Thorne?"

Terry pulled out a chair. "Mrs. Bowman, we have a lot to go over. Maybe if you—"

Janis did a double take. "Oh my God! Is that what you think? No, no. I'm not Mrs. Bowman. I'm Peter's sister."

Terry pivoted toward Alice. "Then *you* must be Mrs. Bowman? Now that I've impressed you with my total incompetence, why don't we all sit down, and I'll break it down for you?" He held a chair out for her.

Alice slowly sat and thanked him, adding, "Don't be so hard on yourself. You're the first glimmer of real hope I've had."

Terry cleared his throat. "First off, this isn't unique. Kidnapping is on the upswing all over the world. Sometimes it's for terrorist purposes. Or maybe they're looking to trade for one of their own who's been locked up. Sometimes it's propaganda. It depends where you are. Down here it's about one thing and one thing only. Money. Kidnapping in Tecala is nothing more than a business. A dirty business."

"Backwater country," Janis grumbled.

"In Peter's case, we're dealing with the *Ejercito de Liberacion de Tecala*. Thirty years ago the E.L.T. was a serious revolutionary movement. But that's all over now. In the 80s they went to work for the drug cartels.

74

They ran protection for the coca farms and factories in the mountains. Bought lots of guns. Took a lot of ground. Got a big payroll going, right?"

Janis made a spiteful, gutteral grunt. "They should open up franchises."

Terry waited for a beat, then continued. "When the cartels came under attack, everything became confused. The army, the CIA, the DEA, they all came in looking for blood. Suddenly the money wasn't there. And the E.L.T. had a lot of mouths to feed. So one day they realized they needed to diversify."

"By kidnapping," Alice said.

"By kidnapping," Terry confirmed, nodding. "It's been extremely profitable for them. They have the terrain, the equipment, the personnel. Best of all, the whole thing looks vaguely political so they can justify their greed."

Janis couldn't go sixty seconds without interrupting. "All this is well and good. But what I want to know is where this leaves my brother?"

Terry Thorne didn't mince words. "In deadly danger. Which is why we can't afford a single mistake. One slipup, and you'll never see him again."

Chapter 6

Just when Peter thought it couldn't get any worse, the next twenty-four hours proved him wrong.

Four rebels had thrown him into a jeep, pulled a burlap hood over his head, and driven from the village in a spray of dirt, the tires squealing. Hour after hour they traveled steadily higher into the mountains. Peter could tell by the constant grades and the constant shifting. When they finally braked, he was seized and roughly dragged out. The hood was jerked off.

Peter found himself in a small clearing deep in the jungle. Facing him was a guerilla platoon of Tecalano Cong in dirty pants or shorts and scuffed combat boots. Each man and woman bristled with weapons.

Peter was passed over to them without ceremony. The man in charge, a stocky specimen who liked cigars, gave Peter the once-over, then shoved the business end of an Fusil Automatico Livano assault rifle into his ribs.

"Do what we say. When we say. Or die."

"Sí," Peter said.

And with that the guerillas trudged off into the jungle, Peter doing his best to hold to the brisk pace they set. They hiked in loose formation, always climbing, moving ever farther from Tecala City, ever farther from safety, ever farther from Alice.

It helped Peter immensely to think of her. To remember the many happy times they had shared. To envision her smile, how she walked, how she felt in his arms. He missed her so much, and he hadn't been gone all that long.

The platoon crossed a verdant ridge into a bowl-shaped valley. Indian farmers were tilling the soil, and, for a few fleeting minutes, Peter thought he might be able to get their attention and maybe one of them would send for help. But they knew better. The Indians never so much as glanced at the guerrillas. Their lives would be forfeit if they did.

In the center of the valley was a village smaller than the first, no more than a collection of grass huts. A few women and small children were the only occupants, the women sewing or preparing food while the children scampered playfully about. They scattered when the platoon made a beeline through the center of the village rather than go around.

Peter had an inspiration. The rebels had emptied his pockets and taken all his personal effects except for a pen in his shirt pocket. It had been beneath their notice. Little did they know it was a company pen and had the QUAD-CARBON logo on it. If he were to drop it where the villagers could find it, they might turn the pen over to anyone who came looking for him. At least the searchers would know they were on the right track.

Peter raised a hand to his pocket, then caught himself. The stocky man with the cigar was watching him, suspicion etched on his swarthy features, fingering the trigger of the FAL. Pretending to scratch an itch, Peter strolled on as if he hadn't noticed. Soon they left the huts behind and were once again climbing toward the clouds.

For Peter to try and get his bearings was a study in futility. In all directions for countless miles all he saw was unbroken forest canopy. Landmarks were nonexistent. All he could say for sure was that they were going west.

The afternoon started to wane. Peter's feet and legs were unbearably sore when the leader unexpectedly called a halt. The guerrillas broke out rations, mostly candy bars and crackers, and the stocky headman came back down the line. Peter was famished enough to eat a cow, but the man didn't offer him any nourishment.

Lighting another cigar, the man squinted at him through a wreath of smoke. "Big Americano, eh?"

"Hungry Americano," Peter said good-naturedly, but the man didn't take the hint.

"Big oil man. QUAD-CARBON." The man spat. "Bastardo."

"I don't work on the pipeline," Peter said. "I don't have any connection with it. I work on the dam. *La represa.*" He didn't know why he wasted his breath. The honchos at the first village hadn't cared. Neither would this one.

"La represa?" the stocky man said, straightening. *"La represa de Chimaya?"*

"Sí," Peter said glumly. What difference did it make? he asked himself. He might as well say he worked on a dam on the moon.

"I did not know," the man said. "No one tells me." He tapped his broad chest and said in Spanish, "I am from Chimaya. My brother, he works on your dam."

Peter clutched at the straw. "Then you know I have nothing to do with the oil. All I care about is building the dam to help your people. To stop the floods that destroy their homes and crops every few years."

"Me llamo Tajo," the man said, a new note of respect in his voice. *"Como se llama?"*

"Peter. Peter Bowman." Impulsively, Peter extended a hand. After a few moments of hesitation, Tajo gave it a quick shake. "Please, Tajo. Can't you help me? Can't you tell your superiors they've made a mistake?"

"So sorry, but no," Tajo said. "The men above me make such decisions. I am but a soldier. I follow their orders."

"But I am not their enemy. I am not one of those they hate. If they see that, perhaps they will let me go."

Tajo took a candy bar from a pocket, unwrapped it, broke it in two, and gave half to Peter. "They never let you go. Not until they get the money. That is the way these things are done. Do as you are told, and you get through this all right."

"I have a wife," Peter said plaintively.

"I have a wife, Pabla, and seven children," Tajo said. Fishing in another pocket, he produced a faded photo of a woman the size of a walrus and a brood ranging in age from ten months to ten years. Chortling, he said, "You want to know the real reason I joined the revolution? To get away from Pabla. She is a shrew, that one. Nag, nag, nag."

"My wife is not like that," Peter said. "She is . . ." He searched for the right word in Spanish. "She is *magnifico*."

"Sí?" Tajo sighed. "I envy you. You have much to look forward to when you go home."

"*If* I go home," Peter amended.

Squatting, Tajo placed a hand on his shoulder. "Listen, gringo"—he used English—"I like you. So I tell you this, eh? You no good dead. We keep you alive for money. Do not cause trouble. Do not talk back. You get by." He looked up and down the line. "Just be careful of the locos."

"Locos?"

"Crazy ones." Tajo touched a finger to his head. "Mucho loco. They like to kill." He slashed the same finger across his throat. "Kill you for fun." Rising, he declared, "We go now."

"Wait," Peter urged, but it was no use. The platoon moved on, and he moved on with it, munching on the candy bar, taking tiny bites so the chocolate would last that much longer. He looked forward to stopping for the night. But sunset came and went and they hiked on under a sliver of moonlight.

The guerrillas were seemingly tireless, but Peter couldn't say the same. He was exhausted. The candy bar gave him energy for a while, but once it wore off he trudged along with his head hung low, his shoulders stooped, his body aching to collapse but his mind fueling it onward, ever onward.

At midnight to Peter's great joy, Tajo finally called another halt. They formed a cold camp, the guerrillas lying on the ground in a ring around Peter, a pair left as sentry guards. Peter coiled on his side, his hands tucked between his legs. A rock was poking him in the thigh and a rough clump of grass gouged his shoulder. He was too uncomfortable to sleep, or so he assumed, but the instant he closed his eyes he was dead to the world.

Terry Thorne returned to the Scorpion House bright and early the next morning. He had spent the previous afternoon going through the same old motions. First he'd contacted the police to let them know he was the K&R rep handling the case. A formality, nothing more, since the police were of no consequence in the greater scheme of things. Next, he renewed some old contacts, seeking news on his own. Lastly, late at night, he submitted an initial report to Luthan Risk via a satellite link.

Terry had slept remarkably well. He'd showered, shaved and dressed, eaten a hearty breakfast, and headed straight for the Bowmans', eager to get to work. He imagined how Peter Bowman must be feeling right about then: alone, scared, maybe roughed up some, and invariably hungry since hostages were never fed enough. Then he thought of Alice Bowman, of her poise, her charm, her strength. He liked her resolve.

His briefcase in hand, Terry bounded up the stairs and rang the bell. Maria answered, all smiles now that she knew who he was. She ushered him into the living room where Alice and Janis were waiting, as prearranged. A cup of coffee had been set out for him, and he took a few sips before beginning.

"Now then, ladies. The latest news is that there is no new news. But don't worry. By now, the E.L.T. have taken him well up in the mountains so it's not surprising we haven't heard anything. I'll warrant he's fine. Sooner or later we'll be contacted. Until then all we can do is wait."

Janis was filling her cup with enough sugar to turn the coffee from a liquid into a solid. "You told us the same thing yesterday, and I still can't accept it. The authorities should be out combing the country for him, not sitting on their asses."

Terry was patient with her. "If we try to locate Peter or rescue him or bring the E.L.T. to justice, we put him at extreme risk. The last thing we need in a situation like this is heroics. Nine times out of ten it gets the client killed." He bestowed his best sunny-side up smile on them. "All we have to do is find a number, a dollar amount, that gets your brother back in one piece as quickly as possible."

"Amen to that," Alice said. She was seated near a window and a brilliant beam of sunlight bathed her in a golden glow, rendering her positively gorgeous.

Terry tore his gaze away. Concern for a client was one thing; entertaining personal thoughts about any of the client's immediate family was a major professional no-no.

"Can we back up here again?" Janis said. "I just got off the plane, remember? Who the hell are these E.L.T. bozos you keep talking about? And how can you be sure they're the ones who have Peter if they haven't contacted us yet."

"There were witnesses, remember?" Alice reminded her.

"As for the E.L.T.," Terry said, "the *Ejercito de Liberacion de Tecala is* one of the few players in all of South America big enough and ambitious enough to come into a capital city and pull off a snatch in broad daylight."

Janis had another issue. "You said yesterday the police are worthless because most have been bought off. But what about the army? Surely the rebels can't buy them off? Why not send in the marines if they have any here?"

"What, you want us to send in a company of Teca-lan Rangers?" Terry shook his head. "They have a scorched-earth policy when it comes to dealing with rebels. Your brother would be caught in the cross fire."

"Scratch that, then," Janis said.

"How about the embassy?" Alice inquired.

"All you'll get from them is a smile and a pat on the back. The U.S. mission here right now is to keep the cartels on the defensive and the oil flowing. You don't fit into their plans."

Janis licked sugar off her spoon. "Okay. Enough background. How long is all this negotiating going to take?"

Terry was honest with them. "The truth is, I don't know. Last year things were more predictable. But there's a lot going on right now. It's all in a state of flux."

"How?" Alice said.

"It's hard to negotiate when the people you need to deal with are on the move," Terry hedged to spare her added anxiety, but she saw right through him.

"When you say 'on the move,' you mean fighting."

Terry liked how she always cut to the quick of every facet of the crisis. "Exactly. The cartels are thinking maybe they're better off partnering up with the army. The E.L.T. are thinking maybe they don't need any partners at all. Everyone is ambitious. Greedy. It's all heated up quite a beat since I was here last year."

"How long would it have taken you then?" Janis quizzed him.

"Best-case scenario? Two months."

"And the worst?" From Alice.

"Much longer." Terry wasn't specific. She was miserable enough. Telling her it could take years would only compound her suffering.

Janis smacked her spoon on the table. "This is all so damned silly to me. Why not just pay the bastards? What's there to negotiate?"

"Everything," Terry said. "Think of it as a game. A game you play whether you like it or not. For you it's emotional. To the people holding Peter this is business. You're in the market and he's the product." He looked at each of them. "The sooner you become comfortable with that concept the easier it will be."

"I've never been comfortable with stupidity," Janis declared.

Her stubbornness irritated Terry. "Try this, then. If we pay too fast, or pay too much, we make it look too easy for them. Instead of giving Peter back, they'll send a new message thanking us for the down payment and asking for more. Is that what you want?"

"I just want my brother safe."

Alice came to Terry's rescue. "Where is Peter through all this?"

"In the mountains. *La cordillera*. Somewhere we'll never find him, not if we looked a hundred years. It's a rough business, but the people who've taken your husband know what they're doing. It's in their best interests to keep him well." Terry pulled a pen from a pocket. "Let's talk about Peter a bit, shall we? I need more information. For instance, how's his health?"

Alice opened her mouth, but Janis beat her to it.

"My brother has always been as healthy as an ox."

"Does he take any medication?" Terry had to know.

"No," Janis said.

"What about allergies?"

"No. None."

Terry glanced at Alice for confirmation. "Is that true?"

"He's allergic to chlorine and strawberries. A blood vessel broke in his eye last month, and he's been taking drops prescribed by his doctor. He's also prone to ear infections in wet weather." Alice looked at her sister-in-law. "I thought you knew about the strawberries?"

"I forgot." Janis's jaw muscles tweaked. Picking up her cup she headed for the kitchen. "Well, I can see you two don't need me. I think I'll try to reach my husband again."

Terry was enormously pleased she had gone, but he was too much the gentleman to mention it. "I hope I didn't say anything to make her mad."

"Janis has the hide of a rhino," Alice said. "She'll get over it."

They smiled, and once again Terry was stirred by her beauty and grace. Coughing, he bent over his file. "Where were we? Oh. How about emotionally? How will this kind of stress effect him?"

"Exactly what kind of stress are we talking about? Being kidnapped? Going without food? Being cut off from everyone and everything he knows?"

"All of the above," Terry said.

"I'm not sure. He's faced challenges before, but nothing to compare to this. I honestly can't say whether he'll handle it well or fall to pieces."

Terry's mouth moved of its own accord. "If he takes after you he'll come out none the worse for wear."

Alice Bowman blushed.

A rocking sensation woke Peter at daybreak. For several seconds he thought he was in his bed in the Scorpion House, and he smiled and turned to embrace Alice. Then he saw the boot on his shoulder and looked up into the spiteful face of a guerrilla. It all came rushing back to him. He sat up, his body so stiff and sore he could barely move his arms and legs.

A fine mist shrouded the mountains. The cries of birds and other creatures pierced the chill morning air.

The rebels were getting ready to head out. Breakfast consisted of more rations and hasty swigs from canteens.

Tajo came over and handed Peter a strip of dried meat. "Salted forest rat," he said, chewing another piece with relish. "Is very good."

"Gracias." Peter feigned taking a bite, and when Tajo turned to bark at the others, he shoved the piece into a pocket. He'd need to be a whole lot hungrier before he'd eat rodent.

"You feel brave today?" Tajo asked.

"Not particularly, no," Peter confessed.

"Your fingers, they are okay?"

"My fingers?" Befuddled by lack of sleep, Peter couldn't understand the significance of the questions.

"Sí." Tajo opened and closed his left hand a few times. "Like this."

Puzzled, Peter imitated him, using both hands. "They're fine." What did his fingers have to do with anything?"

Tajo smiled. *"Bueno."* He growled an order and the platoon headed out, climbing as usual. The mist closed around them, a vaporous blanket that limited visibility to under ten yards.

Peter contemplated making a run for it. Five or six long strides, and the rebels wouldn't be able to see him. Then all he had to do was elude them until they tired of the hunt and find his way back down to civilization. But no sooner had the idea occurred to him than a gun barrel was gouged against the small of his back by the guerrilla behind him. He glanced over his shoulder and the man smirked.

In half an hour the sun was high enough and hot enough to dissipate the mist. Depressed at being foiled, Peter tramped along the narrow trail with his head down, not caring one whit about his surroundings or what went on around him. So he was all the more startled when he nearly collided with the rebel in front of him, who had halted and was gazing at something up ahead.

Peter looked—and his breath caught in his throat. Up ahead the jungle ended. Not just the vegetation, but the ground itself, at the brink of a wide ravine. The other side had to be a good fifty yards away. Linking the span was a fragile rope bridge, which the rebels clearly intended to cross.

"No way in hell," Peter said aloud, and was pushed by the guerrilla behind him. Tajo and the others were securing their backpacks and slinging their rifles and SMGs. Cautiously inching to the edge, Peter leaned out. A thousand feet below were clusters of huge, jagged boulders. "I can't do this."

"What was that?" Tajo had come over.

Peter pointed at the bridge. "I've never done this before."

In Spanish Tajo said, "There is a first time for everything, eh?" He moved to the thick wooden anchor posts. "Just grip a rope in each hand and step carefully on the boards. In no time you will be across."

"In no time I'll be dead." Peter didn't like how the whole bridge swayed with every gust of the breeze, nor how far apart the boards were. The rope itself was old and partly frayed in spots. Crossing was certain suicide.

Tajo reverted to English again. "You must do this. Be brave." Flexing his fingers, he gingerly started forward, gaining speed as he went once he was convinced the bridge would hold.

Another rebel went next. Then a third. A fourth. The whole while, Peter stared into the chasm, his body caked with cold sweat. A single misstep would spell disaster. Yet if he refused, they'd probably bind him and carry him across, which is his way of thinking was much worse. More weight meant higher risk.

"Gringo!"

Peter looked at the man who had shouted.

"Your turn." The rebel gestured.

Swallowing hard, Peter stepped to the anchor posts. His limbs locked up and for a moment he was paralyzed with raw fear. Marshaling his will, he placed a hand on each of the ropes and his right foot on the first wooden slat. It creaked beneath him like a rotten floorboard about to break, but it held when he put his full weight on his leg.

"Rapido!" one of the rebels goaded.

Like hell, Peter thought. He tried the next slat, and the next, taking his sweet time, not giving a damn whether they liked it or not. His life was at stake. He tried not to look down, but he couldn't help it. The gaps between the boards gave him a clear view of the jagged boulders far below. He was ten yards out when whitish objects scattered among them piqued his curiosity. Stopping, he had to study them a bit before he realized what they were—human bones.

"Faster, señor!" Tajo called. "You must go faster!"

Peter glanced at him. *When cows fly,* was on the tip of his tongue. Then he saw Tajo point at the jungle. Confused, Peter surveyed the undergrowth, but saw nothing. "What?" He took another slow step.

"The trees!" Tajo yelled. "The trees!"

Again Peter scoured the jungle, and this time noticed that the tops of the trees were bending to the wind. Simultaneously a blast of air fanned his face. The bridge swung in the opposite direction, him along with it. He clung on for dear life, his knuckles white, his knees rigid. When the wind subsided he moved on, doubling his pace, afraid it would pick up again.

It did.

Peter was smack in the middle when a banshee howl preceded a powerful blast. The boards underneath him swayed and the ropes he was holding shook and shimmied. The bridge itself groaned, and for a heart-stopping minute he thought it would collapse. But the wind tapered, the bridge steadied, and Peter scurried toward the other side, stepping on every other board instead of each one, moving as quickly as the others had done.

Upon reaching the far side, Peter moved to a grassy spot and sank to his knees, grateful he was alive.

"Easy, no?" Tajo asked, and cheerfully clapped him on the shoulders.

From there on the climb wasn't as steep. Peter actually began to relax a bit. Toward sundown tendrils of smoke from a campfire appeared, and in another twenty minutes they arrived at a clearing. Two men and two women were waiting. So were a pair of pack mules and a couple of llamas, tied to stakes. An old, battered coffeepot was on the fire.

Tajo and one of the newcomers consulted with a lean youth with a pockmarked face and a perpetual grin. The youth couldn't be much over seventeen and swaggered around with an FMK 3 submachine gun cradled in the cook of an arm.

Peter was treated to a handful of sardines for supper. He had never been overly fond of them, but he ate with gusto, more famished than he had ever been in his life. Tajo and the lean youth glanced at him several times, the teenager sneering in contempt. The expression on Tajo's face when he strolled over didn't bode well.

"Come morning, you go with them."

Peter had one sardine left to eat, but his appetite abruptly disappeared. "You're leaving?"

"All of us," Tajo said, encompassing the platoon with a wave. "You are with Juaco now." He tilted his head at the youth.

Juaco leered at Peter. Striding to the side of the clearing, he trained the SMG on a tree and opened fire. A 9-mm hailstorm chewed the trunks to bits, Juaco crackled as he emptied the magazine. When he was done he glanced at Peter and said in Spanish, "That is you if you do not do as I say, pig."

The members of the platoon had watched the display in disgust, Tajo among them. Now, bending toward Peter, he whispered. "Be careful, American. He is one of the *muy locos* I warned you about."

Chapter 7

Terry Thorne was at the kitchen table in Scorpion House, sorting through the big box of photographs Norma had brought down from upstairs. Terry held up a photo that showed Alice and her husband in front of an ancient stone temple. She was gorgeous, standing in a plain T-shirt and shorts. He glanced over at her, busily whipping up a meal.

"So who are you?" Alice asked without looking over. "I mean, the people who do this? Are you lawyers, foreign service, what?"

"Some have backgrounds in law enforcement," Terry said. "Some come out of intelligence. Mostly it's former military."

Alice turned. "Which are you?"

"I was a soldier."

"Whose side?"

"Excuse me?" Terry dropped the photo in the box and selected one of Alice in a skimpy outfit, leaning against a tree and grinning happily.

"What kind of soldier?" Alice took the salt shaker from the table and added a dash to the chicken simmering in a large frying pan.

"Oh. I was in the British Army." Terry spotted a

recent photo: Alice in a stunning dress, dancing with a Tecalan in a tux. "Who's your dancing partner?"

Alice bent over his shoulder. "Him? Oh, that was taken at the country club ball last week. A friend dropped it off yesterday." She resumed cooking. "You sound Australian."

"I am." Terry saw she wanted more background so he fleshed it out. "We're a bit short of action down under. All dressed up and no place to play, if you get my drift. So I went to England for that." He paused. "S.A.S. Special Air Service."

Alice's curiosity knew no bounds. "Special means what? Like Special Forces?"

"Right."

"Jesus," Alice said softly. "This is all so heavy."

From out of the living room rose Janis's voice in stern rebuke. Terry glimpsed her pacing like a drill sergeant, the phone to her ear.

Alice chuckled. "She's a trip, huh? Wrestling her family into line from two thousand miles away."

"How do they get along?" Terry inquired.

"Peter and her?" Alice grinned. "Janis drives him crazy. Sometimes I think we've been bouncing around the world just so he can avoid her."

Terry nodded. "I see that." She glanced at him, and he tapped the dossier. "The bouncing around, I meant. You were in Egypt last, right?"

For some reason the question seemed to rattle her. Alice moved to a cupboard and brought down a long-stemmed glass. "I need a little something to calm my nerves." She took a bottle of wine from the fridge and poured, her hand shaking slightly. "We were supposed to go home. We were in Africa and the plan was to go back to the States. Peter's father has been ill, and, well, there have been some other things, really."

Sympathy filled Terry. She was talking to hear herself talk, rattling off words a mile a minute.

"So we were all set to go home and then this project came up. Peter's dream project. It's very competitive, the field he's in. Projects like the dam don't come along very often." Alice sheepishly looked over at him. "I just realized. I didn't think to ask if you want any."

Terry imagined Ian Havery frowning in disapproval and heard Havery's voice in his head: *Never become attached to a client or the client's family, Terry, my boy.* Terry nodded. "I'd love some, thanks."

Alice fetched another glass. "He knows better than to go off alone like that," she lamented, her voice nearly breaking.

"You can't think about that," Terry advised, but she acted as if she hadn't heard him.

"It wasn't Sandro's regular day off. And that stupid goddamm car of his!"

Terry tried to calm her down. "People get comfortable. They forget. It's only natural."

Alice gulped down wine. Her body trembled, and she gripped the bottle as if ready to fling it against the wall.

At that juncture, Janis passed the doorway again, saying, "I don't care. You have them clean their rooms or they'll be grounded for a month when I get back. Honestly, Harold, you're worse than the children."

Terry saw Alice on the verge of tears and desperately sought a way to dispel her sorrow, if only for a little while. "What I'd really like to know," he said, getting her attention, "is what's with all the bloody scorpions?"

Alice stared at the walls, at the floor. "Oh, God.

This place. I know. It's insane, isn't it? Some busted drug guy. 'El Escorpion,' I think they called him. He built this for one of his mistresses." She laughed and downed more wine. "Peter called and said he'd found the perfect house, but it was supposed to be cursed. What should he do? I was completely determined to have a decent kitchen down here, so I told him to take it, sight unseen."

"Uh-oh," Terry joked.

"Exactly. Live and learn. Anyway, maybe it is cursed. Cinta, one of our maids, she brings holy water every Monday and sprinkles it around. All that bad juju." With no hint she was shifting gears, Alice looked at him and said, "So this is what you do, right? This is your life? You go to people's houses and tell them how it is and—"

"That's part of it."

"—try to figure out what they're like?" Alice didn't miss a beat, her tone growing firmer, "How they're going to be? How they'll hold up? That's what you're doing, right?"

"I'm on your side, Alice," Terry said softly, and resisted an inexplicable impulse to rise and take her into his arms.

"Yeah? So how am I doing? You know, for the bereaved spouse and all?" Alice was close to tears again.

"Your husband is alive. He's alive, and we're going to do everything we can to bring him home to you."

Alice's forehead knit. "You've done a lot of these, haven't you?"

"I've been doing this for nine years." At times, Terry mused, more like nine hundred.

"And it always works out?"

Terry hedged by responding, "This is as good a place as any to be kidnapped."

"Really? But what about those two Brazilians they found dead last month? They were hostages, I believe. And the rebels killed them." Alice's gaze speared him to the chair. "What happened there?"

"First of all, one of them was Venezuelan. Second, they were arms dealers. They were doing a gun deal when they were taken. It's a little different."

"This won't work if you bullshit me," Alice told him, not mincing words.

"I can see that." More than ever, Terry admired her grit, her tenacity.

"So we'll be straight up then, from now on?"

"That's how we'll do it," Terry agreed. Frankly, he wouldn't have it any other way. The moment lingered, their eyes joined, and Terry experienced a feeling he knew he shouldn't entertain. He was spared from having to excuse himself by the timely entrance of Janis, who was so typically self-absorbed she didn't notice anything out of the ordinary.

"Sorry. God, you'd think I've been gone for a month! My husband is hopeless. He couldn't keep the kids in line if his life depended on it." Janis plopped down into a chair. "So, where were we?"

Peter couldn't sleep. Most of the guerrillas had turned in, including Tajo. The four newcomers were still up, though, getting ready to leave at first light. Juaco was bossing the two women around as if they were his personal slaves, while the other man, about the same age as Juaco, busied himself with the llamas.

Peter had learned the names of the women: Cara and Linda. More teenagers in scruffy camouflage, but deadly teenagers. Both women wore pistols. Both had a hard, life-weary glaze to their features that told Peter they were as tough as the men. Maybe tougher. They endured Juaco's abuse stoically. They were used to it, Peter supposed.

A myriad of stars filled the night sky, more than Peter had ever seen. Perhaps the altitude was a factor. He had the illusion he could reach up and brush them with his fingers. Silhouetted against the glittering spectacle were stark, towering peaks, a clue as to why the llamas were needed. The guerrillas were taking him to what the Tecalanos called "the ramparts of heaven," which was a poetic way of alluding to the uppermost reaches of the mountains.

Resting his forearms across his knees, Terry gazed eastward. At the limit of his vision a solitary light gleamed. Was it a village? he speculated. Or just another campfire? He looked beyond it, hoping against hope for a glimpse of Tecala City. But they had traveled too far. It was a world away now, and he felt as if there was very little chance he'd ever set eyes on it again.

A shadow fell across him. Peter started, and twisted. "Sí?"

Juaco was between him and the fire, as cocky as ever, the submachine gun held at an angle so all he had to do was squeeze the trigger to riddle Peter with bullets. "I hear you speak our language, *gringo.*"

"Enough to get by," Peter said.

"Then understand. I am not Tajo. I hate Americanos. Were it up to me I would kill you all." Jauco patted the SMG. "I am skilled with this. Give me trouble, and I will show you just how good."

"I will behave. I promise."

Juaco spat. "That is what I think of *gringo* promises. Your kind, they rape our country. They take our oil."

"I'm here to build a dam—" Peter began and recoiled when Juaco hiked a hand to hit him.

"I do not care why you are here. I have been ordered to take you to a special place and hold you until your people pay the money, and that is what I will do." Juaco had a knife in a belt sheath and he slowly drew it, holding the blade so it reflected the firelight. "But hear me. I would as soon gut you as look at you. You do well to remember that."

The hothead stalked off, leaving Peter to contemplate the unfairness of it all. Through no fault of his own, he had gone from the proverbial frying pan into the fire.

But the worst, Peter feared, was yet to come.

Terry had overstayed his welcome. He should have left hours ago, but he couldn't bring himself to leave. Only when Janis yawned and gave him a look that implied he was an uncouth clod who had overstayed his welcome did he bid the two ladies good night.

Before leaving, Terry figured a security check was in order. It was highly unlikely the E.L.T. had men posted near the house, but it wouldn't hurt for him to have a look around. Music wafted from the dwelling next door, a lively salsa number, as he prowled along the driveway to the north corner of the Scorpion House. The patio and the pool were secure. He pivoted toward the fountain, then caught a hint of movement on the second floor.

Alice was framed by a window. She was lighting a cigarette, her fingers quaking. Despite her fear, despite her predicament, she was undeniably beautiful, so stunning that she brought an ache to Terry's chest.

The right thing to do was turn and leave. But Terry stood rooted to where he was, unable to say whether

her beauty or her vulnerability mesmerized him so. A yearning overcame him, a yearning long denied.

You damned fool, Terry berated himself. Havery had been right. He had already let himself become much too emotionally involved. The wisest course was to steel himself against attachment and to treat his clients as dollar and cent signs, not real, live human beings.

Alice was stretching, bending backward with her hands on her hips, her eyes closed, fatigue oozing from every pore, yet at the same time radiating enough sensual allure to melt a candle. Or a man.

Suddenly a dog cut loose with a series of savage barks and growls. Terry spun, thinking it was after him, but the animal was on the next roof over, securely chained. He backed toward the gate, hoping it would quiet down. When he glanced at the window again, Alice was gone.

"I can take a hint." Terry made for his rented sedan and drove straight to the Intercon Hotel. He was halfway across the lobby when familiar voices pricked his ears from the fern bar to his right. Old habits died hard, and he glided into its murky confines with his back to the wall. The place was packed with hotel guests, locals and ex-pats. His interest was in a pair of rough-and-tumble types at the far end of the bar. One was Italian-American: sharp, aggressive, whipcord-and-nails in a business suit. The other was English, softer, yet clearly iron underneath, with a capacity for alcohol to rival most three men. They were nursing near-empty glasses, leaning with their elbows on the bar, their backs to the doorway.

Terry crooked a finger and the bartender came right over. He whispered what he had in mind. The American and the Englishman were suitably horrified when the bartender presented them with two fruity tropical concoctions complete with tiny pink umbrellas. When the bartender pointed at him, Terry laughed and sauntered down the bar.

The American, whose name was Dino, recovered first. *"Bienvenidos, hermano,"* he said with affection and levered Terry's hand with vigor. "We've been waiting for you."

Wyatt, the besotted Englishman, went Dino one better. He hugged Terry and clapped him soundly on the back. "We heard a rumor you had checked in. We were beginning to think you had gone all civilized and unsocial on us." Stepping back, he flicked a finger at the bandage. "What's this, then? A face-lift?"

"Yeah, I'm doing one side at a time." Terry was genuinely glad to see them. Among his rarified peers they were the two closest friends he had. Men he had shared danger with. Men he trusted. Men he would give his life for. "You're good?" he asked Wyatt, who last he knew had been unceremoniously given the boot by an employer.

Dino snickered. "He looks like shit, but he's working."

"Correction," Wyatt said, feigning indignation. "I look like shit *because* I'm working. This line of work would turn a priest into a lush."

"What are you ladies celebrating?" Terry asked.

"Life, liberty, and the ability to purchase happiness." Dino tipped his glass to them. "Not that we need an excuse to imbibe, you understand."

"Hear, hear." Wyatt winked at Terry. "Thank God you're here, old friend. I tell you, the quality of conversation has been just bloody appalling." He chortled. "So where'd you get the face-lift, anyhow? I seem to recall someone saying you were in Turkey."

Dino rolled his eyes. "He'd forget his name if we hadn't tatooed it on his stomach. It was Chechnya, right? The Frenchman Lenoir?"

Terry nodded. "You always did keep up on things."

"My guys turned the job down," Dino revealed. "They said it was too iffy." He glanced at Wyatt. "Sounds like something your outfit would do, though."

"Up yours."

The barb rolled off Dino like water off a goose. To Terry he said, "What in hell was Ian doing sending you out there, anyway? Trying to get you killed?"

"We've been busy," Terry said lamely.

"So is everyone else," Dino said. "Christ, if Wyatt here is working, you know the world's in a boatload of trouble."

Wyatt was about to take another swallow. "Did I say up yours already?" he asked Dino, and drained the dregs of his glass.

"I thought you were retiring, mate," Terry addressed the Englishman.

"I was. But Inherent Risk rang me up with a sob story. Could I please bail their asses out of the fire? And like a great bloody lump, for old time's sake, I agreed." Wyatt held the empty glass aloft for the bartender to notice, but the man was busy with another customer. "I am just too bloody noble for my own bloody good."

"And bloody well drunk," Dino quipped.

"Who's the lucky bastard?" Terry wanted to know, referring to Wyatt's client.

"A Canadian fellow. A provincial. A geologist who traipsed off hunting for minerals in the wrong place at the wrong time."

"I hear that," Terry said. It was how half of all

100

kidnap victims wound up being snatched. "What about you?" he asked Dino.

"Come on, man. Where have you been? I'm working the biggest thing down here at the moment."

"And since he's much too modest to tell you what it is," Wyatt said, "I'll spare us having to hear him brag and spill the beans. It's Calitri, the Italian banker. Our boy is quite pleased with himself. He's made the A-team at last."

"Up yours," Dino said.

Wyatt scratched his chin and made a show of trying to recall something. "Now where have I heard that before?"

Dino polished off his own drink, then arched an eyebrow at Terry. "And Ian sent you off to fucking Chechnya. Alone, yet. Astounding." He also wagged his glass for attention, but the barman had his back to them. "Say, have you heard about Clyde and Jenkins?"

Terry remembered Havery telling him they had bailed, but he feigned ignorance to see if his friend had more information. "No. What happened?"

"They're back working for us. They say Luthan Risk is too damned cutthroat for their liking. And after hearing about Chechnya . . ." Dino shook his head. "What is Ian thinking, man? Does he keep you under a rock? You've got to get better informed. I'm taking it on myself to open your eyes while you're down here."

"You think I go around with my eyes shut?" Terry said.

Dino became deathly serious. "I think you trust too much. You believe certain people have your best interests at heart when they don't. If you don't wake up soon, you'll learn the truth the hard way."

Wyatt snickered. "Don't beat around the bush like that. Give it to him straight."

Terry appreciated his friend's concern, but he could handle his own life without help. "Tell me," he said to Dino, "do you still have those boys on the police force on payroll?" Dino had spent much more time in-country in the past couple of years and had developed an extensive network of crucial contacts.

"Tighter than ever."

"Will you run a few names for me?" Terry requested. "I want to check out my client's driver and a few other people."

"No problem," Dino said. "But I guess that means you're buying tonight, doesn't it?"

Wyatt was sadly staring at his empty glass. "That's if we can get a fucking drink. I think someone's gone and kidnapped the bloody barman."

Alice still wasn't sleeping well. Ten days had gone by and still no word from the kidnappers. Terry Thorne kept assuring her it was par for the course, but she couldn't stop worrying, couldn't stop tying herself into emotional knots. It didn't help that Janis was beginning to fray her nerves with all that constant carping.

The next morning Maria took a phone call from Ted Fellner's secretary. Fellner needed to see both of them in his office as soon as possible.

An hour later Sandro dropped Alice and Janis off in front of the QUAD-CARBON building in downtown Tecala City. Alice craned her neck back and coldly regarded the glass-and-steel monolith. So huge, so pretentious, like QUAD-CARBON itself. The company had spent money like there was no tomorrow, and now there *was* no tomorrow. A bigger outfit with deeper pockets had come along and gobbled them up.

Alice resented the fact her husband had devoted so much of his life to QUAD-CARBON, and for what? His dream project had been ripped out from under him. His future—and their marriage—had been put in jeopardy. And now Peter was in the clutches of fanatics who would kill him if they didn't get what they wanted.

Ted Fellner came out of his office to greet them. Alice stiffly shook his hand and suffered a hug she didn't reciprocate. She never had liked Fellner much. He was too glib, too suave, and much too devious.

"Ladies, I thank you for coming on such short notice. I flew back in late last night and we've had everyone working the phones."

Alice was surprised to see Jerry Winsted and several men she didn't know already there. She nodded at the others and said, "Morning, Jerry. How have you been?" An inner alarm went off when he mumbled something and averted his gaze.

Fellner moved around to his chair. "We've been going full-out here, trying to access the information we need to make informed decisions and make them quickly. The right decisions for everyone."

Janis got right to it. "I thought this meeting was about my brother. Where's Mr. Thorne? Shouldn't he be here?"

Fellner looked perplexed.

"The man from Luthan Risk," Alice clarified.

"Ah," Fellner said, and gave a little cough. "There's been a change in plans, ladies."

"What kind of change?" Janis asked.

"We think it's best for all concerned, under the new circumstances, for us to go with a local representative."

"Not use LRI?" Janis said.

Alice had picked up on something else. "What new circumstances?" she interjected, and caught a quick look between Fellner and Jerry. It was a half a minute before Ted Fellner answered her.

"There's no insurance."

For an instant Alice's heart seemed to stop and the room seemed to spin.

"None of us, no one at QUAD-CARBON, has been insured against kidnapping for months. Apparently there's been a clerical glitch somewhere along the line, and Luthan Risk wasn't aware of the change."

"No insurance," Alice said, striving to come to grasp with the implications.

"QUAD-CARBON stopped paying the premiums, if you can believe it." Fellner smiled as if it were a great joke. "Some idiot in New York was trying to cut costs and didn't know what they were doing." He shrugged. "I'm sorry."

"But that's crazy," Janis said.

"That's one way to describe it," Fellner said, trying to sound sympathetic and not entirely succeeding. He looked at Alice. "Please try to understand. This could be any one of us. We're doing what we can. I've been talking to Octonal, trying to get their input, and we're hoping they'll step up to the plate. But at this point . . ."

Janis sat forward. "Don't they have to?"

Fellner gestured, palms out. "Well, their position is that they've just taken over, so they can hardly be responsible for mistakes of the past."

"This is absurd," Janis declared. "Where's QUAD-CARBON in all this?"

"Evaporating as we speak." Fellner shrugged. "It's just Peter's luck to be taken when all this is going down."

Alice was fit to burst. QUAD-CARBON had screwed up royally, and her husband was being left in the lurch. They were treating him as if he were an expendable commodity.

Janis shifted toward her. "Can you believe this? We need to speak with an attorney right aw— "

Alice held up a hand, silencing her. "So what you're saying is that my husband is being left to fend for himself?" she demanded of Fellner.

"Not entirely, no." His eyes darted toward a Tecalan who had been listening intently to their exchange.

"And who are you?" Alice asked, taking his measure. He was fifty, maybe fifty-five, too well fed and wearing a cheap suit. She was *not* impressed.

Fellner motioned. "Alice, this is Arturo Fernandez."

Fernandez bounced to his feet and politely bowed.

"He's been our local security coordinator for years," Fellner explained. "He's very well connected. Very experienced. I think if you give us a couple minutes to talk it over, you're going to realize just how lucky we are to have him working with us."

"I can't wait," Alice said.

Chapter 8

Terry Thorne was paying his bill at the Intercon Hotel when he saw the desk clerk glance beyond him and stiffen. He turned, not knowing what to expect, certainly not expecting Alice Bowman. The look on her face was one of fury and disappointment.

"Boy, did you have me fooled."

"I was just about to call you," Terry said. He had received a call himself from Havery at six that morning.

"Where? From the plane?" Alice's voice dripped venom. "You stood in my house and told me I didn't have to worry anymore." She shook from head to toe. *"You stood there!"*

Terry reached for her, but she pulled away. "We all thought QUAD-CARBON was still a client. Luthan Risk has so many accounts, the update got lost in the shuffle. It's not a perfect system."

"What about us? Can't we be the client?"

"It's not that simple." Terry wished it were. God, how he wished it were.

"You get ten thousand a week plus expenses," Alice said. "We've checked it out. Why can't we pay you instead of QUAD-CARBON?"

"There are other factors." Not the least of which was Terry's employer had ordered him back to London. "Really, I'm sorry, but this isn't a good situation for us, either.'

"Us?" Alice uttered the word with savage incredulity. "Let's talk about you! You stood in my kitchen and told me my husband was coming home!"

"QUAD-CARBON is out of business, okay? Octonal spends forty million a year on K and R insurance around the world. The company I work for has thirty percent of that business. And Octonal doesn't like conflict."

"But Peter doesn't work for Octonal!" Alice said it so loudly she turned heads throughout the lobby.

"That's the whole point," Terry said, struggling to keep his own voice down. "That's how they want it. No QUAD-CARBON confusion. No Octonal exposure. No Octonal liability." He picked up his briefcase. "Technically, I'm not even supposed to be speaking to you."

Alice was like a pit bull thirsting for blood. "So, what? This is you being brave?"

"No. This is me doing my job." Terry withered at the hurt and betrayal in her eyes. His heart went out to her, but he reminded himself he had a weakness for becoming emotionally involved.

"Well, it's good I came by then, right? Let you get that off your chest."

"I'm sure it's going to work out," Terry offered encouragement, when the truth was there were no guarantees in the K&R business.

"They're giving us some local security guy," Alice revealed. "They're giving us exactly the kind of guy you warned me about, remember?"

Inwardly Terry squirmed. "I don't know what else

107

to tell you. I don't make policy." And, again, Havery said they needed him to be on the next flight out.

"Great. So when this is over and my husband is dead, and I'm suing the shit out of these scumbags, you can tell the judge you did everything you could to help me out!"

Stung by her rebuke, Terry headed for the entrance. She pursued him, flitting from side to side, her eyes moist.

"Wait. *Wait.*" Alice snatched at his sleeve. "Please, just listen. Please? You can't go. Listen to me, all right?"

Terry kept walking. He was a cauldron of conflicting desires. On the one hand he wanted nothing more than to help her—on the other he had a responsibility to his job.

"I'm sorry to be like this," Alice said, "but you're the first, the *only* person I've met who knows what they're talking about. I'm begging you—I'm totally fucking *begging* you to help me. I don't care about the rules. I don't care about the liability or being right or whatever it is. And if it's the money, really, we can pay. Peter's father isn't poor."

Almost to the door, Terry stopped. If she only knew what she was doing to him, how she was tearing him up inside. "You asked me once not to bullshit you, right?"

"Right," Alice said with a glimmer of hope.

Terry couldn't bring himself to look at her. "I have a plane to catch. I am so, so sorry, but that's the way it is." He walked briskly out the door, still refusing to look at her. But he caught her reflection in the glass. She was stunned, crushed, heartbroken. A lump formed in his throat, and he walked faster to a waiting cab outside.

The driver looked around.

"Get me to the airport," Terry growled. Fists clenched, eyes narrowed, he told himself he was doing the right thing, told himself he was doing what a professional would do, what Havery and Luthan expected him to do.

Why, then, did he feel so bloody awful?

Juaco's small band had been on the go for days. Climbing, always climbing, and just when Peter thought they would keep climbing until they reached the clouds, they came to a rocky plateau, a barren wasteland more reminiscent of a lunar landscape than planet earth. There was not a hint of vegetation anywhere.

Peter trudged in their wake, more miserable than he had ever been. He scratched his chin. A beard was growing, and it itched constantly. He'd asked for a razor, but Juaco had laughed and given him a blunt rock. The kid was a natural-born sadist and seemed to delight in tormenting others.

They came to a ledge. Below was a barren, bleak valley. Juaco and Cara began arguing, and Peter had a hard time grasping what it was they were arguing about. He turned to Linda, always the nicest of the bunch. *"Aqui. Esta? Para nosotros."*

"Sí. We stay here."

"How long?"

Linda shrugged.

The argument ended. Peter saw Juaco come toward him, leveling the FMK. Juaco pulled the bolt and sneered.

"What are you doing?" Peter asked, scared the kid actually intended to kill him. *"Por que?"*

Juaco pressed the stock to his shoulder and aimed squarely at the center of Peter's face.

"*Por que*? What are you doing?" Peter tried to back up, but he had nowhere to go. Growing frantic, he appealed to Linda. "Please. What is he doing? You won't get any money for me if I'm dead."

Smirking, Juaco waved the barrel back and forth, drawing out the suspense, drawing out his pleasure. Suddenly he tensed, leaned forward, and stroked the trigger.

Peter cried out. But the young guerrilla had merely placed the muzzle close to his ear and fired past him, three times in swift succession. The noise was painful enough, but it was the humiliation that drove Peter to his knees, his whole body shaking. It had only been a signal, and someone below answered in kind with three shots.

Juaco cackled. He directed the women to bring the llamas and strode off.

Peter rose mechanically and shuffled after them. As they carefully descended it dawned on him that they were in the basin of a long-dead volcano. Volcanic rocks were everywhere. Overhead scuttled wispy clouds. A couple of tents had been sloppily pitched next to a ribbon of a stream. Several goats were tethered nearby, and a flock of chickens had the run of the place. Two more teenaged boys appeared, their clothes rumpled, cigarettes dangling from their mouths, rifles slung over their shoulders.

"Alex and Berto," Linda said, nodding at each in turn.

Peter made a mental note of which was which. "They're the only ones here?" he said, but she didn't respond. Linda was a puzzlement to him. Quiet and considerate one minute, she could be cold and aloof the next.

Juaco waved the SMG as if he wanted to shoot someone. "Where's the fire?" he fumed. "We've been walking for days, and you can't have a fire going for us? You lazy faggot bitches!" Alex and Berto shriveled. "Look at you! Put down those guns and make a fire!" Juaco glanced at Cara. "You, get those animals unpacked!" Then at Linda. "And you, get the damn *gringo* in his place. Now!"

Everyone hastened to obey. Peter was confused when Linda handed him two folded sheets of plastic. "What am I supposed to do with these? *Para que? Para mi?*"

"Sí. You make your house." Linda pointed at a flat spot. "You make it there."

"With these?" Peter was dismayed. They had tents, yet they expected him to get by with lousy strips of plastic? "It's cold out, and tonight it will get a lot colder. How am I supposed to keep warm?"

"That is your problem," Linda said and turned her back to him.

Harry Luthan made a good living. Some would say an exceptional living. With his seven-figure salary came prestigious perks, among them a yacht worthy of a Greek shipping magnate. On a sunny afternoon ideal for a party, Terry Thorne stood on the forward deck of the *Luthan I* and observed the seventy-odd partygoers enjoying themselves.

Terry couldn't bring himself to share their festive mood. He had been back for two weeks and he couldn't stop thinking of the Bowmans. Specifically, Alice Bowman, and the devastated look on her face when he walked out on her at the Intercon Hotel. She had trusted him, and he had let her down. Failed her spectacularly. Never mind the bond he had sensed they shared. Never mind that he liked her more than he had any right liking the wife of a client.

Time for a drink, Terry thought, and threaded through the revelers to the bar. Alcohol had a marvelous amnesiac effect he sorely needed right then. He was about to order when Ian Havery materialized at his side, holding two glasses brimming with champagne.

"Here you are! I was hoping to get a private minute together," the chief of K&R operations declared.

Terry accepted a glass.

"I wanted to thank you for a job well done down in Tecala," Havery said and took a drink. He'd already had close to his limit and was not as stiff-backed as usual.

"I didn't do anything," Terry said. Which had to be the understatement of the century. "Except bail out on those people."

"Here's to dodging bullets," Havery said. Clinking his glass against Terry's, he drank down some more bubbly. "Can you believe we almost lost a twelve million dollar account over that QUAD-CARBON fiasco?"

"Have you heard anything new?"

Havery shook his head. "I can't be bothered. Octonal was quite put off by the whole misadventure. I'm sure you were, as well. And rightfully so. I'll make it up to you, though. Right quick, too."

"What will happen to them?" Terry asked.

"To who?"

"The Bowmans. Our former clients."

Havery swished what was left of his champagne. "What does it matter? It's out of our hands. They'll find a way, I assume. In any event, it's past history, of no concern to us. On to bigger and better things."

Terry set his glass down. "So we just leave them there hanging high and dry? Is that it?"

"Here you go again," Havery said. "Getting all emotional on me. What did I tell you about remaining detached? What did I have to say about being professional?"

"It's just not right."

Some of Havery's good mood dissipated. "Since when does right and wrong matter? We're a business. We must conduct ourselves in a businesslike manner. QUAD-CARBON was no longer a client. What were we to do? Have you work for free? You know how long those things can take. A year, maybe longer."

Terry gazed across the Thames. He was so sick at heart he couldn't stand it, and nothing Havery was saying helped.

"Listen, the Bowmans will be fine." Havery draped an arm across Terry's broad shoulders. "Look, the real reason I wanted to talk is because I have a trip lined up to Bangkok. Two, three days at the most. Strictly management assignment. All you have to do is wave the flag. Talk to a few people. Afterward, I thought you might want a week at the beach in Phuket. What do you say?"

Terry looked at him.

Havery smiled. "To sweeten the trip, I'm thinking of sending Yasmine along. To back you up, so to speak." Havery winked. "She's expressed an interest in working with you, you know. So how about it? What do I tell Mr. Luthan?"

"I haven't let him down yet, have I?" Terry rejoined and downed his champagne in a single gulp.

*　　*　　*

113

Alice Bowman was sound asleep, the first real sleep she had enjoyed since Peter had been taken. Half a dozen gin and tonics had helped. She was adrift in inky limbo when a loud noise intruded on her slumber. Struggling up through a thick haze, she groped for the light switch and flicked it on. On the floor beside her bed was her broken glass. It had shattered when she'd let go, and she was careful not to step on the sharp shards as she rose and unsteadily moved to the hallway.

Someone was ringing the doorbell.

Alice glanced at the wall clock. It was three A.M. Whoever was out there began pounding on the door. "I'm coming!" Alice said, pulling her bathrobe tighter around her. She turned on more lights as she went, as much to illuminate the way as to offer security. "Who's there?" she called out, but no one answered.

Janis rushed up. "What is it? What's going on?"

"Hush," Alice said, waving her quiet. "Who's out there?" she asked again. "What do you want?"

"It's me!"

Me? Alice thought, and recognized the voice. Eliodoro, her neighbor. She opened the door and saw Norma hurrying toward them, wearing only a nightgown.

"Señora, I'm sorry," Eliodoro said. "We had a call a few minutes ago about Peter. They told me to look in my car. I found this." He extended a cell phone.

Norma arrived breathless. "They're calling back in a while. They want you to be ready for the call."

"In the middle of the night?" Janis said.

Alice held the phone as if it were a stick of dynamite ready to go off. "Call Mr. Fernandez on our own phone. Have him get over here. This is what we've been waiting for."

"After over a month," Janis complained, rushing to comply.

Inviting Eliodoro and Norma in, Alice padded to the kitchen to put on a fresh pot of coffee. She needed it more than they did. She needed a gallon. But she had to settle for two cups before Arturo Fernandez arrived, wearing a sweatsuit and sneakers. Eliodoro filled him in, and then Arturo asked for the cell phone.

Five minutes later, the call came. Alice lit a cigarette and hung on every word even though she didn't understand much of the conversation. Fernandez sat in a living room chair, hunched over, furiously jotting notes. Eliodoro and Norma were on the couch.

"Sí, sí, comprendo," Fernandez said for what had to be the hundredth time. *"Ire yo mismo si es necessario."* He listened awhile. *"Sí, hablamos."*

Alice straightened when he placed the phone down. "Well? What did they say?"

"He says Peter is alive," Fernandez reported. "A prisoner of war, they called him. They want five million dollars for his release."

"Oh my God!" Janis blurted.

"No, no," Fernandez said. "It is always a big number to start, but it is negotiable, yes?" He checked his notes. "The man says to make a better condition for Peter's food and care, and to prove for us he's still alive, they want to make a first transfer. Like a good faith payment, as soon as possible."

"The first transfer being what?" Alice asked.

Fernandez glanced at his notes again. "Six hundred thousand pesos. Is maybe fifty thousand dollars."

Alice wondered if she would be able to get the money together quickly. "Can we talk to him?"

"To this guy? On the phone?"

115

"No. To Peter."

Fernandez mulled it over. "I don't think so. I doubt he is near a phone. This guy who called, he's going to make one more contact, okay? He's going to tell us where to go for the transfer." He paused. "But this is good news. Peter is okay. The call, it's very fast for a case like this. Very fast."

Janis tapped Alice's arm and crooked a finger. "Will you excuse us a minute, Mr. Fernandez? We need to talk this over."

"Surely, señora, surely."

"What's to discuss?" Alice asked as her sister-in-law guided her to a nook just off the kitchen.

"I don't trust that man with fifty thousand dollars. Hell, I wouldn't trust him with five thousand under armed guard."

"What's our alternative?" Alice countered. They had none, and they both knew it. "If we screw this up we might never see Peter again."

Janis peered into the living room and lowered her voice. "Do you feel good about this? About him? Is that what you're telling me?"

"No, I don't," Alice confessed. "That's not the point."

"Because it feels . . . I don't know how to describe it." Janis described it anyway. "It feels thrown together. Out of control. Off-kilter." She lowered her voice even more. "Slick Willy in there isn't the only person who does this sort of thing. We should find someone else. Someone who doesn't raise the short hairs on my neck."

Alice shared the same sentiments, but was hesitant to do so now that they had finally heard from Peter's captors. "You've been on the phone for days now.

What do we have to show for it? Who have you found to replace him? No one."

"There's that guy in Miami. He's on a job right now, but I say we wait—"

"For how long? Five days? Two weeks? Another month? You want to comparison shop when Peter's life is at stake? Fernandez is with us here and now. As much as I hate to use him, he's all we've got."

Janis sighed. "I'm just trying to be smart about this." She took Alice's cigarette and took a long drag. "I gave up smoking four years ago, but what the hell."

"I know how you feel," Alice said. It was like their backs were up against the brink of a steep cliff, and they had nowhere to go but over the edge.

Rain had been falling for almost twenty-four hours. Peter was huddled in his lean-to, his arms wrapped around his legs, his teeth chattering from the cold. He had a small fire going, but it wasn't giving off much heat.

Fog was rolling in. Heavy fog, the kind where a person couldn't see their hand in front of their face. Peter couldn't wait for it to cover the camp. His moment had come. He would make a dash for it. He didn't give a damn how far he had to travel, or about the odds of making it back alive. He couldn't take being held captive another day.

The flap to one of the tents parted and out stepped Juaco, the SMG tucked at his side. Linda dogged his steps, carrying something Peter couldn't quite make out until they were almost to the lean-to. Then he stiffened and started to rise.

Juaco trained the submachine gun on him. "Stay where you are, *gringo*. We have a present for you."

The "present" was a length of steel chain, a metal stake, and a large padlock. Linda did the honors.

"This isn't necessary," Peter said as she worked. "Where does he think I'm going to go?" The fog was close, so very close.

Linda translated and Juaco exploded with a string of obscenities. She relayed the gist of his tirade. "He says you wear the chain. The rainy season has started. The fog comes. This is how it goes."

Juaco glared, challenging Peter to defy him, but Peter stood, crestfallen, and watched the fog bank roll in around them. "Ask him something else, then. Ask him if he knows how long I'll be here." He faced the arrogant, teenaged psychopath. *Cuanto tiempo aqui? Yo? Cuanto tiempo?*

Leering, Juaco said, "Until they pay the money or you die, Americano pig."

Terry and Yasmine stepped from the glittering casino at Heathrow Airport, Yasmine stuffing the money he had won for her into her handbag. She was provocatively dressed, her body a walking centerfold that turned heads as the two walked through the terminal.

"We still have half an hour before our flight," Yasmine mentioned and pointed at a bikini shop next door. "Do you mind? I won't be long. I need something to wear when we're sunning ourselves on the beach."

"Have fun," Terry said, unaffected by the enticing sway of her hips as she dashed inside. He stood alone, a motionless island amid the ebb and flow of waves of people, wrestling with his conscience, his heart, his very soul.

Bangkok. The playground for the decadent, the city where all inhibitions were put aside, where pleasure was king. Most would give a year's wages for a week there. Terry gazed through the shop window at Yasmine, busily examining a rack of thong swimwear. She was stunning. A man would have to be insane to pass up an opportunity to be alone with her in so exotic a locale.

Terry turned and headed for the phones. He found one not being used and placed a local call.

"Havery here."

"Ian, this is Terry."

"What's up, my boy? Isn't your flight due to leave shortly?"

"I won't be on it."

An awkward silence prevailed until Havery responded, "You don't say. Care to tell me why not?"

"You know why."

Havery seldom swore, but he did so now. "Think, man! Think of what you're doing. Pissing your career away, and to what end?"

"To help two people who need it."

"Damn you and your self-righteous attitude."

"That's the spirit," Terry said, and began to hang up.

"I'm asking you to reconsider, friend to friend," Havery said. "You've worked so hard, so long, and you're on the verge of great things. You stand to earn twice as much money as you're making now."

"Money isn't everything."

"Spare me the tired cliches," Havery snapped. "We're both seasoned veterans of the trenches. We've both seen enough of the real world to know differently. But if the money won't persuade you, then how about a position as third man on the totem pole at Luthan Risk International."

"Third, eh?"

"Mr. Luthan plans to make the announcement at our Christmas bash. I've dropped enough hints the past few months—you know I'm not bullshitting you." Havery paused. "Think of all you're passing up. The chance of a lifetime. And for what, Terry? Tell me, please. What do you get out of it?"

"I get to look at myself in the mirror again."

"Come now. Is that really worth throwing everything out the window?"

"If you have to ask, you're worse off than I thought," Terry said and hung up. Pulling the ticket to Thailand from an inner pocket, he ripped it to pieces and discarded them in a waste bin. Then, squaring his shoulders, he hurried to catch the next flight to South America.

Chapter 9

The Tecala National Bank was the oldest banking institution in the country. The building boasted a grandly elegant lobby and a bronze-gilt spiral staircase that led up to the plush offices of the bank's executives. Among them was the lavish office of Victor Santos, Senior Vice President. An expensive suit, gold watch, and a ruby ring testified to his prestige and income, and the slightly bored, slightly antagonistic look on his flawless face testified to his opinion of Americans. "So you want to wire some monies into Tecala, but you need to waive the normal forty-day holding period?" He consulted the application form in front of him. "Correct, Mrs. Bowman?"

"Yes," Alice said. They were there at Arturo Fernandez's insistence. He claimed he knew Victor Santos personally and that Santos was as decent and honest as the year was long. But based on her initial impression, Alice had grave doubts. Santos was a weasel. A well-dressed weasel, but a weasel just the same. And what did that say of Fernandez?

"Who is this C. H. Bowman?" Santos asked, a finger on the form.

"My father-in-law," Alice said.

Janis involved herself in the conversation. "He's my father. The money is being wired from his bank in Denver, Colorado."

Santos bent lower, his brow puckered. "You have a choice on this form. Two boxes. One states that the money is for living expenses, the other that the money will be used for investment." He looked at them. "You have checked both boxes."

Alice was becoming royally ticked off. Fernandez had supposedly explained the situation, yet here Santos was nitpicking them to death. "We made a mistake. If you'll look closely, you'll see that we crossed off living expenses and checked the box for investments."

"We wanted to get another form, but that one you have was the last one available," Janis elaborated. "They ran out, and the girl couldn't find any more." She motioned at Fernandez. "Don't just sit there like a bump on a log. Explain it to him."

Fernandez and Santos exchanged a flurry of Spanish. Alice keenly regretted not bothering to learn the language. For all she knew, the pair were somehow in cahoots and were planning to fleece them. "Look, if you have another form, we'll be glad to fill it out."

Santos rose and made for the door, taking the form with him.

"What the hell is going on?" Janis demanded.

"So sorry," Fernandez apologized. "He wants to help you. He feels for your plight. The forty-day waiting period can be waived. But there will be a fee, a commission. You understand?"

"A commission?" Janis said. "Don't you mean a waiver fee?"

Alice never ceased to be amazed at her sister-in-law's inability to grasp the obvious. "No, he means a bribe."

Arturo Fernandez shrugged. "Call it what you will, señora. But it is how things are done. We do as he asks, and he will bend the rules so you get the money you need to bring your husband back to you alive. You should be grateful, not mad."

"Arturo?" Alice said, smiling sweetly.

"Yes, Señora Bowman?"

The fury that had been roiling in Alice ever since Peter was kidnapped burst from her in a throaty snarl. "Don't ever tell me how I should feel. You got that?"

Fernandez never batted an eye. "Of course, Mrs. Bowman. Please forgive me if I overstepped myself."

Alice suppressed an urge to slap him silly. She had never felt so helpless, so useless, so completely dependent on others. And it was all Terry Thorne's fault. If he hadn't bailed out on them they wouldn't be at the mercy of every two-legged piranha they encountered. *Wherever you are, Mr. Thorne,* Alice thought, *I want you to know I hate you.*

Six hundred thousand pesos was a lot of money. A lot of bills. Especially when it was all in small denominations as the kidnappers had requested. Or should that be *supposedly* requested? Alice wondered as she helped Janis and Arturo Fernandez stuff the payment into a plastic bag. She didn't like any of this—didn't like the setup, didn't like having to trust Fernandez, didn't like the assistants he had brought along, Raymo and Nino, two young toughs who reeked of macho and malice. Nor was she happy about the shoulder holsters the three wore under their jackets.

"Only a few more stacks," Janis said.

The bag was bulging at the seams. They took turns

123

shoving the money in, and soon enough, the side of the bag ripped wide open and bills cascaded over the living room table and onto the floor.

"Damn!" Janis exclaimed.

Fernandez didn't appear any too happy either. He barked at his assistants, who were lounging in nearby chairs.

"This is ridiculous," Janis said. "We need something else to hold this much money."

Alice stared at the stacks scattered about her feet. A fortune by Tecalan standards. "I'm sure I can find something better, something sturdier."

"Please do," Fernandez said. "We must deliver it on time or the kidnappers will think we do not bargain in good faith."

Alice took a step, then stopped in her tracks when the front doorbell chimed. Everyone else also froze, the assistants giving their boss a worried look.

Fernandez reached under his jacket and unsnapped the strap on his holster so that he could draw his weapon quickly if he had to. "You have someone coming?"

"Not to my knowledge, no," Alice said. "I gave everyone the evening off just as you advised."

"No one knows what we are doing?" Fernandez asked as the chimes pealed a second time.

"No one."

One of the assistants had a hand on his revolver and whispered urgently to Fernandez, who motioned for him to be quiet. "Perhaps you should go see who it is and send them away," he suggested.

Alice walked through the living room and down the hall to the front door. Through the glass she beheld the last person she had ever expected to see again.

Resentment seized her. Without opening the door, she snapped, "What are you doing here?"

Terry Thorne appeared somewhat embarrassed. "I wanted to apologize."

"I thought you did that already," Alice said stiffly. For the life of her she couldn't imagine why he had returned. Not after so much time had gone by, and not now, of all moments. It seemed unreal.

Janis came up behind her. "Oh my gosh. It's you!"

"Hello, Janis," Terry said warmly. "I'm sorry to catch you both off guard like this, but I—"

"What do you want?" Alice demanded. He would get no respect from her after what he had done.

"I want to tell you how sorry I was about the way things went."

"That's great," Alice said. His sincerity was evident, but that still didn't excuse his betrayal. "It's just that we're kind of in the middle of something here."

Terry didn't take the hint. "I understand how you might be reluctant to hear me out, but I wanted to offer my services."

A spark of hope flared in Alice's breast, but she smothered it before it could swell unchecked. "I thought your hands were tied."

"They were," Terry said.

"What about your company?" Alice reminded him.

"I'd be doing it on my own."

Alice finally met his gaze head-on and a bolt of lightning seared her. *He had come back. He had come all the way from England at his own expense.* She heard Fernandez say something, heard Janis tell him everything was okay. It was plain Fernandez wanted Terry out of there. But instead of asking him to leave, she unlocked the door and opened it.

Terry glanced down the hall. "What's all this, then?"

"We're putting together a payment," Alice said.

"What kind of payment?"

"For Peter. A good faith payment."

"Good faith?"

Janis moved up beside Alice. "We're getting a proof of life. Isn't that what you called it? It's all been arranged."

"Really?" Terry's tone spoke volumes. "Who put this together?"

Arturo Fernandez chose that instant to intervene. Gesturing, he said, "*Señora*, I must insist. Right now is not good for visitors."

Terry glanced at Alice. "Is this your guy?"

Alice nodded, sensing a certain tense alertness in him, so immeasurably glad he was there she almost embraced him when he abruptly brushed past her.

"Hey, how are you doing?" Terry had both hands out and was shaking before Fernandez could object. "Terry Thorne. Nice to meet you."

"I'm sorry. Come back later, señor," Fernandez said gruffly. "We can't have people in here right now."

Terry breezed on by him toward the living room. "Come on, man, where's all that good faith?" he said, genially, smiling at Raymo, who barred the end of the hallway.

"*Señora*," Fernandez persisted. "Please!"

Alice came to Terry's defense. "It's all right. We know this man." They drifted after him, Alice amazed at how relaxed he was, at how he nonchalantly strolled past Raymo as if it didn't matter Raymo's hand was on his gun.

"*Que tal?*" Terry said to the assistants. "*Como estan? Como andan?*"

Raymo was understandably baffled and was looking to Fernandez for instructions. Fernandez went to speak, but Janis placed a hand on his arm and said, "No, really, it's okay. This is what he does."

Alice couldn't take her eyes off Thorne. She followed him into the living room, dazzled by the innocent act he was putting on.

"Whoa! Look at all the money!" Terry started toward the table and Nino moved to intercept him. A hand flashed, and Nino was holding a pistol. "Sweet Jesus! There's a guy in here with a gun!"

Fernandez shoved past Raymo and bawled, "You! *Oiga!*" He patted his holster. "You stop right here, okay?"

Terry halted. "Hey, I don't want any trouble."

Alice faced Arturo Fernandez. "Tell your man to put his pistol away!"

"We told you we know him!" Janis reiterated.

Fernandez paid no mind to either of them. He was only interested in Terry. "I asked you not to come in, okay? These ladies, maybe they don't understand so good. But you, I think you understand, right?"

"Definitely." Terry nodded. "I definitely get what's going down."

"I have my job to do. If you want to talk to these ladies, come back later," Fernandez directed.

"When the money is gone," Terry said.

"There you go." Fernandez smiled.

Terry smiled, too, and took another step. "See, here's the thing," he said, talking fast, gesturing smoothly, so slick Alice had no idea what he was up to. "You guys, you're probably well aware of this." Terry glanced at Fernandez. "And I promise I'll be brief." He looked at Raymo while taking yet another step closer to the table and Nino. "Good faith is for losers." He smiled at Nino. "You don't buy proof of life." His gaze drifted to Fernandez. "You don't pack money in a client's house unless it's an emergency." He focused on Nino once more and resorted to Spanish. *"Y yo creo que ustedes saben perfectamente de lo que estoy hablando."* He quickly glanced at Fernandez. "You don't flash weapons around people you're trying to help."

Alice saw a blur of motion, and suddenly Nino was on the floor, clutching a spot above a kidney and gritting his teeth. Terry now had Nino's weapon, but he made no attempt to raise it.

Fernandez and Raymo drew their guns and adopted two-handed grips, their pistols trained on Thorne.

"No!" Janis cried.

"Stop it!" Alice commanded, but she was wasting her breath.

Fernandez glowered at Terry, his finger curled around the trigger. "Okay, asshole. What are you going to do now?"

Terry was amazingly calm. "Ask them to leave," he told Alice.

"What?" So much had happened so fast, Alice was having a hard time coming to grips with it all.

"Thank him for his trouble, and tell them you want them both to leave."

"Me?" Fernandez butted in. *"You're* telling *me* to go?"

Alice looked from one to the other. She still couldn't get over the fact that Terry had come back. She would rather have him handle the negotiations, but he had crushed her heart once, and she was hesitant about trusting him a second time. "You're taking the case?"

"Yes."

Fernandez still had his weapon leveled and was fuming at the turn of events. When Nino began groaning, he snarled, "Get up off the floor, idiot!"

Janis moved to Alice's side. "How much for your services?" she asked Terry.

"Expenses only."

Arturo Fernandez had had enough. "Silence!" he hollered. "Put down the gun, señor, or I will blow your head off."

Slowly, carefully, Terry complied, smiling congenially. He didn't appear to be nervous or scared or upset at all, handling himself with collected professionalism.

Alice, though, was terrified. "Mr. Fernandez, I'd like for you to go. Now."

"You heard the lady," Terry backed her up.

Fernandez chuckled, the sound like the sinister rattle of a sidewinder about to lash out. "I'm not going anywhere. You think you can waltz in here and have me thrown out on my ear. Big man, eh? *Muy macho.*"

"May I make a suggestion?" Terry asked.

"Please. I would love to hear you talk your way out of this." Fernandez and Raymo were poised to cut loose at the slightest provocation.

"I think, first of all, you need to take a deep breath." Terry took his own advice and loudly inhaled and exhaled. "Then, very slowly, very nice and easy, I want you to turn around and meet Dino, an old friend of mine."

Alice looked beyond the two men. A dark-haired man had a shotgun fixed on Fernandez and Raymo. At that range, he could cut them in half if they twitched wrong.

"Arturo and I are old friends, too," Dino said amiably. "We go way back. He knows me. Knows what

129

I'm capable of." The metallic click of a hammer being pulled back was unnaturally loud in the sudden stillness. *"Arturo, no deberias andar contando tus asuntos de plata por todos partes, hermano."*

Alice let out a tense breath as Fernandez and Raymo complied to Dino's request, slowly lowering their guns to the floor.

Terry's first order of business was to escort Fernandez and the two goons off the property. While Dino led the other two off, he offered a few parting words to their boss.

"We'll forget this ever happened, right? We both know you were going to keep the money for yourself, but I won't hold it against you. Unless"—Terry swung around in front of the Tecalan, his face a mask of raw savagery—"unless I hear that you've bothered these women again. Then I will personally slit you from your crotch to your throat and leave you in a ditch for the scavengers to eat."

Fernandez backed up a step, his Adam's apple bobbing. "I believe you, señor. I didn't know you were Dino's friend when you came in. He likes to pull the trigger, that one."

"He's not the only one," Terry said. Grabbing Fernandez by the arm, he propelled him into the car and slammed the door.

Going back inside, Terry had Alice and Janis fill four plastic bags with newspapers and trash and line them up near the front door. They wanted to know why, and he explained that if the rebels were watching the house, he needed to trick them into thinking the money had been taken back to the bank. To that end, he phoned Sandro, their driver, and asked him to come over; Dino's friends on the police force had run a thorough background check and Sandro had come out clean.

For the next bit, Terry was left with nothing to do. Dino was on the phone again, checking with some other contacts of his. Janis was out on the patio indulging in her umpteenth cigarette since the confrontation with Fernandez.

Terry decided to find Alice and go over the steps they should take. She wasn't in the kitchen, and he didn't see her in the living room. He headed toward the stairs to call to her and heard soft sobs coming from a shadowed corner. Not wanting to intrude, but feeling a need to console her, he ventured nearer. "Alice?"

In the blink of an eye she was on her feet, crying uncontrollably, her arms around him, her face buried against his chest. Terry went rigid. He started to return the embrace, started to loop an arm around her waist, but changed his mind and put both hands on her shoulders. "Listen," he said gently, "Dino and Sandro are going to take the dummy bags into the city. Make it look good just in case. We'll keep the cash stashed here." Her fingers found his neck and a warm tingle spread down his body. Struggling to remain detached, he continued. "I need to know if there was any sort of plan. Were there any future contacts scheduled?"

Alice's breath fluttered across his neck. The tears had slowed, but were still trickling down her flushed cheeks. "Not that I know. We didn't—" Her voice broke, but struggled to go on. "There was nothing. We were just waiting." She was fused to him, their two bodies one, her lips brushing his throat. "I'm sorry. I haven't cried since this started. It's just the tension."

"You've got to let it out," Terry advised her.

Pulling back, Alice threw a curve ball at him. "Tell me the truth. Why are you doing this?"

"No one else is going to take your case," Terry answered. "No one any good." But was that the real reason? he asked himself. Or was he deluding both of them?

"I know. But you came back. You came all the way back."

Her wonderment, her affection, weakened Terry's inner resolve. With a conscious effort he pried himself loose. "And we're going to do this my way, right? Even if it's tough on you. You've got to learn to trust me."

Alice frowned. "You're something—you know that? I'm trying to thank you, and you're giving me shit."

Suddenly Terry sensed they weren't alone. He glanced sharply toward the hallway and there was Dino, a knowing smile on his face. "Do you want something?" Terry said more harshly than was called for.

Dino's smile widened. "The driver is here."

Two months, Peter Bowman thought. Two fucking months and there hadn't been one word, one ray of hope. Two months of freezing his ass off morning and night. Two months of subsisting on mere mouthfuls of food a day.

"I hate this," Peter said aloud. He had taken to talking to himself a lot of late. With one exception the others rarely said a word to him. More of Juaco's doing. Out of sheer meanness, the bastard had announced that no one was to converse with their hostage.

Raucous laughter rippled across the basin. Juaco, Alex, and Berto were seated around a large, flat rock, the "rock table" they called it, merrily cackling. They were indulging in their favorite pastime: getting wasted on brandy and cocaine.

Every day it was the same. The rebels slept in until eleven, then had one of the women cook a meal. The afternoon was spent drinking and smoking. By nightfall they were so blitzed they couldn't stand straight. Usually they stayed up until two or three in the morning, joking, arguing, and playing cards. Eventually sleep claimed them, and at noon the next day the whole cycle began anew.

A flap to one of the tents parted and out walked Linda, pulling a ruana around her to ward off the chill. The glance she bestowed on her male counterparts wasn't flattering. She had been increasingly unhappy of late. Why, Peter didn't know, but she'd had several heated exchanges with Juaco.

It was Linda's job to tend the llamas. Each day she fed and watered them; each day she walked right past Peter's lean-to.

Today Peter tried to get her attention. "Linda?" he said, and when she gave him the same raw look she'd given the others, he clasped his hands to his upper arms and trembled to convey how cold he was. *"Madera. Por favor."* He nodded at a pile of sticks and broken limbs just beyond the limit of his chain. *"Para el fuego."*

Linda turned away. She was in one of her sour moods. Wringing kindness from her would be the same as wringing water from a stone. She was almost to the llamas when automatic fire thundered off the walls, followed by peals of hysterical laughter. Juaco and his boys were taking out their boredom on another empty bottle.

Peter tried once again to engage her in conversation

regarding the guerrillas' political affiliation. *"Escuchando esta cojudez toda la noche."* She wouldn't take the bait and reply. *"Diles que Japon."* Her head began to turn but stopped. Construing that as a sign of interest, Peter rattled off in English, "Japan isn't a communist country. Never was. And while we're at it, there's no more communism in Russia, either. Or Germany or Hungary or basically anywhere, except maybe Cuba, and even that's seriously debatable. So you see? You're devoted to a lost cause."

Linda started leading a llama to the stream.

"Que tal revolucion que estan haciendo ustedes!" Peter sought to get a rise out of her by goading her and her beliefs; but he was not successful. Oh well, he thought. Occasionally it worked, and she would whisper to him in secret for a while. But not today.

Dejected, Peter hunkered under the lean-to. He couldn't understand why it was taking so long to earn his freedom. He knew QUAD-CARBON had K&R insurance, a fact he'd always kept from Alice for fear of adding to her emotional burdens. At a briefing he'd attended, they'd told him that in the advent of a kidnapping, an expert in the field would be brought in to negotiate and payment arranged as soon as feasible.

So what was the delay? Peter puzzled it over while watching a few stray tendrils of mist writhe across the basin. Were the guerrillas asking more than QUAD-CARBON was willing to pay? Did they overrate his importance to the company? He wished he had been able to get it through their thick heads that he wasn't connected to the pipeline.

Peter had another, more troubling, notion. What if the delay was caused by Octonal's buyout of QUAD-CARBON? What if he had been lost in the shuffle? He had no clue what Octonal's corporate position on ransom might be. Some companies flatly refused to pay under any circumstances, and Octonal might be one of them. Maybe the rebels had contacted whoever was now in charge and been told to taking a flying leap.

What would they do in such a case? Would they kill him?

Peter refused to give up hope. Maybe Octonal had abandoned him, but Alice never would. It wasn't in her nature. She would do whatever it took to get him back. Move heaven and earth, as the saying went. She was one tough lady when she needed to be, and he had unbounded confidence she would succeed.

Peter touched the collar of his shirt. God, how he missed her! In his darkest moments it always helped to think of her, to remember the joy of holding her in his arms, the rapture of making love, the many fun times they'd shared.

"Alice won't let me down," Peter said softly. "Not her. Not in a million years."

Chapter 10

The famed Saint Tecala Cathedral was enshrined on postcards and featured on the itinerary of every Tecala City tour bus. An imposing stone-and-stained-glass edifice five stories high, it gleamed brightly in the afternoon sun.

As the taxi Terry Thorne was in screeched to a halt at the curb, he spotted Alice Bowman midway up the wide stone steps leading to the central arch. He was out the door before the cab stopped rolling, the urgency in his stride matched by her dire expression. "Who talked to them?" he asked, bounding toward her.

"Janis answered the phone. I was in the shower."

An image popped unbidden into Terry's head of Alice standing under a cascade of water, droplets running down her bare skin, of her hair plastered to her head, her lips upturned. Catching himself, he glanced at the majestic spires high overhead. "Let's go in."

"Thank God Maria was there to translate," Alice said, taking his hand.

The interior was awash in the musty scent of ages and the reverence of dozens of parishioners attending a Mass now being delivered by a gray-haired priest.

"They said we should check the altar below the black Jesus," Alice disclosed.

"Stay here." Terry was unsure what to expect. The kidnappers had only told them they would find something important. It might be proof of life. One of Peter's fingers, maybe, or an ear. He'd rather spare Alice the horror if he could.

The cathedral was immense. Terry prowled down one aisle and across another. Nowhere was there a black Jesus. A few parishioners, on their knees in the pews, studied him as he went by. Turning a corner, he roved toward the rear.

A dusky statue loomed before him, an exquisite black Jesus sculpted in intricate detail. On a pitted table below it lay a tattered cloth.

Terry wasn't taking anything for granted. Crouching, he peered underneath the table, checking for booby traps. A few years ago a K&R associate had gone to pick up a new ransom demand and been blown to pieces when he hastily opened a cardboard box that contained a bomb rigged with plastic explosive. Apparently the kidnappers had decided he wasn't bargaining in good faith and had eliminated him.

No wires or relays were attached anywhere. Terry pulled a pen from his pocket, gingerly slid it under the end of the cloth, and raised the cloth high enough for a peek. All he saw was a slip of paper.

Satisfied it was safe, Terry flipped the cloth off and studied the sheet. At last they had made headway. He was smiling when he rejoined Alice, and he waved the paper, saying, "Great news. They sent a list of radio frequencies, times to call, that sort of thing. We're on for this Friday night."

"At last," Alice said.

"We'll need someone to translate," Terry mentioned.

"Why? I thought you were fluent in Spanish."

"Not fluent enough. We need someone who speaks it like a native. Someone sensitive to shades of meaning and nuances I might miss."

"Sandro?" Alice proposed as they emerged from the cathedral.

"I was thinking your good friend Eliodoro," Terry said. "His wife would do just as well, but as a general rule the rebels don't like to deal with women." He'd had the couple checked out, and they were as clean as Sandro. The only difference was that Eliodoro's English was much better than Sandro's and precise translation was crucial in such delicate situations.

"I'm sure he won't object."

They walked to the curb, where the taxi was waiting. So was Sandro, over by the jeep.

Alice lingered. "Thanks for coming so quickly. I was afraid you wouldn't be in. It's a pity you're not closer."

Terry didn't want to touch that one with a twenty-foot pole. "I'm always just a phone call away." He tapped his cell unit. "And I never turn it off, even when I go to bed."

"Did you ever hear from your former bosses in London?"

"They've tried to convince me to go back, yes," Terry admitted. A week ago he had let the circumstances of his parting with Luthan Risk slip out, and he had regretted telling her about it ever since.

"I can't get over how you didn't mention it sooner," Alice said. "It was so decent of you, so noble."

"Oh, please," Terry responded. "I lost my halo decades ago. What I did, I did for me. Don't build it up as more than it was."

"If you say so," Alice said, her eyes belying the

statement. "But I can never thank you enough." She grinned self-consciously. "I mean, Peter and I can never thank you enough. He's almost as decent a man as you are."

With that she was gone, whisking away to the jeep. Terry stared after it, her one phrase "almost as decent" ringing in his ears. If she only knew. Ever since he had arrived back in Tecala City, he found himself thinking of her constantly.

And it had nothing to do with saving her husband.

Another wonderful day at Camp Insanity, as Peter had nicknamed his volcanic prison bivouac. For once the day was warm, and he had taken the occasion to strip to his shorts and fully wash his filthy clothes. They were presently strung across a rope, drying.

Close by, Alex was guarding him. Or pretending to be. Alex had the submachine gun slung over his skinny shoulder and was kicking a soccer ball in a circle while at the same time smoking a joint. Most of his kicks went astray.

Juaco was at the rock table sucking on a pipe as if his lips were permanently attached to it. In the pipe was brown cocaine paste, *basuco* the locals called it, and he was as wasted as a man could be and still be conscious.

Linda and Berto had gone off down the stream to bathe, an occurrence that hadn't sat all that well with their leader.

"Who needs a soap opera?" Peter commented to himself, and moved toward the rope to check his clothes. The chain rattled against his ankle, his skin chafed from where the links constantly rubbed against his foot.

The next moment the basin rocked to the blast of three evenly spaced shots from the rim far above.

Juaco jumped up, spilling the *basuco* into his lap. Alex tossed the joint aside as if it were a hot ember. And out of a tent rushed Cara, buttoning a blouse.

Figures were silhouetted against the sky. More rebels, Peter guessed. Maybe with word of his release.

Juaco lurched toward Alex, his eyes dilated, a pantywaist Frankenstein trying to act the part of a military commander. "Give me the gun!" he ordered, and when the other youth fumbled with the sling, he screeched, "Give me the fucking gun!"

Alex wasn't any too eager to obey, but he did.

Swaying unsteadily, Juaco pointed the SMG at the clouds, set the selector to single shot, and banged off three rounds. Pleased with himself, he puffed out his string bean chest. "Now get the *gringo* back into his little tent."

Peter wanted his shirt. Motioning at the clothesline, he said, "*Mi camisa, mi cuchara.*"

"Okay, okay, *muevete,*" Alex granted permission.

His chain clanking, Peter took another step, only to be brought up short by a roar from Juaco directed at hapless Alex.

"What did I fucking tell you?"

"But he only wants his shirt!"

Juaco never liked having a command questioned. He liked it even less now. Glowering at Peter, he hissed, "When I give you an order, you stinking faggot *gringo,* you do what I say. I am the boss here. Me!"

"*Quiero mi camisa, mi cuchara,*" Peter pleaded.

Growling like a beast, Juaco weaved forward, his eyes and the blue-black submachine gun both glittering. He was close to the breaking point, and everyone realized it.

"Juaco, por favor," Cara tried to calm him.

"Callate!"

The hothead waved for Peter to move toward the lean-to, but Peter had been bullied for the last time. He held his ground, staring back daggers, and taunted, "Do you know what I'd love? Five minutes alone with you without that gun. Just you and me, you obnoxious prick, and we'll see who's the last man standing."

Incensed, Juaco stopped. "You don't tell me—you got that? I tell to you."

"I'd take you apart without breaking a sweat," Peter predicted and grinned to rub the point home. *"Comprende?"*

Juaco was beet red. "I tell to you!" he screamed. "Move, you fucking *gringo* pig! Move your ass! Move now!"

Peter braced himself. "I want my shirt, and I'm not going anywhere until I get it."

Violence was imminent. Cara yelled for Juaco to stay calm, and Linda and Berto were racing back from the stream, Linda shouting, wanting to know what was going on. Alex simply stood there, either too stoned or too scared to say anything.

Juaco stopped swaying. "I told you to move, ass-hole." He sighted down the barrel.

Peter was past being intimidated, past fearing for his life. "Point that thing at me one more time, and I don't care how bad ass you think you are. I'll make you eat it." He jabbed a thumb at the clothesline. "I want my shirt."

"You want your stinking shirt?" Uttering a feral screech, Juaco began firing at the clothesline, round after round, the slugs tearing through the faded cotton in erratic patterns, stitching right, then left. In his fury he continued to shoot even after the shirt was hanging by threads. He shot at the stream, at the sky, at the tents, at the ground around Peter's feet, firing in a frenzy until the magazine went empty. Still, his finger pulled back on the trigger.

Peter never moved. Never gave way. He had called the other's bluff and won. His only regret was that he hadn't done it sooner.

Juaco was shaking like a reed in a gale, ashen, spent, defeated.

"Look!" Alex said, more a whimper than a word. "Look at what you did to me!" He pointed at his foot.

The kid had been hit. A stray slug had bored through his foot leaving a hole the size of a walnut. Blood gushed like a fountain from the wound.

Cara was horrified. "Juaco!" She had always been the quiet one of the bunch, the timid one. But now she yanked the SMG from Juaco's grip and slapped him across the face with all her force.

Alex started weeping. Linda and Berto arrived and gaped, speechless, at the spreading crimson pool.

As wasted as Juaco was, the enormity of his blunder was sinking in, and he glanced apprehensively at the figures scuttling down the side of the basin—an E.L.T. platoon, all adults, all hardened veterans.

Peter hoped they skinned the vicious runt alive.

But no such luck.

After Cara had explained and Alex had been bandaged, the head of the platoon took Juaco into a tent and closed the flap. No sounds leaked out, no voices, nothing. They were in there a long time and when Juaco finally came out he was visibly pale, sweaty and so shaken that he staggered over to the rock table and collapsed, his head in his hands. No one extended any sympathy. The new arrivals treated him with contempt, and his old companions avoided him as if he were a rabid cur.

Still, things were looking up. About an hour later Linda approached the lean-to carrying a bowl heaped high with food. "By orders of the sergeant," she said.

Peter's stomach rumbled. He'd noticed the other guerrillas were eating and had expected the usual pittance for himself, but finally, this was a real meal. "Thank him for me."

Linda wasn't finished. "You leave. In the morning. With the soldiers."

"Where to?" Peter asked, but she wouldn't say. She held out her other hand. In it was what was left of his shirt. Tossing the tattered garment down, she departed.

As hungry as he was, Peter set the bowl aside, shifted his body so that his back was to the rebels, and pried at the seam of the collar. The loose threads easily came undone. Eagerly, he inserted a forefinger and pulled out the photo of Alice. It was faded and worn, but intact. None of the bullets had hit it. He touched his finger to her face, choking back tears.

"God, I miss you."

The communications relay station, as Dino referred to it, was a small warehouse perched on a ridge overlooking Tecala City. "Welcome to my hideaway," Dino greeted Terry at the door and ushered him inside.

The place wouldn't win any *Good Housekeeping* awards. Footlockers, ammo cases, weapons of all kinds, a tripod, surveillance devices and communications equipment, a computer, and much more were scattered willy-nilly, with no rhyme or reason. In a corner stood a refrigerator, purring noisily.

"What's all this?" Terry said in mild surprise.

Dino grinned. "I think of it as my CNN relay station. My little roadhouse on the information highway."

"So how's your case going?" Terry idly asked, examining the assorted collection of equipment.

"Slow. But better than Wyatt's. He lost his cargo."

"Sorry to hear that." Terry glanced toward a beach chair where his English friend was sucking on a beer, drunk and oblivious to the world. He stepped over a backpack filled with flares and skirted a crate containing a dozen pistols. "Christ, mate, when did you turn into such a bloody packrat?"

"What can I tell you?" Dino shrugged. "Tecala has become the kidnaping capital of the world. Out of my last six assignments, four were down here. I was tired of buying gear every time I came. So I started collecting stuff. And it hit me that I could make a few bucks on the side by selling my surplus to other K and R guys."

"What about a scramble phone?" Terry asked.

"Check the table in front of you."

Sure enough, Terry found one and was examining it when Wyatt sat up.

"Terrence! A breath of fresh air if ever there was one. Have you heard the earthshaking news?"

"Dino just told me."

Wyatt focused with definite effort. "Can you believe it? I haven't had a client die on me since '91. And that was Mexico, where a third of them die anyway." He downed more beer, dribbling some on his chin. "I had no idea Canadians could be so bloody emotional. They were keening away like a bunch of bloody Brazilians."

"How did it happen?"

"A heart attack," Wyatt said and snorted. "He just up and had a massive coronary. No one's fault, actually. He just couldn't take the strain."

Terry wagged the scramble phone. "Dino, this is my old one. Remember? I lent it to you three years ago."

"Ah, yes, back when life in Tecala was oh-so-simple," Dino waxed nostalgic, then became serious. "So, what, you're expecting a discount?"

Wyatt was still absorbed in his personal calamity. "The kidnappers demanded twenty-five thousand for the body. They had no clue what a bargain that is. Those teary-eyed Canadians would have paid ten times as much." He swilled the last of the beer. "Well, I'm well out of it, mate—I'll tell you that. You poor bastards are in for it down here." He gazed out the door. "This place, I'll tell you, it's taken on a decidedly hinky-dinky-stinky feel to it. Everyone stroking everyone else's private parts. It's a damned kidnapping orgy."

"You'll be back, Wy," Terry said. "You'll see."

Wyatt was looking around for more beer. "No, I'm afraid not, mate. I'm out of the business for good this time. I'm retiring."

Dino rolled his eyes at Terry as if to say, How many times have we heard this before? To Wyatt he said, "Get over it, man. You're going to wake up on a job in the Philippines and not even know how you got there."

Wyatt had found another bottle. "Why is it no one ever believes me when I say I'm kicking the K and R habit?"

"Because you were born to it, just like us," Dino said. "What else would you do? Sell used cars? Be a security guard at a shopping mall?"

"The only thing I was born to do is see how much alcohol I can imbibe in one lifetime," Wyatt said, opening the beer with a flourish. "Everything else is superfluous." He cocked an eye at them. "And that goes for life itself."

Peter Bowman hiked along a winding jungle path humming to himself. From time to time some of the E.L.T. platoon members shot puzzled glances at him, unable to fathom why he was so happy. But to Peter's way of thinking he had a lot to be glad about. For starters, Camp Insanity was many miles and many days behind them. He had seen the last of that miserable volcanic basin, and he wouldn't miss it one bit. Then there was the joyous fact that the chain and padlock were gone. The sergeant in charge had ordered they be removed and instructed Linda to apply ointment to reduce the chafing and swelling.

Peter was also eating regularly again. Decent, hot meals. He estimated he had lost forty pounds in captivity and was as close to being skin and bones as a man could get without being a cadaver. Which the sergeant didn't like. Juaco had been reprimanded a second time, only in public, in front of all the rest, and Peter had heard every word.

The sergeant had gone on about how important it was to keep captives fed and in good health. Juaco, being his usual brainless self, had sniped, "Why go to so much bother over a stinking *gringo*, eh?"

With a quick bound, the sergeant had his fingers clamped around the younger man's throat and began throttling the life out of him. "You just won't learn, will you, stupid? This Americano and others like him, they are valuable, yes? They are worth a lot of money to us so we must make sure nothing happens to them." The sergeant had shaken Juaco like a terrier shaking a rat, then shoved him to the dirt in contempt. "They are worth much more than you, who goes around shooting his own people."

The sight of Juaco gurgling and groveling was one Peter would relish for a long time.

Now on the way to a new camp, Peter was in better spirits than he had been in months. He was sure it wouldn't be long before the ransom was paid and he was freed.

Suddenly everyone halted. The guerrillas tilted their heads skyward to the east, and in another moment Peter heard it, too: the repeated *whomp-whomp-whomp* of rotor blades. The sergeant barked instructions and everyone scrambled for concealment. The mules and llamas were pulled into deep shadows.

A muscular rebel pushed Peter toward a log and shoved him down beside it. Peter peered up through the forest canopy as a pair of army helicopters, gunships on routine patrol he assumed, flew overhead. They blitzed in low over the greenery, the machine gunner probing the vegetation, but not spotting the platoon or the animals through the dense foliage.

Peter was tempted to call out, but he knew the men in the choppers wouldn't hear him. And valuable or not, he wouldn't put it past the guerrillas to stick a knife or machete into him to silence him if their own lives were at risk.

Within seconds the choppers had banked and were gone.

Peter didn't care. He was going home soon. He was sure of it.

The first contact wasn't going well. Terry Thorne stood behind Eliodoro in the Bowman study and listened to the tirade coming from the speakers in fiery Spanish.

"What kind of bullshit game do you think this is,

anyway? That we're stupid about this? That we're not serious? Because I tell you, if you think this is how things are done, it's clear you are not serious people and that this can only be a waste of our time."

The Bowman study had been converted to a radio room. Dino had supplied most of the equipment. The rest Terry had scrounged on his own.

Alice was there, endlessly pacing. Janis hovered expectantly. Norma was watching her husband at the microphone.

Terry bent over Eliodoro and said quietly, "Tell him the people he spoke with before didn't represent the family. Tell him the family wants to do this in a way that's good for everyone. So nobody feels stupid."

Eliodoro pressed the transmit button and did as Terry had directed. *"Esta gente no era la familia. La familia quiere que todo salga bien. Para que nadie se sienta como un estupido."*

The voice at the other end wasn't appeased. "We had an arrangement, and you pull this bullshit? Forget it. Where's the family? Put the family on to talk."

"Tell him to forget it," Terry said. "Tell him we speak for the family now." When Eliodoro hesitated, he gripped the man's arm. "Just do it."

The voice on the radio switched to English. "You're going to put his wife on, or we're going to forget the whole fucking thing."

Terry snatched the microphone. Learning that the man on the other end of the line spoke English made things a whole lot easier. "Who is this? What's your name?"

"Who is this?" the man snapped back.

"Tio," Terry said without missing a beat. "You can call me Tio, okay?" He smiled at Alice, who had stopped and was gnawing on her lower lip. "You're not setting all the rules here. We have to work together to get this going. And we want to work with you. But we need proof of life, and we're not going to pay for it. If there's good faith it can start with that."

"So you, Tio," the man said angrily, "are you the one in charge here now?"

"That's right."

"Then you'll be the one with this man's blood on your hands."

The transmission at the other end was terminated and static crackled like bacon in a frying pan.

"God, no!" Janis cried.

Alice took a step toward the radio. "He's gone!"

Terry turned off the radio, conscious of their accusing stares. "Get used to it. This is how it's done."

Eliodoro sagged in the chair. Norma came over and began rubbing his shoulders. Janis lit another cigarette.

Alice closed her eyes a moment, then wheeled and bolted.

"I'll be back," Terry told the others and went after her. She wasn't in the living room. She wasn't in the kitchen, either. She had fled out onto the patio and was lighting a cigarette of her own. When she dropped the pack onto the table, Terry helped himself.

"I've never seen you smoke," Alice commented.

"I do when I play cards." Terry leaned against a chair a comfortable distance away from her.

"Is that supposed to be reassuring?"

"It's how these things go."

"Peter isn't a game," Alice declared.

"Remember when I told you to trust me? Remember you telling me you could? Was that all hot air?"

Alice faced him. "Who do you care about?"

I care about you, Terry almost said. Instead, he curtly responded, "Are you implying I don't have your husband's best interests at heart? I deserve better than that." Terry spoke more gently, "Look, we're on track here. They've come to us. We've established radio contact. This is all positive."

For a long while Alice didn't say a thing. Then out of the blue she mentioned, "Dino says you have a thirteen-year-old son."

"Imagine that. An ogre like me. Were you shocked?"

"A little."

"Think how I feel." To Terry it seemed his ex-wife had just given birth a few days ago. Time flew by so incredibly, terribly fast.

"What if it was him? What if it was your son up there in the mountains?"

Her tenacity was extraordinary, Terry thought. "I'd get someone I trusted to handle the negotiations and do whatever they told me to do."

"Touché," Alice said, and softened. "Is your son going to be a soldier like his dad?"

"A pilot. So he can get all the girls."

"And you never remarried?"

Terry was uncomfortable discussing his private life. "I took up the veil," he said, making light of his often profound loneliness.

"A confirmed bachelor?"

"I prefer 'man of the world.'" Terry smiled. "You do this kind of work, you get into a rhythm. It just takes over."

"And your wife?"

"She never liked my being away so much. Not that she's a paragon. She's on husband number four at the moment." Terry looked at her and said what she really wanted to hear. "They know what he's worth, Alice. They're not about to do anything rash."

"I hope to God you're right."

Chapter 11

After three weeks of slogging through the jungle, of hiding from random army patrols, of sleeping on the hard ground every night, Peter's good mood had long since evaporated. He was beginning to think the guerrillas intended to keep him on the move forever when one sunny afternoon the platoon emerged from the dank jungle and before them unfolded a narrow valley. In the center was a rebel encampment. Camouflage netting covered buildings and sheds scattered among the trees. Maybe thirty rebels were present at the camp, and when the platoon leader hailed them, they rushed to meet him.

Presently two soldiers steered Peter toward a shack. To the west a farm terraced a slope, a large adobe farmhouse on the crest; to the south clouds roosted on a sawtooth ridge. All very picturesque, but of no consequence compared to Peter's new home.

The shack had wooden walls and a thatched roof. Fresh straw bedding had been provided, and to one side was a small table and a gourd. To Peter it was the Grand Hilton. It even had a door for privacy's sake, which the two soldiers closed after one of them said, "You stay here, understand? We bring food later."

Peter sat and tugged at his shredded boots. Neither would last much longer. His feet were in nearly as bad shape. Bloody, swollen, they needed to be soaked in a bucket of ice. Peter closed his eyes and leaned back, so tired that he longed to sleep for hours on end. Suddenly, something hissed. Startled, he pushed away from the sound, fearing it was one of several species of deadly snakes the guerrillas had warned him about. But it was a man standing outside, his bearded face pressed to a gap in the planks.

"Don't make noise! Quiet, ja? We must whisper."

Peter's heart was pounding like a jackhammer. All he could do was nod.

"You just came from the mountains, ja? I am Kessler. Erich Kessler." A matted white beard covered the fellow's broad face. His clothes seemed to be in a little better shape than Peter's. "I am German missionary."

"Bowman. Peter Bowman."

"You have heard of me, maybe, yes? About my situation? Some news, ja?" Kessler was so anxious he was pitiable. "Any news at all?"

"No," Peter said. "I'm sorry. Nothing." He slid closer. "You're a hostage, too?"

"Nothing?" The missionary pressed his forehead to the plank and groaned. "Yes, I am hostage. There is another, an Italian up at the farm. He came a week ago. He's your friend maybe?"

"I've never heard of him, either. I came alone."

Kessler looked up. "He is sick, I hear. They won't let me see him."

"What kind of camp is this?" Peter inquired. His hope was the rebels would only keep him there a few days, then move on, lower down the mountains toward the city.

"It was once for only drugs," Kessler said. "To make cocaine at the river. Now from the fighting, it's all soldiers. And us."

"How long have you been here?"

Kessler stiffened at the sound of footsteps. "I must go," he whispered. His eyes darted to Peter's feet. "You need soap, bandages, my new friend. Maybe tomorrow I can bring them. We'll see." He was about to leave but he glanced back and grinned. "They think I'm crazy."

"Please." Peter moved to the crack. "How long have you been here?"

"Nineteen months."

The missionary skulked off, leaving Peter to his new prison and an acute sense of foreboding.

The very next day something unusual occurred.

Exhaustion had taken a heavy toll and Peter slept in late. When someone pounded on the door, he assumed it was a guard bringing his morning meal, and he sluggishly rose and shuffled to open it.

Outside stood the two soldiers who had brought him to the shack. Mono and Rambo, he had nicknamed the pair. With them were half a dozen others. One was an E.L.T. officer. Another held a camera with a flash.

"What is this?" Peter asked in Spanish.

"Step out here," the officer commanded and thrust a newspaper at him. "Take this and sit there." He pointed.

Not knowing what to make of it, Peter did as he was bid.

"Open the newspaper."

"Like this?" Peter said. No sooner had he done so than Rambo stepped up and kicked him on the right foot. The pain was excruciating. Peter grimaced, suffering waves of anguish, and it was then the soldier with the camera pressed the shutter and the flash lit like the sun. "What the hell was that for?" Peter said through clenched teeth. "Of all the stupid stunts!"

"*Llevenselo,*" the officer said.

Before Peter could object, Rambo roughly grabbed hold of him and lifted. Furious, hurting, Peter pushed the soldier away. "Get your goddamn hands off me!"

Rambo clenched his fists, and other guerrillas moved in to help. Peter was willing to take them all on. But around a corner of the shack dashed Erich Kessler, waving a Bible.

"*En el nombre de Dios, dejenme a este hombre! Ya basta, basta! Que venga conmigo! Sueltenlo!*"

Unfazed, Rambo told the bearded apparition to leave.

"*Esta enfermo!*" Kessler railed. "Defy me and you defy the Almighty! I am his instrument. And I tell you to leave this man alone."

His face twisted with hate, Rambo made as if to pounce on the German missionary.

Peter prepared to help Kessler, but assistance came from another source: the officer.

"No. He is not to be touched. Word has spread of him, and the people say he is blessed of God. Harm him, and we harm the revolution."

Kessler smiled, grasped Peter's arm, and tugged. "Take some exercise with me."

Limping badly, Peter blistered the air with his opinion of Rambo.

"Let it go," Kessler said. "It's nothing." He nodded at the opposite slope. "You see? Up there at the farm-

154

house? That's where they've got the Italian. They figure he'll bring a lot more than either of us, so they treat him like royalty."

"He'll likely get out of here long before we do," Peter noted.

Erich Kessler smirked and winked. "Not if we can help it, ja? As soon as your feet are better, we are both of us getting out of here."

Alice didn't expect much to come of their visit to the U.S. Embassy. She'd let Janis drag her there against Terry's advice and the three of them had been cooling their heels in the waiting room of one Dover McLoon, the Assistant to the Deputy Chief of the Mission, for the better part of an hour.

"I don't understand why Mr. McLoon has kept us waiting so long," Janis griped. "I told him how important this was, and he assured me he would give it the attention it deserved."

Alice saw Terry's mouth twitch downward. She was getting to know him so well, she flattered herself she could guess what he was thinking. "Maybe this *is* what he thinks we deserve."

"We're U.S. citizens," Janis said. "We have a right to be heard and to demand that our government aid us to the best of its ability."

"Governments do what's best for them, not for the average schmuck off the street," Terry remarked.

"I refuse to believe the U.S. government would turn its back on one of its own," Janis argued. "It's not the American way."

"The land of the free and the home of the brave," Alice recited. "Is that what you're saying?"

"Our country has a long history of helping the underdog," Janis said. "We're the land of Washington, Jefferson, and Lincoln."

"Times have changed, I'm afraid," Terry told her.

Without warning the door to McLoon's office burst open and out hustled a balding man wearing thick-rimmed glasses. He angled toward the hallway, treating them as if they weren't there.

Terry rose. "Hello, Dover."

McLoon stopped. "Terry? You're involved with these people? I didn't know. No one informed me."

"This is Alice Bowman, the hostage's wife," Terry made the introductions, "and his sister, Janis."

"I talked to her on the phone," McLoon said, gaining speed again, forcing them to rise and fall into step with him or be left behind. "I know we were scheduled to meet, and I'm really, really sorry. But something has come up."

"We've been waiting for forty-five minutes," Janis complained.

"I'm not at fault here," McLoon said, veering into the corridor. Other embassy personnel were converging on him. "I want to hear about your progress. Honestly I do. I'm sympathetic to your plight. We all are." He walked even faster. "But the thing is, we've had a situation develop, and I'm needed elsewhere."

"What kind of situation?" Terry asked.

McLoon came to a door that bore a large sign: EM-BASSY STAFF ONLY. He paused before pushing on through. "The E.L.T. just lit off three car bombs around the city. They've threatened the embassy will be next. It's a mess. The ambassador wants me to issue a statement. So under the circumstances . . ." He turned his back to them. "I'm sorry. So sorry."

For a while neither of them moved; then Janis

summed up what each of them was feeling. "Well, he was a big help."

Alice trailed the other two outside. Extra Marines were en route to the main gate. People were scurrying around like mice in a maze. Off in the distance sirens shrieked. Coils of black smoke roiled into the sky half a mile away. Tecala City had become a raving madhouse and fate had trapped her there with the rest of the inmates.

Alice saw Terry scan the street. He was always alert, always the professional. She walked around to the jeep's passenger side while he unlocked the doors and opened the rear one for Janis. Upset they had pursued another dead end, she didn't pay much attention as she started to slide in. Then she noticed Terry staring at her seat, and she glanced down.

An unmarked white envelope lay where she was about to sit.

"Where did that come from?" Alice blurted. "It wasn't there earlier." She started to pick it up, but Terry snatched it out of her hand. "Hey! What's the big idea?"

Without answering, Terry stuffed it into his pocket and revved the engine. He checked the rearview mirror and looked right and left.

"What are you doing?" Alice demanded.

Janis leaned between them. "What is it? What's going on?"

"They might be watching us," Terry said. Expertly working the shift, he whipped the jeep from the curb and merged into the flow of traffic.

"Is it from them?" Alice asked, excited. "Why aren't we opening it? What are you waiting for?"

"Not here. Not yet," Terry said, changing lanes like

a racing pro. "We'll do it in private." He shifted again, and the jeep leaped ahead.

Alice couldn't grasp what difference that made, but she reasoned he knew best. The next seventeen minutes were an agony of suspense. When they squealed up in front of the Intercon Hotel, she was out of the jeep first. The desk clerk called to Terry, but he breezed by the front desk without breaking stride.

"Where are you taking us?" Janis wanted to learn.

"My suite," Terry said. "We won't be disturbed."

Alice hadn't been in a man's hotel room since before she married Peter. She wondered if Terry was as slovenly as most males and was pleasantly taken aback to find the suite tidy. He had set up an office of sorts in the living room that included electronic apparatus and other items she was unfamiliar with.

"I want you to sit down," Terry directed. "Both of you." He poked a finger at a sofa. "Over there. Go on."

Alice felt her impatience mounting to new heights. She watched him open a desk drawer and remove a small tool kit. "Can you please just open the thing?"

"Is it the proof of life we asked for or not?" Janis quizzed.

"Sit down."

His tone brooked no dispute. Alice pulled Janis down next to her as Terry wrapped a handkerchief around his hand, carefully pulled the envelope from his pocket, and sniffed it. "What are you doing that for?" she inquired. "What do you expect to smell?"

"You never know," Terry said, still sniffing. "Blood, explosive." He produced a folding knife. "Normally I'd try to see this first. On my own, right?" Inserting the blade, he slit the envelope open and two items fluttered onto the desk.

Janis was squirming like a worm on a hook. "It is, isn't it? It's proof of life?"

Terry bent low.

"How did they slip it into the jeep?" Alice marveled. "How can they do that? God, it's like they're everywhere."

"In a sense they are," Terry said. He was frowning. "Listen to me. Right? This is important." Unfurling, he came toward them. "You never get a pretty picture. This is meant to shake you up. Weaken you so you'll give in to their demands. That's why we couldn't let them see us when we opened it. Understand?"

Alice nodded, too nervous to say anything. He extended a photograph, which she accepted, her fingers trembling. It was Peter, all right. Her Peter. But Peter as she had never seen him. With a mottled beard. Emaciated to the point of near-starvation. His clothes were in rags, his feet were blood-covered ruins. He was in front of a tent, reading a copy of *La Verdad*, a local newspaper. "Sweet Jesus."

Janis shook the photo at Terry. "My brother looks terrible! His feet are awful! I thought you claimed they'd take care of him? That they realize how valuable he is to them?" She paused. "What in hell are you doing now?"

Alice looked. Terry had dashed to a corner. Newspapers and magazines were stacked as tall as he was, and he was rifling rapidly through them. "It has to be here somewhere."

"What does?" Alice prodded.

"Here we go!" Terry spun, holding a copy of *La Verdad*. "This is it, right? This is the one he's holding?"

Alice nodded. The headlines matched.

"What do you do? You save all the newspapers?"

Janis said, contriving to make it sound like the silliest thing she'd ever heard.

"This was last Tuesday's edition," Terry said, pursing his lips. "Hmm. So three days to get it up there, three days back." He blinked. "Peter isn't that far away."

"What else was in the envelop? A letter from him?" Alice prayed.

"No. New radio frequencies and times." Terry tossed the newspaper back onto the pile. "Some bullshit threats. The usual."

"Read it," Janis said.

"Why fret yourselves?" Terry countered. "The proof of life is all that counts. It's what we've wanted. We're in it now. We're in play. And we've all got work to do."

"Oh?" from Janis. "What do you need from me?"

Terry faced her. "The money."

Janis nodded.

Alice was lost in the photo. She wondered what Peter had been thinking when the picture was taken, wondered if he knew what purpose it would serve. She touched the image, remembering all the better times they had shared and scared they would never know such moments again.

The Tecala International Airport was bustling with passengers about to depart on a flight to the States. Terry and Alice were there to see Janis off at the departure gate, and Terry took it on himself to offer some last-minute advice.

"When you get back home, you're going to want to talk about your brother. It's natural. But it can only hurt. If word leaks to the media, the publicity might persuade the E.L.T. to dispose of him."

"I never thought of that."

"Tight lips," Terry stressed. "Don't bring him up in idle chitchat. Don't discuss him with friends. Not even with your own kids."

"My kids will be fine," Janis defended her brood.

Terry patted the carry-on she held. "You turn on the scramble phone when you get home." He had given her one so they could keep in touch regularly, without having to worry about the line being tapped. "We'll test it straight away." Smiling, he pecked her on the cheek. "You're doing great, Janis. I mean it. So hang in there, okay?"

"I'll try."

Terry politely stepped back so the two women could say their good-byes. But he stayed close enough to protect them should the need arise and couldn't help overhearing their exchange.

"This is it," Alice said sadly.

"I guess." Janis did not sound happy about leaving, but she had been gone too long as it was, and Terry knew she missed her family terribly.

"I'll keep you posted," Alice promised.

Janis managed a chuckle. "How many soccer moms get their own encrypted phone?" She dropped to a whisper. "It's a lot of money, Alice. Six hundred thousand dollars. And he's not even sure."

"He's the expert. We have to depend on his judgment."

Terry was flattered by her faith in him, but he kept it to himself.

"What if it's not enough?" Janis said. "We've scraped up more than Peter's inheritance. And I've got four college tuitions coming up in the next five years. You know that."

Alice wasn't offended. "I do. And I appreciate the sacrifice you've made for your brother's sake."

They embraced. Janis heard her flight being called and shouldered the carry-on. "Peter is lucky to have you," were her parting words.

Terry moved to Alice's side, and they watched until her sister-in-law boarded the plane. "Well, now it's just the two of us," he commented.

"Just the two of us," Alice softly echoed.

Terry didn't look at her again until they were in the jeep. He was afraid of what he might see reflected in her eyes—and what she might see in his.

The next radio contact was four days later. At the appointed time the same voice as before came on, saying, "I am here, Tio. From now on you will call me by the code name Marco. Sí?"

"Marco. Got it," Terry said. Eliodoro was beside him, Alice and Norma were over by the doorway. Maria had stayed on late to supply coffee and food as required. "Are you ready to get serious? No more threats? No more theatrics?"

"You are the ones who need to be more serious," Marco said. "You are the ones who offer a pittance."

"I keep telling you he's an aid worker," Terry responded. "He's not a businessman. It's the family doing this alone. A working family. And they're not millionaires."

"They can do better than they have. So far they have been wasting our time."

"The guy is here to build a dam," Terry mentioned. "He's not a big, important CEO. His family could never scrape together three million dollars. So you tell me who's wasting time?"

Marco was peeved. "Come on with this. You treat

it like it's a game. My side is saying concrete things, and you are having us suck cocks here with this bullshit."

"Great bargaining skills, toilet-mouth," Alice muttered.

Terry motioned for her to keep quiet, but the harm had been done.

"What was that?" Marco said. "Who else is there? You are to keep this quiet, remember? The more people who know, the less chance of you seeing the package again."

By unspoken agreement, they never referred to Peter Bowman by name. It was always possible their negotiations were being monitored and neither side wanted the world at large to know of Peter's abduction.

"We are holding up our end," Terry assured him. "The only people here are the package's wife and me." Which was a bald-faced lie, but he wanted to get them back on track.

"Very well. Let us get down to it. How much is the family willing to pay? The maximum amount?"

"One hundred thousand pesos" Terry said.

Over a minute of quiet at the other end was broken by, "That was a joke, right? You insult us with so low a figure. Does the family think we are a charity?" Marco paused. "But I tell you what I will do. Since it is in our best interests as well as yours to conclude this as soon as practical, we will be gracious and lower the asking price to two and a half million dollars. How would that be?"

Grinning, Terry turned to Alice, covered the microphone with his hand, and whispered, "We're on the right track now." To Marco he said, "That sounds good, but it's still much too high. Why don't we compromise and settle for two hundred thousand?"

Marco's laugh was short and brittle. "You call that a compromise? I call that blowing air out your ass." He sighed. "You vex me, Tio. You truly do. This is going to take a long time, and I'm not so sure the people I represent are willing to wait that long."

"They'll wait if they want the money," Terry said flatly.

"You are very good at this, Tio."

"So are you," Terry repaid the compliment. "Now can we quit blowing smoke and get down to cases?"

"Two and a half million and not a centavo less."

By the end of the hour they were no closer to resolving their differences. Another session was slated a week later, but it concluded in the same vein.

And so it went. Day after day crawled by, blending into weeks, the weeks in turn blending into months. Terry spent a lot of time at the Bowman's. More time than was necessary, more than he'd ever spent with other clients. He ate supper there almost nightly. Soon he was eating lunch, also. Then showing up for breakfast now and then.

Terry learned all about Alice, about her childhood in Ohio, her "boringly ordinary life," as she labeled it, until she had met Peter.

"What about you and your ex?" she asked him one evening. "Was it love at first sight?"

"In my case, more like lust at first sight," Terry admitted. "In her case, it was more complicated. Her father is a highly respected general in the English army. They never did get along, and when he told her she was to have nothing to do with me, that a lowly Aussie soldier was beneath her station, she married me to spite him."

"Oh my."

"My grandmother used to say that out of all bad fruit come a few good seeds," Terry said. "In our case she was right. I'm so proud of my son. I don't get to see him nearly as much as I'd like, and Lord knows I'm not the best dad in the world, but I've done the best I could under the circumstances."

"If you're tired of all the globetrotting, why don't you find a good woman and settle down somewhere near him?"

"Because I haven't met a woman I've cared for that much un—" Terry stopped, dismayed at his lapse. He had almost said, "until now." He had almost stepped over the invisible line he knew he must never cross, no matter what. For his sake. For hers. For her husband's.

Alice suddenly developed an interest in the kitchen clock. "My, look at the time. I'd better get supper on, or we won't eat until midnight."

"I'll go wash up," Terry said. But what he really did once he shut the bathroom door was turn on the cold tap and hold his head under the water until he had counted to a hundred. The pity of it was, it didn't help.

Chapter 12

More endless days of endless inertia stretched on. Terry and Marco feinted verbally every couple of weeks, Marco agreeing to lower the asking price in small increments, Terry offering to raise it by equally small amounts.

"I told you it would take time," Terry said to Alice one morning on their way back from the market. He had both hands on the steering wheel and was scanning the road.

"I never realized how much," Alice responded. She was peeling an orange they had just bought. Prying off a slice, she automatically held it to his mouth for him to bite, just as she would do for Peter. When he bit down his lips brushed her fingers. The contact sent a tingle up her arm, and she jerked it away, embarrassed by her reaction.

"Are you okay?"

"It's nothing," Alice said and glanced out the window. They were passing the QUAD-CARBON building. A ceremony was underway. The QUAD-CARBON sign had been taken down and a huge crane was raising a new sign that read OCTONAL

PETROLEUM. But it wasn't the sign that caused her to stiffen and grind her teeth. "Stop the car!"

Terry was still gazing up ahead and hadn't seen what she did. "In the middle of the block? Why?"

"Stop the damn car!" Alice shouted, seething. The second he applied the brakes she flung her door wide and leaped out, barreling into the thick of the crowd that had gathered for the formal change in ownership. A ribbon was about to be cut. Gathered in front of it were Ted Fellner and Jerry and Ivy Winsted, along with a group of Octonal executives. Also present, rubbing elbows with Fellner, was Dover McLoon, the man from the U.S. embassy.

Alice felt like ripping their eyes out as she forged toward them, pushing people out of her way.

"What do you think you're doing?"

A strong arm looped around Alice's waist. She twisted to fight back, but Terry was too strong. "They're in this together, the sons of bitches! Let go of me!"

"Not bloody likely." Terry lifted her bodily and carried her toward the street. "We don't want you arrested."

Tears of pure fury blurred Alice's vision. "Don't you see? They don't give a damn about Peter! They never have! Even that embassy snot."

"I tried to tell you," Terry said.

Alice struggled to break free. "It's as if Peter doesn't matter to them!"

"He doesn't. He only matters to us."

Alice was about to lose it, about to break down and bawl in front of dozens of strangers. She was glad when he shoved her into the jeep and slammed the door. Her face in her hands, she didn't hear him climb in.

"Think, Alice, think! If you attacked them it would be in all the papers. The E.L.T. would hear, and they wouldn't be pleased. I've told you before, but I'll tell you again. Publicity can kill a client as quickly as stupidity."

"I hate them," Alice said. "I fucking hate every one of them."

"You're entitled."

The jeep was gaining speed. Sniffling, Alice sat up and dabbed at her eyes with a sleeve. "I'm sorry. Seeing them there set me off. Thank you for keeping me from making a terrible mistake."

"Yet another reason to have me around," Terry said, smiling.

Unconsciously, Alice put a hand on his. "I don't need a reason."

Terry moved his arm to work the shift, and out of nervous tension, he did something he had never done before; he ground the gears.

Peter had fallen into a fit of depression with no end in sight. After the photo-snapping episode so long ago, he had entertained high hopes of the ransom being paid sometime soon, but months later, he was still stuck at the rebel encampment, his hope souring to bitter despair.

On a better note, his feet were almost healed. Kessler insisted on changing the bandages every few days, though, and on one such morning, as the missionary was wrapping them in clean strips of gauze, a bell commenced clanging.

"What's that?" Peter asked.

"They go to fight," Kessler said. "The bell is the signal."

Through a gap in the boards, Peter saw rebels scurrying to the southeast. Some were dressing on the run,

others locking and loading weapons. Only a few guerrillas were left in camp.

"The army is that close?"

"Just over that mountain, I am told." Kessler
pointed. "But they could be on Mars for all it helps us.
The rebels, they hold this territory for a long time."

Peter was eager to try and escape, but the missionary kept telling him they should wait a bit yet. It didn't
help that the rebels always posted a guard outside
his door.

About noon, a different bunch of rebels showed up,
bearing wounded. They were tired, worn, and dirty.
Several were carrying pieces of what appeared to be
a helicopter.

"That was a Gazelle. French made," Kessler commented. "France sold some to Tecala as part of an
arms deal."

"How would you know that?"

The missionary scanned their immediate vicinity,
then rolled up his right sleeve. On his forearm was
a tattoo, a military fleur-de-lis, along with the words
Marcher ou Mourir. "Everyone is something else before they turn to God, yes? I was in the French Foreign Legion."

Peter began to understand how Kessler had sur-
vived as long as he had. Legionnaires were famed for
being tough and resilient. "Why haven't you stolen a
gun and fought your way out?"

"Two reasons. It is difficult for one man alone to
make it through the jungle. Very difficult, yes?"

"And the other reason?"

" 'Thou shalt not kill.' "

Another night, another fencing match between
Terry and the man who called himself Marco took

place. "Three hundred thousand is already at my limit," Terry said. "It gives me nowhere to move. So maybe what you want to do is take it back to your people and see if we can close on this."

Alice was sick of the whole thing. The rebels treated her husband as if he were an old scarf being haggled over at a flea market. All he was to the E.L.T. was merchandise, like a new car or an appliance. Sometimes she thought Marco just liked to dicker endlessly.

"We keep moving from the issue," the guerrillas' spokesman commented. "I keep telling you that the maintenance for this product is more than you are offering."

Product, Alice mentally repeated. It showed how right she was.

"Marco, look." Terry sighed. "You keep talking as if this were a company. There is no company. There's no insurance. There's no one here but the family."

Into the room walked Cinta, Maria's helper. Maria was busy cooking and had sent Cinta with a tray of beers. Eliodoro claimed one. So did Norma. But Terry waved her off, and she started for the doorway.

"This family is bullshit," Marco groused. "They need to start thinking harder, like around two million, or they'll never see him again."

Alice was facing Terry and didn't see Cinta trip, sending the tray crashing to the floor, making everyone jump. Two beers spilled. Cinta bent and fearfully gathered them up, as if she were afraid Alice would punish her.

"Don't worry," Alice said. "Accidents happen."

Norma translated as the young woman dabbed at the beer with her apron, terrified.

From the speaker drifted Marco's wry wit. "Are you having a party there, Tio?"

"We won't celebrate until the package is here to celebrate with us," Terry responded. "Accept our offer of four hundred thousand, and we can have that party before the week is out."

Alice leaned forward on her chair. Four hundred thousand was the highest Terry had gone. She studied him, the tilt to his handsome features, his broad shoulders. The night was unbearably hot, and all he wore was a pair of shorts. Perspiration dotted his tanned skin. When he moved to adjust a dial, his taut muscles rippled like those of a tawny panther. She noticed old scars networking his back and wondered what they were from.

Eliodoro was beside him, as always, and when Eliodoro turned, Alice quickly tore her eyes away, ashamed at the thoughts she harbored.

"So it's four hundred thousand now?" Marco said. "How generous. Maybe I should have had a cake baked for the occasion?"

His sarcasm sickened Alice. Obviously the negotiating was nowhere near an end.

"I am losing faith in you, Tio," Marco stated. "And I must tell you, our mutual friend, he is losing faith, too. In his family, in his wife, and the whole thing. We try to say how this is going. We try to tell him we are doing our best to get him home, but it's very bad for him now."

Alice couldn't take any more. Rising, she sidled past Cinta and on out to the patio for some fresh air. She was confident Marco was lying. Peter would never lose faith in her. But it hurt just the same. Fishing a cigarette from a pack left on the table, she lit up and sank into a chair.

Unbidden, Maria brought a glass of wine and the

bottle, set them down without saying a word, and considerately retreated indoors.

Alice sipped at the wine a few times and frowned. The constant worry was taking a severe toll. She had heavy bags under her eyes from chronic lack of sleep, and she was always jittery, always one negotiating session away from a nervous breakdown.

A cool breeze from the northwest soothed Alice's hot brow. She relished the sensation. The quiet solitude was also a welcome respite, and she sat savoring the serenity, losing all track of time until the patio door slid open.

"We're done for the night," Terry announced. "He's coming down slowly, but surely."

"I couldn't listen any longer," Alice said.

"It's all right. We're making progress, though, real progress." Terry sat in the chair next to hers. "Are you okay?"

"I don't know," Alice confessed. "What's okay? Being happy? Or does just being alive count? Know what I mean?"

"That's why we keep going, right? One foot in front of the other."

Alice crushed out the cigarette. "I'm not up for a pep talk. I get enough of that from everyone else."

Terry nodded, grasped the wine bottle, and treated himself to a slug.

"People say things happen for a reason," Alice said, feeling a need to unburden herself. "But I know now that's not always true."

"Are we talking about Peter here?"

"Not entirely, no." There was more, so much more, all the awful feelings Alice had pent up since that dark day in Africa, a day she'd never discussed with anyone except Peter. "I had a miscarriage last year. It wasn't anybody's fault, really. It sure wasn't Peter's fault, but that didn't stop me from blaming him." She tried to smile and couldn't. "People don't know what to say when you lose a baby. It's like you were sick, and now you're on the mend or something. Or they blather on about how you can always try again."

Terry was listening with fierce intensity.

"You're lonely enough already, you know?" Alice said. "Nothing that anyone says really helps. None of their advice makes sense." She contemplated the heavens. "People who think things happen for a reason have never had anything bad happen to them. Things just *happen*. My daughter just died. Why try to pin it on a higher power?"

"What was her name?" Terry inquired.

"Mali. Mali Jasmine Bowman." Alice refilled her glass. "No one ever asks me that."

"It's a beautiful name."

"It is, isn't it?"

And for the longest while they sat and drank, just the two of them alone in the shadows of the night.

Ten days later contact was reestablished. Terry knew a crucial stage had been reached the moment Marco acknowledged his call.

"I'm here, Tio. Not that it will do our mutual friend or his family any good."

"What's the matter?" Terry goaded him.

"My people are very unhappy at the slow progress. Very unhappy. They say the family should have agreed to an amount by now and have sent the money."

"First we agree. Then the family will collect the funds. Keep in mind they're going to try and borrow it from friends. That will take a while."

173

"I am tired of all the bullshit, Tio," Marco said. "I'm telling you. I say let's just fuck it. Let's forget the whole deal."

Terry had been slouched in his chair, but now he was all attention. In most negotiations a point was reached where the kidnappers ultimately realized their outrageous demands were never going to be met, and they began to bargain in earnest. That moment was always marked by resignation and threats. "Do that and your friends are out four hundred thousand dollars. All we need is new proof of life and the money is theirs. We need something to show the people who will lend the family the money." Static hissed and he thought maybe Tio had broken contact. "Do you copy?"

"Yes, I copy. I think maybe we should just put a bullet in his head and sell you the body. Do you think we won't do it? For what you're offering? Tell the family they can buy his bones."

"They are trying so hard for you," Terry said. "What if they tried to borrow another fifty grand? That brings us to four hundred and fifty thousand. Is that anywhere near a limit you could accept?"

"Only if I had shit for brains."

Again static filled the room. Terry tried to carry on, but he was talking to himself.

Mario was no longer there.

"More troops, they come," Erich Kessler declared from his vantage point near the doorway to Peter's shack. "Reinforcements from deep in the jungle."

Peter stepped over to see for himself. Word was that the battle on the other side of the mountain had temporarily ended in a stalemate. Guerrillas and equipment had been pouring into the encampment for several days. A mule train trailed the latest additions, and slogging along beside the animals was someone Peter could have gone a lifetime without encountering again.

Juaco listlessly surveyed the buildings. His gaze fell on the shack, on Peter, and a familiar sick smile twisted his cruel countenance Pointing a finger, he pretended to be firing a pistol.

"Do you know that one?" Kessler asked.

"He's the one I told you about."

"The blowhard who made your life so miserable at that other place?" The missionary scowled. "Now I see what you must have gone through. He has the look of a viper, that one. Beware. He will do whatever he can to make your life miserable."

"Just what I needed." Peter figured the sadistic hothead would pay him a visit before long, but the morning passed without incident. At noon Kessler got a fire going and put soup on to boil. Most of the reinforcements had already moved on, and the camp was largely deserted.

"So as I was saying," Peter resumed a conversation they had begun earlier, "I was a control freak. I thought that if I didn't keep control, everything in my life would fall apart. I timed everything out. Scheduled my life from the moment I woke up until the moment I went to bed. Hell, I even scheduled the nights my wife and I were intimate." He pulled a folded strip of cloth from under his belt. Secreted inside was the photo of Alice, worn, frayed, faded. "She always claimed I wasn't spontaneous enough, but I never believed her."

"May I?" Kessler asked.

Peter gave him the picture.

"She is lovely, this one."

"And smart. She was right about me all along, and I was too pigheaded to see it."

The missionary gave the precious photograph back. "And now that nothing is under your control?"

"It's like I was wearing blinders, and they've been removed." Peter gently replaced his sole physical link to Alice. "All the stupid stuff I worried about. All the nonsense I put her through. God, I was an idiot." He stared into the crackling fire. "I've got to get through this. I've got to make it home. I have so much to apologize for."

Kessler ladled out the soup. As they ate, more soldiers emerged from the jungle to the south, three whole companies led by a colonel. The soldiers were permitted to rest while the officers gathered for a strategy session around a table placed in the shade of a nearby tree.

Peter and the missionary were ignored, which was fine by Peter. He became keenly intrigued when the colonel laid out several maps. Reports from the field were read, plans were formulated, and at about two in the afternoon the officers retired into a tent to drink and relax.

The rest of the rebels were napping or chatting, awaiting orders to march.

Rising, Peter whispered, "Keep an eye out and signal if you see anyone coming."

"What are you up to?" Kessler asked.

No one was near the table. Peter casually ambled toward it, shamming interest in the trees and the mules and the farm up on the slope, in everything except the maps, pens, and pencils carelessly strewn about. Pivoting so his back was to them, Peter reached behind him, swiftly rolled a large map up, and slid it down his pants, then palmed a pen. Willing himself to remain calm, he took a roundabout route to his shack.

Kessler entered moments later. "Do you realize the risk? If they find it missing, they come here first."

"Then we don't have much time." Peter spread the map flat. Tecala City was in the lower right corner. In the upper left a large black X marked the valley where the stronghold was located. The rest consisted of current rebel and army positions, along with trails, roads, and towns. "This is just what we need. Let me have that Bible of yours."

"My Bible?"

"There are a couple of blank pages at the back," Peter recalled. "I'll copy the map and put it back on the table before the officers are done with their siesta."

"You are crazy, friend," Kessler said, but he handed the Bible over and moved to the doorway to stand guard. "If we are caught . . ."

"Here's where some prayer would come in handy." Peter knuckled down to the task, sketching rapidly, unable to add the detail he would like. "With this we can find our way back to civilization, no problem."

"Hurry. I am nervous wreck."

"Makes two of us." Peter tried to match the map's scale, but the page in the Bible was considerably smaller. He noted distances where they were given, invariably in kilometers. A river close to camp deserved special study, but he lacked the time.

Kessler wrung his hands and tugged at his beard in an excess of anxiety. "Faster, my friend. Faster."

Peter gave himself five minutes. Any more and he was playing with fire. Ticking off the seconds in his head, he stopped when he reached three hundred. "Any sign of them?"

"Not them, no."

Rolling the map up, Peter stood. "You wait here. I'll sneak this over." He stepped toward the entrance but the missionary had other ideas.

"Give me the map. Is better for me to do it."

"Why you?"

Kessler wriggled a finger at someone or something outside.

It was Juaco. Perched on a stump forty yards distant, dripping malevolence from every pore, he watched the shack like a hawk about to swoop down on unsuspecting prey.

"He wasn't there a while ago," Peter said.

"Now he is. Now I take the map." Kessler stuck it up his left sleeve and strolled out.

Juaco paid no attention to the missionary.

Peeking out between the rough-hewn planks, Peter saw his friend circle wide of the tents and approach the table from the other direction. As slick as could be, Kessler dropped the map and the pen and strolled off whistling to himself.

Peter opened the Bible to his sketch. He was tired of waiting for the ransom to be paid. At the first opportunity that came along, he was going to escape. Or damn well die trying.

Once more into the breach, Terry thought. He was alone in the radio room. Alice was throwing a dinner party at his insistence. She needed something to do other than worry, needed to socialize and laugh. Dino, Eliodoro and Norma, and several Tecalano friends had been invited. The tinkle of mirth filtered through the partly open door.

Terry checked his watch again. Marco was over an hour late. The rebels' mouthpiece had always been extraordinarily punctual for their previous negotiating sessions. Terry didn't like it.

To compound the situation, the lights unexpectedly dimmed. Terry glanced up, expecting them to brighten any second, but they stayed dim for more than a minute, then flickered wildly before returning to normal.

A hum preceded the muted sound of a voice that slowly swelled in volume and clarity. "Tio? Tio? Are you there? Do you copy?"

"Sí!" Terry answered. "I was beginning to think you had taken the night off."

"Conditions are most unstable at my end," Marco said. "Communicating with my friends is very complicated now."

Terry had seen the latest newspapers. The E.L.T. and the army were embroiled in a full-scale battle for a sizable chunk of Tecala. "I understand. So let's forgo rehashing the same issues over and over again." His main concern now was that all contact with the guerrillas might be lost during the conflict, translating into many more months of confinement for Peter Bowman.

"Yes, go ahead," Marco said, his voice fading slightly. "Do you have a better offer for us now?"

"As I recall your last demand was an even one million."

"And yours was five hundred thousand," Marco reminded.

"Then let's cut to the chase," Terry proposed. They were about to come to terms. He felt it in his bones.

"That would be advisable. Let me confide in you—"

The transmission broke up. Simultaneously the lights dimmed once more and the speakers went dead. "Marco, do you copy?" Terry said. It would be just their luck to have a power outage foil them when a resolution was minutes away. "Marco?"

"I copy." The signal was weak, the voice disembodied.

"I didn't catch what you said last. We're having a problem with the electricity at this end."

"The same here," Marco said.

Terry glanced out the window as the lights flickered anew. The entire city was affected, but not, he saw, lights on a mountain a mile away. With a start, he realized Marco must be somewhere in Tecala City. "What did you say?"

"It would be advisable to end this soon. My friends have much to occupy them. They cannot guarantee the safety of the package for much longer. I am serious when I say this might be your last chance."

For once, Terry believed him. "Let's settle the thing right now then. The highest the family can go is six hundred and fifty thousand. That's absolutely all they can raise. If it's acceptable and your people will provide additional proof of life, we can finally end it."

"I'll take that back to my people. But remember, reaching them is not easy. If they agree I will contact you again on a different frequency in—"

Static drowned out Marco's voice. Terry turned the volume all the way up. When that failed to work he twitched the tuner. "Marco? Do you copy? I didn't catch that last part. When do you want to talk again?"

From the living room pealed Alice's giddy laughter, clearly enjoying herself for the first time in a long time.

"This is Tio? Do you copy, Marco? Come in. Come in. I need to know the time and the frequency." Without it, Terry didn't have a snowball's chance in Hades of wrapping things up. "Marco? Do you copy? This is urgent. Do you hear me?"

The lights blinked completely out. The radio sputtered and was still. Terry was left holding a useless microphone, thwarted and furious. It had all gone to hell. Months of work down the drain. How was he to break the news to Alice that, despite his many assurances, she might never see her husband again?

Chapter 13

Three nights later, Peter made his bid for freedom.

Almost all of the guerrillas were gone. The colonel and his men had stayed for two days, then marched off to reinforce comrades beset by a new military offensive. The next afternoon a runner arrived, tottering and breathless, to relay an urgent request for more help. The Tecalan Army was making a concerted push to drive the guerrillas back. If the military succeeded, the E.L.T. would be forced to retreat into the remote provinces. Nearly every last able-bodied man and woman rushed off to the battlefront.

It was the moment Peter had been waiting for. Shortly before sunset, he announced his decision to Erich Kessler, who greeted it with less enthusiasm than Peter had anticipated.

"I advise against it, my young friend. We are better staying put, ja?"

"This from the man who's spent almost two years of his life here?" Peter was incredulous. "We'll never have a better chance. There can't be more than a dozen rebels left. We'll wait until most of them have bedded down for the night, then slip out."

"Through the jungle? In the dark?" The missionary

shook his head. "Much too dangerous, I think. These are traps, yes? What you call booby traps? And in the jungle are animals. Jaguars and worse."

Peter refused to be persuaded. "I'm offering you your freedom on a silver platter, and you're quibbling over the small stuff?"

"I don't want you hurt. You have much to live for."

"You think I don't know that?" Peter stepped to the doorway and made note of where the remaining rebels were and what they were doing. "She's the reason I'm doing this. She must be half out of her mind with worry by now. I've got to get back." He looked at Kessler. *"I've got to."*

"I understand."

"Then are you with me or not?" Peter asked. "I'll go alone if I have to. And once I start I'm not turning back."

Kessler ran his fingers through his beard, pondering. "I think you make a mistake. But I go anyway. Tecala City is a long way. You maybe need my help."

"All we have to do is find an army outpost or a town the rebels don't control," Peter said.

"Harder than you think."

"I don't care." Peter spotted Juaco over by the mules. "I have a feeling that if I don't get out soon, I'll die. Call it a premonition. Call it silly. But I can't shake the feeling my days are numbered if I stay."

"We go together then."

Peter gratefully clasped the missionary's hand. "Thank you. I'll meet you at the east edge of camp half an hour after the last of the guerrillas turn in."

"By the trees with the vines?" Kessler suggested.

"That will do fine."

Peter was left alone with his thoughts. He dwelled on Alice, on how marvelous it would be to see her

183

again, to hold her in his arms, to feel her lips on his. The wait was unbearable. He paced. He watched the rebels. He paced some more. The sun took forever to dip below the horizon. Shortly thereafter the wind increased, rustling the trees nonstop, as low clouds scuttled in from the west, bearing with them the scent and promise of rain.

Peter smiled. For once Lady Luck was on his side. Rain was just what they needed. It would limit visibility, and would smother whatever sounds they made. Best of all, it would wash away their tracks so the guerrillas couldn't hunt them down.

Sitting just inside in the doorway, Peter doodled in the dirt with a finger, marking time. More clouds drifted in and soon the sky was completely overcast. Scattered raindrops fell, huge drops that patterned on the shack and the tents and sent the few guerillas out in the open hastening for cover.

The rain fell faster, soon becoming a liquid sheet, hitting the earth in steady rhythm. Peter couldn't have been happier. But would the rain last until the rebels turned in? Even more important, how would he know when they did since he couldn't see them through the deluge?

Over by the string, a mule brayed. Peter had lost sight of Juaco, but it didn't matter because now Juaco couldn't keep tabs on him, either.

Peter poked his head out and looked toward the missionary's shack. Only a vague outline was visible.

Why wait until later? Peter asked himself. It was dark enough already, and the guerrillas had all sought shelter. Rising into a crouch, he crept into the open and was instantly soaked to the skin. Hugging the front of his shack, he moved to the corner. Rain cascaded mercilessly, the drops pelting him like tiny barbs. Raising a hand to his eyebrows to shield his eyes, he launched himself toward Kessler's shack. Water inches thick covered the ground. But the splashing sounds his feet made couldn't be heard above the downpour and the howling wind.

Suddenly a darkling shape hove out of the murk. It was the side wall of the missionary's humble abode. Peter moved to the front and around to the doorway. The interior was mired in shadow, but even so Peter could tell Kessler wasn't there.

Peter turned. Where could the man have gotten to? Was it possible the missionary intended to betray him and had gone to report his plan to the rebels? He dismissed the notion as paranoid. Kessler wanted out of there as much as he did.

The next heartbeat a man-sized shape materialized, lumbering straight toward him, and Peter started to backpedal into the shack to hide.

"Pieter? It is you, yes?" Water dripped from Kessler's bulbous nose and cheeks.

"Where did you go?" Peter asked.

"I thought maybe we should leave now so I went to get you." The missionary's beard was plastered to his neck and chest. "We have the same idea, ja?"

"Yes." Peter peered into the downpour. "Have you seen any sign of our captors?"

"Nein."

"Then's let go for the gusto," Peter said, and hurried past the shack, bearing eastward, or what he hoped was eastward. Landmarks were lost in a watery limbo so he had to rely on his inner sense of direction. The rain and the dark tended to disorient him, but he was confident he could do it.

Kessler shuffled at his side, his hairy head bent to ward off the rain.

185

As Peter recalled, they had to cross approximately forty yards of open space to reach the jungle. He counted off his steps and at forty-seven an inky wall of vegetation reared. Halting, he gripped the missionary's wrist. "Listen," he said, shouting to be heard above the roar of the wind. "If one of us goes down the other is to keep on going. Agreed?"

"I will not leave you."

"You have to!" Peter disputed him. "No matter what, one of us *must* make it out to send help."

"I don't know if I can."

"Give me your word," Peter persisted, and when the older man hesitated, he said, "Erich, it's the only way. If we're recaptured, they're liable to do anything. Maybe beat us or fit us with chains. We won't stand a prayer of escaping ever again."

Kessler was hunched over, his back bearing the brunt of the downpour. Reaching under his shirt, up under his left arm, he slid the Bible out just far enough for Peter to see. "It goes against all I now believe."

"Your word, damn it!"

"I promise," Kessler said, not pleased at all. As he tucked the good book back under his arm to keep it dry, to their rear a strident shout pierced the night. *"Was ist los?"* he whispered.

To Peter it sounded like someone screaming their lungs out, but the words were indistinct, muffled by the elements. "They're on to us!" he exclaimed and dashed into the jungle. Swiftly weaving through the undergrowth, he sought to put as much distance behind them as he could.

"How can this be?" Kessler said, keeping pace, but breathing heavily. "So soon?"

Peter knew the answer: Juaco. The little sadist had been spying on him all along and must have tumbled to the fact something was up. Now the whole camp would be aroused and every last guerrilla would be after them. Panic welled up, but he dispelled it with the thought that the rebels could never find them in the rain.

A large log appeared and Peter barely avoided falling on his face. Scrambling over it, he shifted to help Kessler, who was slower, more ponderous. Suddenly the rain slackened dramatically and the wind virtually died. Another shout rang out.

"It is the one who hates you," Kessler said. "He has found footprints. In the mud."

Peter had never wanted to kill another human being in his life, but he wanted to now. He wanted to wrap his hands around Juaco's scrawny throat and squeeze until the pyscho was dead. "Let's go," he urged.

According to the map, over the ridge to the east lay a river. Following it to the southeast would eventually bring them to a small settlement. Whether the guerrillas or the army controlled it was unknown. Thirty miles farther, though, was a town safely in government hands. Once there, they would be clothed and fed and escorted under guard to Tecala City.

The thought of being reunited with Alice spurred Peter on. He had so much to say to her, so much to atone for. Screw Octonal. Screw his career. His marriage was more important. Once they were reunited, pleasing her would be his number one priority. He'd start with a vacation to somewhere exotic, Hawaii perhaps, or Tahiti, and afterward they would settle down in the States. Wherever she wanted would be fine by him. He would do his best to make her happy, do his utmost to make up for being a horse's ass for so long.

"Pieter?"

Peter stopped in midstride and glanced back. Off

through the trees shadowy figures moved, trailing them. *How the hell were they doing that?* "We don't give up, remember?" He resumed running. He wasn't in the best of shape, but he had the best incentive in the world to spur his worn body on whether it wanted to or not.

The ground sloped steadily upward. The rain had tapered to a light drizzle, increasing visibility by a dozen yards. Peter spied what he took for a game trail and slanted toward it, only to be grabbed by Kessler and nearly yanked off his feet.

"Careful! *Gefahr!* Look there!"

A trip wire glistened with moisture. Attached to the far end were three hand grenades.

Peter shuddered. Another couple of feet and they would both have been blown to bits. He wished he knew how to dismantle the wire so they could use the grenades, and he was going to ask if Kessler could when the missionary shoved him and hissed a warning.

"They come! Run! Run!"

The figures were much closer. Peter spotted the toothpick-thin figure of his nemesis, out to stop him at all costs. He chugged upward, losing his footing a few times, but always regaining it and going on. The grass was slippery, the ground treacherously slick. Toward the top he had to drop onto all fours just to find purchase.

Kessler was wheezing like a blacksmith's bellows. "We must reach river!" he cried.

Peter agreed. Its average depth was seven feet, deep enough for swimming. They could dive in and let the current sweep them along until they were out of rifle range. It was unlikely the rebels would follow suit, not when most Tecalan waterways were infested with piranha and anacondas. The missionary had told him piranha were mostly inactive at night and that anacondas rarely went after humans, so they should be safe enough. Peter hoped their luck held.

Their exertion was taking a toll. Peter's legs were lanced with torment, his weakened muscles protesting after months of inactivity. Willing himself not to give up, he clawed at the earth, pumping higher and higher until he burst onto the top of the hill.

Kessler joined him seconds later and sank down next to him, gasping for breath. "Is . . . crazy!"

Peter sucked in air. "We can do it! It's downhill all the way from here."

"I hope so."

A harsh yell galvanized them into rising and moving to the rim. An oath escaped Peter's lips. The upper portion of the slope was practically bare of plant growth, and the rain had turned it into a slick tract of mud.

"We are doomed," Kessler lamented.

"Like hell." Peter jumped, landing heels first, and let gravity take over. Tucking at the knees like a skier, he sped downhill, gaining speed quickly, mud sloshing up over his feet halfway to his knees. He teetered when a bump threw him off-stride, but managed to recover his balance.

Kessler wasn't as agile. He tried to stay upright, but plopped onto his posterior. His arms wrapped across his barrel chest to protect the Bible, he slid toward the bottom like a flesh-and-blood toboggan.

Peter desperately looked for sign of the river. It had to be there! The map said it was! He began to slow down, but not intentionally. Waist-high weeds had replaced much of the muck, weeds that coiled around his legs as if they were alive. Moving toward a flat spot, he scoured the base of the hill. He didn't pay much attention when his foot brushed against what he took to be another weed until a low *twang* proved him wrong.

Suddenly Peter was falling and sliding, his body ripped by a painful spasm. He clamped his hands to a hardwood shaft jutting from his thigh. He had set off a booby trap! A short spear had penetrated clean through, scraping the bone, and there was blood everywhere. Gritting his teeth to keep from screaming, Peter thrashed to a stop.

"Pieter? Pieter?" Kessler gripped his shoulder, rolled him over, and gaped in horror. *"Mein Gott!"*

"Go!" Peter cried. "Get out of here!"

"No." Kessler tried to lift him. "Get up. Come, we go together or not at all. This changes everything. You will need me to mend you."

"You promised!" Twisting, Peter looked for the river. He couldn't understand why it wasn't there until he saw it much lower down and realized they weren't at the base of the ridge, they were on a shelf midway down.

"They are close," Kessler said, gazing up toward their pursuers.

"Quit talking and go!" Peter was almost beside himself. "We agreed, damn it! *Go!* Go now! Send help back!"

The missionary frowned, then moved toward the brink of the shelf, seeking a way down.

Peter clutched his ravaged leg, fighting to stay conscious, the agony unbelievable. He heard footsteps and swiveled.

Juaco had caught up with them. Raising a submachine gun, he sighted on Peter's torso and smiled his executioner's smile. He was really going to kill him this time, and they both knew it.

Peter tensed for the jolt of impact, then saw other guerrillas arrive, saw two of them take hasty aim at Kessler. He glanced toward the missionary just as they fired, his heart sinking as Kessler was punched backward, plainly hit. Staggering to the brink of the cliff, Kessler flailed his arms a few times, then keeled over the edge and disappeared from view without uttering so much as a peep

"No!" Peter wailed. "God, no!" He glanced up into the muzzle of Juaco's weapon and past it at the leering face of doom.

It had been a terrible day.

In the morning Alice talked Terry into taking her to the market. He'd tried to dissuade her by pointing out the rebels had escalated their terrorists attacks on the civilian populace. In the past several days alone there had been ten more bombings and half a dozen random drive-by shootings. All in an attempt by the rebels to force the government to withdraw the army units besieging their stronghold.

"Be that as it may," Alice had said, "I need to get out. I need some fresh air. Either you come with me, or I'll go alone."

Terry had tagged along, always watchful, always primed to ward off any and all threats. Alice enjoyed herself at first. She tried to get him to lighten up by buying him a shirt and treating him to tamales, but it didn't work. Then her own good mood took a turn for the worse when she spied the stand where the little girl had given psychic readings. The stand was empty, the divinia gone, but it reminded her of her loss, of her enduring heartache.

Abruptly, bursts of gunfire shattered the air. People screamed and ran for their lives. Almost immediately soldiers materialized, firing wildly across the plaza, as careless about who they hit as the rebels.

Alice was rooted in consternation until Terry grabbed her and raced into an alley. Pressing her against a wall, he shielded her with his body, his chest molded to hers, his gaze on the unfolding bedlam. Her eyes were locked on him: on his wide shoulders, on his handsome features, on the short hairs framing his ears. His chin was tantalizingly close to her lips, and she had to restrain herself from kissing it.

"This city is a bloody madhouse," Terry said, spiriting her down the alley. "I'm getting you home, and you're to stay until I say otherwise."

Annoyed with herself, Alice brooded until they braked in the driveway. She was a married woman, she kept telling herself. She shouldn't indulge in the sort of thoughts she found herself constantly having. But she was also human, the same tiny voice said, and Peter had been gone for such a very long time.

"Don't let anyone in you don't know," Terry said, reaching across to open her door. "If anything suspicious happens, call me at once."

"Will do." Alice slid out and bleakly smiled. "Sorry I talked you into the market. Sometimes I wonder how you put up with me."

"I wonder, too," Terry impishly responded. "Now get inside and lock the door."

Alice meekly complied. Only after she had thrown the bolt and waved did he drive away. She watched until the jeep was out of sight, then went to the kitchen to ask Maria about lunch. Only Maria wasn't there. Nor was Cinta.

"Odd," Alice said aloud, and snatched up the telephone.

The line was dead.

Alice pressed the plunger a few times with no result, then slammed the handset onto the cradle. Maria was always there by ten. Always. Without fail. And it was almost ten-thirty.

Calming her frayed nerves, Alice put coffee on to brew and went out onto the patio. From all points of the city sirens blared, broken by intermittent gunfire. It was a war out there, a city-wide kill zone, and innocent lives were being caught in the cross fire. She fervently hoped Maria wasn't one of them.

Alice went back in and switched on the portable TV on the kitchen counter. Usually a game show was on that particular channel at that time of day, but now a grim announcer was intoning grave news while in the background smoke poured from a building and the rattle of small arms fire was heard.

Once again Alice regretted not taking the time to learn more Spanish. From what she gleaned, the E.L.T. had gone on an orgy of bombing and killing. Citizens were being urged to stay in their homes. The president was expected to announce martial law and impose a curfew.

The news was too depressing. Alice went upstairs and changed from her shorts and a halter top into a blouse and jeans. Why exactly, she couldn't say. Unless it was the unconscious thought that she might need to leave in a hurry.

The lights flickered. From then on, for the rest of the afternoon, they constantly dimmed, sometimes for only a few minutes, sometimes for much longer. It reminded her how fragile so-called civilization was, how everything depended on electricity, how without it everyone would be at the whim of factors over which they had no control.

Alice tried the phone every half an hour, but it was

always the same. No dial tone. At four she made herself a sandwich and sat on a stool at the counter. A new but equally somber announcer was droning on about the latest drive-by. Men, women, and children were shown lying in their own blood. A bawling woman held a bullet-riddled body to her bosom.

At five-fifteen the roar of aircraft drew Alice to the patio. Four jets were streaking in low over Tecala City. They banked in tight formation, veering to the south, and she was amazed when one of the pilots launched a missile at a hilltop to the southwest. Smoke spewed in a thin trail, the missile flashing to its target in less time than it took her to blink. On the hill, a fireball erupted in a roar.

Shaken, Alice went back in. She needed company, needed someone to talk to. Dashing to the front door, she threw the bolt and headed across the street to Eliodoro's and Norma's. No one else was out and about. The street was deserted, the entire block as empty as a graveyard. To the west a dark plume of smoke spiraled toward the clouds.

Alice hammered on their front door with her fists, her skin prickling. No one answered. No one came to admit her. Venturing to their carport, she discovered their station wagon was gone.

A noise out in the street startled her, the rasp of metal on metal. Every nerve jangling, Alice surveyed the block from end to end, but saw no one. She headed for the Scorpion House. A low growl from an adjoining roof demonstrated she wasn't the only living thing left. The guard dog at the next home had bared its fangs, its hackles raised. But was it growling at her or someone else? Unwilling to linger to find out, she darted inside and slammed the door.

Alice felt more alone than she ever had before. She

tried the phone for hundredth time. The lights kept flickering. Static spiked the TV, and the image broke apart every few seconds. As near as she could tell, the president of Tecala was being interviewed by a swarm of reporters, homegrown and foreign. Government troops were shown repelling guerrillas. A tank was seen blasting away at emplacements on a mountain. A phalanx of police stormed a building held by the E.L.T.

"Where's Terry when I need him?" Alice said aloud. He had never left her by herself for so long. The possibility that he had been hurt, or worse, speared fear deep through her. She paced in front of the kitchen counter, watching image after horrifying image fill the screen. So much bloodshed. So much carnage.

On an impulse, Alice went up to the second floor and gazed out over the city from her bedroom window. It was worse than she had imagined. Eight or nine fires blazed. Smoke rose from a score of others. A cacophony of sirens keened like demented specters and hardly a second went by when guns weren't firing.

Alice sat on the edge of her bed, her hands in her lap, feeling small and insignificant, neglected, sorry for herself, and, she admitted, very scared. Frightened to death that the fighting would spread to her neighborhood, and that she would be trapped in the thick of it.

The sun dipped over the rim of the earth and night made its advent.

Again the lights flickered, only now they faded completely. Alice looked up, waiting for them to come back on, but they didn't. She went back downstairs. The TV screen was blank, the house as silent as a tomb. Remembering that there used to be a flashlight in one of the kitchen cabinets, she groped around for it without success.

The dog next door began barking. Alice walked to the patio door and looked toward the neighbor's roof, but she couldn't see a thing. The dog was barking like mad, snarling and snapping as if it had gone berserk. She started to open the door, but froze when the dog gave a high-pitched yelp and was quiet.

Alice saw someone slinking along the edge of the roof nearest the Scorpion House, as if looking for a way down. Panic-struck, she backed away from the glass, whirled, and raced to the front door. She needed Terry, needed him and the safety he provided more than she had ever needed anyone. But when she jerked the door open, she paused. She didn't have a vehicle. Sandro had taken the jeep, and the police had never returned Peter's Volkswagen, claiming it was evidence.

It would take an hour to reach Terry's hotel on foot, an hour adrift in a bloodred sea of mayhem.

From the back of the house came a sharp scraping sound.

In a rush of adrenaline Alice was out the door, fleeing into the fire-splashed nightmare of a city in the throes of self-destruction. She didn't look back. She just ran and ran and ran, and when she was so tired she could scarcely stand, she pressed herself to run some more. Only one thought was on her mind: *She had to reach Terry.*

Chapter 14

Terry Thorne had taken three cold showers that day, and it still didn't help.

All afternoon Terry wrestled with a desire he could no longer deny. That morning in the alley, when their bodies were pressed together, it had been all he could do to concentrate, all he could do to keep from taking Alice into his arms and kissing her with all the passion pent up inside of him.

She was a client's wife. As taboo as taboo could get. In the K&R trade, there were certain things a negotiator never, ever did, and up there at the top of the list was becoming romantically involved with the client or any of the client's immediate family.

It just wasn't done.

But to Terry's profound unease, knowing that and convincing his heart were two different things. He couldn't stop thinking about her, couldn't stop envisioning the two of them locked in a passionate embrace. So he had stayed put. He had spent the afternoon in his hotel room, taking cold showers and pacing and sometimes lying on his back on the sofa and staring at the ceiling fan.

Terry wasn't unduly worried for her safety. He'd

kept the radio on all day, tuned to a station that broadcast news updates every fifteen minutes. The fighting wasn't anywhere near the area where she lived, and the bombings were all at strategic points: government buildings, police and fire stations, major intersections—anywhere the blasts would disrupt services and communications and sow widespread panic.

Now night gripped the city, and still Terry couldn't bring himself to go see her. He was afraid of what he might do. He was even more afraid of how she might respond. So he refused to budge, even when the lights went out.

The Intercon Hotel was one of the finest in the city. Along with a four-star restaurant and an Olympic-size swimming pool, it also boasted its own generator. The lights were only out a few minutes before they flared to life again.

Terry placed a forearm over his eyes and attempted to doze off, but he was too wound up to sleep. When the phone rang half an hour later he was grateful. Anything to take his mind off of *her*. Hoping it was Dino, he got up and stepped to the desk.

It couldn't be Wyatt. Their English friend was no longer in-country. They had seen him off the day before. Or, rather, packed him off, since he was too besotted to stand, and they had to carry him onto the plane.

"Thorne here."

"It's me. Hey."

Alice. "Hey," Terry said, the mere sound of her voice rekindling his desire to a fever pitch. She sounded out of breath and scared.

"Maria never showed up today and neither did Sandro. Norma and Elio never came back from their weekend trip. The phone went out, but I kept trying to call." Alice was spitting words out like a Gatling gun. "The lights kept dimming. The power went off. And then, honest to God, I think someone killed the dog next door. He was going nuts and I—"

"Is Cinta there with you?" Terry interrupted, inwardly cursing his reluctance to go over to the Scorpion House.

"I'm not at the house. I left. I was completely freaked and I—"

"Where are you?" Terry cut her off again, afraid she was stranded in the middle of the city, where some of the heaviest gun battles had occurred.

"I'm here."

"Here where?" Terry asked. The obvious eluded him.

"Downstairs."

Terry looked for his shirt. He had taken it off and thrown it somewhere. "Okay. Hang on. I'll be right down."

"Forget it," Alice said. "I'm coming up."

She hung up before Terry could talk her out of it. "Bloody hell," he said. He had to convince her to go home. He would drive her. It was safer for both of them. As he moved toward a pile of clothes the lights went out again. The hotel generator had run out of fuel.

Forgetting about a shirt for the moment, Terry hunted for his flashlight. Alice would need it if she were coming up the stairs. Suddenly a thought hit him, and he sped out the door and down the hallway. He was taking for granted the fact that she wouldn't use the elevator, not with all the power outages. But he had to remember she'd never been in a situation remotely resembling strife-torn Tecala. She might not know what was safe to do and what wasn't.

"Alice?" Terry said, playing the flashlight beam over the empty corridor. "Alice? Where are you?"

"Terry?"

Her tiny cry brought Terry to the bank of elevators, their control panels as dark as everything else. "Which one are you in?"

"Here! This one!" Alice thumped the door. "I'm stuck! It won't open!"

Her fright was understandable. Terry set the flashlight on the floor and applied his fingertips to the crack. The door parted a hair, but that was all. "Are you okay?"

"I can't see a thing. God, what a night! The whole city is out." Alice was pressed to the crack, her breath fluttering over his fingers. "I'm sorry. I couldn't stay there. I just couldn't do it."

"You have nothing to apologize for. Hang on." Terry braced his feet against the doorframe, bunched his shoulder muscles, and pulled. His sinews rippled and bulged, but nothing happened. Locking his knees for added leverage, he exerted himself to his utmost, his teeth clenched, his head thrown back. Inch by gradual inch, the door opened. Her hand fell on his, but still he strained, his back arched, his fingers about to crack.

The next second the door jerked wide, allowing Alice to squeeze through. Terry let go and straightened to comfort her, but she had other ideas. Just like that she was in his arms, kissing him, embracing him, as starved for him as he was for her. He resisted for all of three seconds. Then he was matching her ardor, his hands exploring her body, his need overwhelming, a tidal wave irresistible in its intensity.

Terry hooked an arm under Alice's legs and lifted. Their mouths fused. He headed for his suite and kicked the door shut behind them. The gunfire outside, the explosions, the fires—none of it mattered anymore. There were just the two of them alone in the dark, and there was no denying their need.

The bed was unmade. Terry gently deposited her on the crumpled sheet, and she pulled him down beside her, her hot lips roving over his face, his throat, his shoulders. He reciprocated, his hands everywhere, exploring, fondling, caressing. She yielded, a rose opening its petals. And when, after an eternity, their two bodies became one, she cried out in the flush of ecstasy.

Cast adrift from time and space, they soared to pinnacles of mutual release.

Neither wanted the night to ever end.

Terry came awake, conscious of being stared at. He rolled over in bed and saw Alice in the chair by the desk. Her hair was wet and had been combed out, the comb still in her hand. He had the impression she'd been watching him for quite a while. "Morning."

"You're a good sleeper." Alice smiled half-heartedly. "I took a shower. I've been trying not to wake you."

"The power is back on?" Terry sat up and saw Peter's dossier on the desk where he had left it lying open, Peter's photograph on top.

"Yup." Alice looked at the photo, too, her guilt as blatant as her despair.

Terry swung his legs over the side of the bed and retrieved his underwear. "Are you all right?"

"I don't know. What happens now?"

"I don't know either," Terry admitted. He had guilt of his own to contend with, a sense of shame at having taken advantage of a vulnerable woman.

"Have you ever done this before?"

Terry wasn't offended. She had every right to ask. "No. It's sort of the cardinal sin."

"I guess we're breaking all the rules, huh?" Alice listlessly ran the comb through her hair. "I've been sitting here, thinking how it would be if we'd just met. If it wasn't like this. If it was just, you know—"

"Somewhere else."

"Another place, another time, that sort of thing," Alice said. "What would that have been like? If I was just in my life and you came through. Like we could know that, right?" She turned the photo of Peter over. "This is just so not like my life, that's all. Nothing that's happened is like my life anymore. So I'm a little lost here. Maybe for you it's not that confusing. I mean, this is your life, right?"

Terry snagged his pants. "Is that what you think?"

"No. I don't know." Alice gestured. "And I'm not saying that I did it because I was stressed out, or I was drunk, or it was late or anything. I'm not trying to let myself off the hook. Because this was me. I know that. You never would have made a pass. I know that, too. So obviously I'm just—" She caught herself. "Oh, God. I don't know what I am anymore."

Her sorrow, her confusion, ate at Terry like acid. In one respect she was wrong. He was as much at fault as she was. He could have stopped it if he'd really wanted to. "Don't be so hard on yourself. None of us are saints." Terry stood. "And we're not hurting Peter. That's not what this was about."

Alice's eyes brimmed with tears. "I can't stop thinking about him. I can't help it. Where is he right now, do you suppose?"

Terry said the one thing that would soothe her guilt. "It sounds to me as if he's right here."

Alice smiled, sniffed, and rose. "I was looking for a hair dryer. Don't you have one?"

"They can send one up. I'll call down." Terry watched her pad into the bathroom and close the door. There was so much more he wanted to say, but he dared not voice his feelings. To do so would mean destroying a marriage. It was best for everyone involved if he erected a wall around his emotions until the whole affair was over.

When the hair dryer was delivered by a chambermaid, Terry handed it in to Alice. Ten minutes later Alice emerged, so breathtakingly beautiful that an ache formed in Terry's chest at the thought she could never be his.

Alice couldn't bring herself to meet his gaze, which stung him severely. Terry walked her down to the line of taxis always waiting for fares in front of the hotel. She finally looked at him as she was about to climb in, her expression inscrutable. Instead of hugging or kissing him she clasped his hand and gently squeezed.

"Thank you."

"For what? Losing control?"

"For being there when I needed you most."

Alice slid in and the cabby whisked her away. Terry stood watching until the cab was lost amid the flow of traffic; then he inhaled deeply and turned to go back in.

Tecala City lay quiet under the bright glare of a new day. The sirens were stilled, the smoke was gone. Both sides in the conflict were taking a breather. But it wouldn't last long.

Terry showered and shaved and made a few calls to local contacts. He had to reestablish communications with the E.L.T., and by sending out feelers he was optimistic they would contact him. That afternoon he went to the Scorpion House. Alice remained reserved around him, and when he went into the radio room and fired it up, she didn't tag along. For hours he tried to reach Marco, vainly trying frequency after frequency, saying, "This is Tio calling Marco. Do you copy?" It was a lost cause.

That night Terry couldn't sleep. He tossed and turned, flushed with vivid images of Alice, of their passionate lovemaking. He craved more. Several times he sat up and reached for the phone, but he couldn't bring himself to dial her number.

Toward dawn Terry finally dozed off. He slept until nine. Still unable to keep Alice out of his mind, he donned his swimming trunks, threw a towel over his shoulders, and headed for the Olympic-size pool. He hoped an hour of exercise would help since cold showers were obviously overrated.

Terry had the pool pretty much to himself. Hostilities had yet to resume, but most people were staying off the streets and out of public places. Martial law had been put into effect, and there was a ten P.M. curfew.

Terry dived in and began swimming laps. The mere act of doing something physical felt good. He concentrated on stroking cleanly, smoothly. For a while he was able to shut Alice out and forget about the mess he had made of the whole affair. For a while he was spared the guilt that had been gnawing at him since the morning before. But only for a short while. On his third lap, as he came up after swimming the entire length of the pool underwater, he saw Dino waiting for him, holding a towel.

"You'd better get out." Dino, wearing a grim look, extended a hand.

"What's up?" Terry asked, his intuition telling him that something really bad had happened.

"Kessler. The German."

"The missionary?"

"He's out. He escaped from the rebels. My friends on the police force contacted me. He's at St. Tecala Hospital. I've seen him."

"What's he got to do with me?" Terry wondered.

"Your boy was being held with him. They made a run for it." Dino hauled Terry out. "It doesn't look good."

The police had already contacted Alice. She was in the kitchen with Norma, both of them crying, when Terry and Dino arrived to pick her up. The only thing she said to him was, "They say Peter's dead. They say he was shot."

"Don't jump to conclusions," Terry cautioned. "Wait and hear what the missionary has to tell you first."

The ride was conducted in silence save for Alice's soft weeping. Norma came along to comfort her.

At the hospital, the nurse led them to a private room. The shades had been drawn. Erich Kessler was bandaged and hooked to an IV, his face badly bruised, one eyebrow swollen. The first words out of his mouth when Terry introduced Alice brought on more tears.

"I am so sorry, Mrs. Bowman. Pieter was a good man."

"You know for a fact he's dead?" Terry demanded.

"Ja," Kessler said. "I was shot. I fell into a river. But before I fell, Peter was hurt. A spear, here." He touched his thigh. "And a rebel, a bad one, was about to shoot him. I heard the shots as I fell."

Alice sat on the edge of bed, broken, despairing. "Tell me more. How was he?"

"He missed you so much," Kessler said. "You were all he thought of." The big German smiled. "For the meals, we could eat together. But the food, it's nothing. Just to keep you alive, ja? Peter would take the bowl. He would say, 'Tonight let's see what Alice has made for us.' And he would make a menu. From his memory. You know, describe the feast we were about to eat. A transformation. A Eucharist." He took her hand in his. "Do you understand? So many wonderful dinners I've had at your table. Bouillabaisse and lentil salad and cold Muscadet."

Alice was quaking. Tears gushed. She reached up, her fingertips brushing the missionary's lips.

"Mrs. Bowman," Kessler said tenderly. "May I call you Alice? You were everything to him. Sitting there with you and your daughter. Both of you so alive for him. He missed you both so very much. He spoke of you all the time. You have to know this."

Kessler patted her, and Alice slumped in abject misery.

Terry longed to take her in his arms and comfort her. Instead, he had to settle for nudging Dino and stepping out into the hall so as not to be overheard. "This is bullshit, buddy. He didn't see the body. He didn't see shit."

"Get real, man."

"I don't buy it," Terry insisted. "The E.L.T. worked hard on our deal. Then they killed the hostage?"

"When was your last radio contact?" Dino said. "I've had nothing but static since the lid blew off. Maybe there are no more deals, man. Maybe it's all coming apart."

"And maybe he's alive," Terry said. He refused to believe Peter Bowman was dead. He refused to accept that fate was denying him the opportunity to redeem himself by saving the life of the man he had wronged.

"Yeah, well, here's what's for sure. My guy is still up there." Dino glanced at the room and plucked at his lower lip, a habit of his when he was in deep thought. "You know, the rebels don't have any idea Kessler made it out. They think he's dead. That could work to our advantage. He knows every inch of that camp, and he's willing to help. He drew me a map."

"*Pendejo,* he's a missionary," Terry reminded him.

"Don't sell the man short. He used to be in the French Foreign Legion. He knows about directions, coordinates, landmarks. The map looks good."

Terry saw where the conversation was drifting, and tensed. "What're you doing, Dino?"

"This has got to stay quiet. She's got to know that."

"Tell me you're not thinking of going up there on your own?"

"Shit, man, all I'm doing is thinking." Dino bent closer. "What else am I supposed to do? Sit around, waiting for the damn phone to ring, like Wyatt? I want my client out alive."

Terry looked into the room at Alice. She was totally crushed. Norma and Kessler were trying to soothe her, but she was inconsolable. "Count me in," he said softly.

Terry drove Alice and Norma back. Alice sobbed on Norma's shoulder the whole ride. In the driveway, Terry hopped out and opened the door for them, saying, "I know this is a bad time, but you can't give up hope."

Alice catapulted out of the jeep as if she couldn't get inside fast enough.

"Hold up," Terry said, but she wasn't waiting, not

for him, not for anyone. He ran to overtake her and tried to catch hold of her hand, but she jerked loose.

"Just leave me alone. I don't want to hear it."

"Alice, we don't know for sure," Terry stressed. "Until we do, until we're positive, it's got to stay in play."

Her contempt was thick enough to cut with a machete. "Do you think Mr. Kessler made it all up?"

"He didn't see it happen," Terry said.

They were almost to the door, and Alice slowed at last. "Why are you doing this?" she forlornly asked, bowing her head.

"Look at me, please," Terry asked, and when she finally did, he said, "I've been at this for nine years. In all that time, all those cases, I've only seen hostages killed twice. Kidnappers don't kill the golden goose before the payoff. It's just not done." She started to turn. "He's worth half a million dollars to them, and they know it."

Alice gestured as if to say it was all hopeless and went to go inside.

Terry had reached the limits of his patience. Seizing her by the shoulders, he swung her around so they were face-to-face. "I'm going to keep it together here. I'm going to stay professional. Stay on the protocol. Until I'm sure, until I *know* he's dead, until I get the cargo back, I'm looking to close this deal. One way or another."

Stifling another sob, Alice pulled from his grasp. She was losing it again. She bolted indoors, Norma rushing after her, and they disappeared up the stairs.

Dejected, wooden, Terry went inside. He figured to stick around awhile and talk to her again after she had composed herself. She had to be made to understand, for her own peace of mind as well as his. He heard more weeping, but from the kitchen, not upstairs.

Cinta, the young maid, was at the table bawling. Maria, the older maid, and Sandro, the driver hovered over her. Sandro appeared mad, and Maria had an arm on Cinta's shoulder as if to protect her.

"What is this all about?" Terry asked in Spanish.

"I am numb from shock," Maria said.

Terry assumed she was talking about Peter Bowman. "I believe everyone is."

"We must remember she is a young girl."

"Cinta?" Terry said, mystified.

Sandro wagged a finger at Maria. "What she did was very foolish. She should have told us sooner."

"Enough!" Maria said. "She was scared. She didn't know any better."

"If she had told us sooner we might have saved Señor Bowman," Sandro said bitterly. "What she has done is despicable."

"It is too late now. So let her be." Maria patted Cinta's back. "There, there, child. You can't blame yourself. Who can say whether it would have done any good?"

Terry stepped to the table. "What would have done any good? I want to know what this is about, and I want to know now."

Maria sighed. "That voice. On the radio. Cinta thinks she knows who it was."

"She knows who Marco is?" Terry said, his whole body tingling with expectation. "How can that be?"

"Her mother does laundry for the man and his wife. Cinta has only met him twice, to say hi to, but it was his voice."

"I need a name. I need a telephone number. I need an address if she has one," Terry said taking a pen from his pocket and snatching a napkin from a holder. He could well be grasping at a straw, but given the news from the missionary, he'd grasp at anything if it increased his chances of bringing Peter Bowman back alive.

The Tecalan Country Club was holding a beauty pageant, and the man Terry sought was among the spectators. Terry studied him from afar, his memory jogged. He remembered seeing the man before in one of the many photos in the box Alex kept, the photo that showed her all decked out in a lovely dress, as gorgeous as a starlet, dancing with a suave local at the Tecalan Country Club.

The swimsuit portion of the competition was just under way, and the man was ogling the young women, a born lecher if ever there was one. Terry wound through the tables and sat down across from him. "How are you doing?"

"Excuse me?" the man said in Spanish. "Do I know you?"

"Here's what we'll do," Terry held to English. "I'll be Tio. You be Marco."

The man blanched. "Look, I'm sorry, my friend," Marco stuck to Spanish, "but I don't speak your language."

Terry smiled cheerfully and pulled a cassette from his jacket. He placed it on the table between them. "Know what this is? A tape of you negotiating for ransom for the E.L.T."

Marco was trying not to crumble. "Look, I'm sorry, but this isn't—"

Terry had no hankering to indulge in mind games. He nodded at several military officers a few tables away. "Maybe I'll take this over and play it for those gentlemen in uniform. See what they make of it." In loud Spanish he declared, "If you think I'm in the mood to fuck about, you're in the wrong line of work."

People at adjacent tables glanced around. So did a couple of the officers. Marco's blood drained from his face, and he whispered in perfect English, "Keep your voice down, Tio. What is it you want?"

"Is Peter Bowman still alive?"

"As far as I know, yes. He tried to escape. He was hurt, but he's alive."

"Is he with the Italian?" Terry probed, seeking intel Dino needed confirmed.

Marco glumly nodded. "You know a great deal. How did you find me?"

"That's the least of your problems." Terry tapped the tape.

"Listen, it's not up to me," Marco said, panic setting in. "I'm just a voice. I have nothing to do with the kidnapping."

Terry wasn't so sure. The dance with Alice was too much of a coincidence. It could well be that Marco fingered prospective targets for the E.L.T.

"Instructions come, I spit them back. That's my part."

"What happened to our deal?" Terry asked.

Marco kept trying to justify himself. "Listen to me. I'm no different than you. We do the same thing. We talk for money. Someone else decides about the hostages."

No, they were vastly different, Terry thought. He talked to save lives. Marco was in it out of pure greed. "I want him back."

"It's too late. I can't make contact anymore, not even by radio. And they couldn't get him down now if they wanted to, not with the army breathing down their necks. The money's not worth the danger. It's a war. They don't care anymore."

"We'll close the deal right here," Terry proposed.

"Didn't you hear me, Tio? Do you think Octonal is just buying the pipeline? No. They're buying the army. They're buying the narcos. And they're out to crush us." Marco shook his head. "We're fighting for our lives. There are no more deals."

"So you're just a voice, eh?" Terry glared. "Now *you* listen. I own you. From this moment on you are mine. Is that clear? You're going to do your best to reach them. Tell them the deal is still on. Tell them to keep him alive. Say one wrong word to anybody and I'll know about it." Terry half rose out of his chair. "The army will get the original of this tape." He shoved the copy across. "Here. Keep it as a reminder that if you do anything stupid, you'll be up before a firing squad."

Wheeling, Terry stalked out. He had a lot to do. It was time to go to war.

Chapter 15

The blazing sun beat down on Dino's warehouse hide-away and on the three Tecalan mercenaries playing dominoes out in front. Terry had met them on his last visit to the city. As he climbed out of his jeep, the friendliest of the trio, Carlo, smiled and cheerfully greeted him. The other two, Rico and Tomas, merely nodded.

Half a dozen maps had been taped to a wall, and Dino was examining the largest. "Here's the camp," he said, rapping a knuckle on a spot in the highlands. "Kessler says they call it Canon Verde. And here's the river." Dino ran a finger along a serpentine blue line.

"Rio Caya," Terry read.

Dino roved his finger over another grid. "See this valley here? It's just over the mountain from Canon Verde. The army keeps trying to push up through it and the E.L.T. won't let them. It's like the guerrillas have drawn a line in the sand. Or in this case, the jungle. Kessler said they'd always muster all their troops whenever the army got too close. Practically the whole camp would go off to fight."

"What makes Canon Verde so bloody special?"

"See this?" Dino touched various points between

213

the rebel stronghold and Tecala City. "The E.L.T. has units all the way from the highlands down to the barrios outside the capital. If they get into trouble they fall back along this route."

Terry comprehended. "Canon Verde is their back door, their way out in a fix."

"Exactly. The E.L.T. has to keep that door open so they're defending it at all costs, throwing everything they can muster at the army."

Terry thought of something else. "Where's the oil pipeline in relation to all this?"

"Right here." Dino touched the map lower down. "Fifteen clicks down the river from Canon Verde."

"So what's your plan?"

Dino hooked his thumbs in his belt. "My plan? Well, let me see." He sat on the edge of a nearby desk. "Plans one through forty-three are pretty much the same. We fly in. We get shot at. We get our guys killed. We limp home in disgrace and quit the business." He scowled. "I have no fucking plan."

Terry studied the large map anew, noting the locations of the camp in relation to the army, and both positions to the pipeline. "What we need to do is get a battle going right around here." He pressed a finger to the pipeline at the point where it was closest to Canon Verde. "Draw the rebels further away than usual. Drain the camp. It would buy us more time."

"Great idea," Dino said enthusiastically. "Let's call the army and schedule a battle. Ask them to launch a major strike. How's Wednesday around three? Is that good for you?"

Terry overlooked the sarcasm. "The army already has units up there. We want them to pour in more, to throw in all they can spare." He glanced at his friend. "Do you have a pilot you trust?"

"One of the best."

"Do you trust those three out front?" Terry didn't, not in a country where loyalty was sold to the highest bidder.

"They're tops," Dino declared. "They're my Panama crew, remember? I trained them. But that's not the point." He stood. "What's the deal here? Are you in love with the woman? Is that why you're going in?" He came over. "Because if we're running options here, let's go all the way. Let's look at all of them." He held up a forefinger. "We go in. It's your raid. He dies, and you come back. She'd never forgive you, which would be bad." He held up another finger. "You die. He comes back. Bad again." A third finger. "You both die. Bad as bad can be."

"You're not telling me anything I don't already know."

Dino wasn't finished. "What are you holding out hope for? That you'll save the husband, and she'll see the light and dump him to run off with you?"

Terry turned from the map. "I outgrew fairy tales a long time ago."

"That's nice to hear. You know why?" Dino was wound up. "Because I want out. I'm looking to cash in. I want my own thing. And if we pull this off, we'll be legends. Word would spread and everyone would want to use us. So don't get me wrong. I'd love to go out on a winner, but come on!" He motioned at the map. "Let's be realistic. This plan of yours could get us completely fucked."

Terry nodded. "So we're on then, right?"

The tennis courts at the country club were filled at that time of the afternoon. Alice walked across them with no regard for the games under way. Players stopped and stared. It made her think of the time when Ivy broke the news of Peter's abduction. Now here she was doing the same thing, but this time the message might save Peter's life.

Alice had been giddy with joy to learn Kessler might be mistaken. Terry had shown up on her doorstep the evening before and had given her a phone number to call. The voice at the other end had startled her. She'd heard it countless times over the radio. It was Marco, and he'd affirmed that Peter might in fact still be alive.

Afterward, Terry took her out onto the patio and confided the plan he had come up with. The risks were enormous. Alice had pointed that out, saying, "Why are you doing this? For me?"

Terry had given her a peculiar look and answered, "It's what I do."

Now here she was, brazenly striding toward Ted Fellner, who had stopped playing tennis and was riveted in astonishment. Fellner, the survivor, the new head of Octonal's Tecalan branch. Fellner, the conniving bastard who had turned his back on Peter when Peter needed help most. Alice would enjoy deceiving him if for no other reason than to enjoy some payback. "Hello, Ted."

"Alice!" Fellner blurted. "What a surprise. Are you okay?"

"Let's skip the bullshit, Ted," Alice said. "I think we're past that. I'm here because the E.L.T. wants a million dollars for Peter. They won't move, and we don't have the money."

Fellner was as duplicitous as ever. "That's a lot of money."

No offer to help, Alice noted. No real sympathy. "If I gave you information that was critical in protecting your precious pipeline, would Octonal step up and do the right thing?"

"What kind of information?" Fellner hedged.

Alice did as Terry had coached her and used it as an excuse to shoulder her bag and walk off in an apparent huff. "Forget it. I should have known better." She was inwardly delighted when Fellner ran after her and caught her by the arm.

"Alice, please, wait. You have me all wrong. Do you think I don't get up every morning and think about Peter? I've had a dozen meetings with the transition team about the whole situation and how wrong it is."

Alice had to hand it to the snake. He deserved an Academy Award. "Fuck you, Ted," she said bluntly and walked on. Terry had told her to make Fellner work for it. If it were too easy, Fellner would become suspicious. She had to be equally part indignant and sincere. But it was a real test of her willpower not to look back to see if he had taken the bait. She strode from the courts and started across the parking lot.

"Alice, hold on there!" Fellner jogged up. "Look, I'm not sure what we're talking about. Give me something to work with, and maybe I can push this the last mile."

Alice stopped. "Do you really think you can talk Octonal into helping?"

"I'll do my best. What do you have?"

In a conspiratorial whisper, Alice said, "The E.L.T. is going after the pipeline tomorrow. I know where. Help Peter, and I'll tell you."

Fellner scrunched up his face like he had just sucked a lemon. "Oh really? I don't know what you think you're trying to accomplish here, Alice. Or what you think you know. Or how stupid you think I am." His smug cockiness reasserted itself. "For your information, I receive three military briefings a week. It's a safe bet that if an attack on the pipeline was planned, I'd know about it."

"Is that a no?" Alice responded.

Fellner was ready to cast her adrift. "How could you possibly know such a thing?"

Alice played her trump card. She pointed at the jeep. Terry was behind the wheel. Beside him sat Erich Kessler, his hair trimmed, his beard shaved. "Know who he is? Maybe you've heard of the missionary who escaped the E.L.T.?"

"He's your source?"

Alice had him. "Can you ask for a better one?"

Insects droned in the heat of the day. Terry could hear them outside the warehouse as he reassembled the M-16 he had selected. Stripping and cleaning one was old hat to him; he could do it blindfolded if he had to. He was almost done. Placing the charging handle into the top of the receiver, he made sure the lugs on the handle were seated in their proper grooves. Next, he slid the charging handle halfway forward and inserted the bolt carrier, with the bolt in the unlocked position. He pushed forward on the charging handle and the bolt carrier until both were fully seated. Finally, he reattached the upper and lower receiver groups and reseated the receiver pivot pin. "Where is he? I'm giving him five more minutes."

Alice had been an intrigued spectator. "I've never seen you nervous."

Terry put down the M-16. "Yes, you have."

A shadow spilled across the doorway. Dino sauntered in, his thumbs hooked in his belt. "You must have done a hell of a job," he complimented Alice.

"I've just had an urgent call from our friend Dover McLoon at the embassy. He wanted to know if I'd heard anything about a rebel push up toward Rio Caya."

"Bingo," Terry said, smiling.

"So lo tragaron completo." Dino chose an M-16 for himself from a rack of machine guns and SMGs.

Terry fed spare magazines into pouches on his camouflage web belt. "Get your fatigues on. Get the boys rolling. I want a full kit check in ten minutes."

"Time to rock and roll." Dino cupped a hand to his mouth. *"Mucháchos, adando! Vamos al baile! Moviendose, carajo!"*

The three Tecalan mercs interrupted yet another domino game to rush inside and claim their gear. A minute later they bustled out on Dino's heels.

Terry lingered for a last moment alone with Alice. He had so much he desired to say, so very much he never could. Embracing her, he molded his lips to hers. For a few heartbeats he feared she wouldn't respond, but she did. He savored it, savored the silken feel of her tongue, savored the delicious taste of her, the fragrance of her perfume. He knew as surely as he was standing there that it was the last kiss they'd ever share.

"Terry! Get the lead out!" Dino hollered. "The sun's going down!"

They broke apart. Terry stared a moment, treasuring the simple sight of her. Then he scooped up his kit and raced for the waiting helicopter.

The grizzled pilot, like the trio of mercs, was Tecalan. Like them, Dino had used him on previous hazardous outings. An old hand at eluding detection, he flew the Bell UH-1 Huey low over the jungle to avoid radar. The copter was an older model formerly in use by the Tecalan Tactical Air Command. It wasn't especially fast, and its warload was minimal, but it could get the job done.

Terry was in the bay, going over the map one last time for the benefit of Dino and the mercenaries. All five of them wore light camouflage fatigues. They had Kevlar vests, Pro-Tec helmets, battle packs, the works. Each man was fitted with com-link earpieces and microphones.

As a professional courtesy, Terry had left the choice of sidearms and heavier hardware up to them. All but Carlos opted for autorifles; the burly merc had chosen an M-60, and at the moment Dino was tearing off strips of gaffer's tape so Carlos could strap extra ammo canisters to his pack.

"Does everyone have his part down pat?" Terry asked.

"Sí, señor," Tomas said.

Rico nodded. He was the quiet one and only spoke when necessary.

Carlos fondled the M-60 as if it were a lover. "Do not worry," he said, chuckling. "I know just what to do."

At the Huey's cruising speed of one hundred and eighty kilometers an hour, they reached the insertion point ninety-eight minutes after leaving the warehouse. Night was in full bloom, moonless but flooded with stars. The pilot brought them in low over a clearing two clicks from the rebel encampment. At Terry's command ropes were lowered from both sides of the chopper. The mercs descended quickly, Carlos with the heavy M-60 slung across his back.

Terry and Dino slid down side-by-side. At a wave from Terry, the pilot banked the Huey and peeled the big chopper toward another clearing seven kilometers north of Canon Verde. The pilot would wait there until dawn, then hopefully be in position to receive the retrieval signal when they were ready to be extracted.

Rico took point. The smallest and wiriest, he hailed from a remote mountain village. He'd joined the Tecalan army after his wife was gunned down by guerrillas for offering water and food to a government patrol. Not satisfied with the amount of action he saw in the army, he took his discharge and became a mercenary so he could hunt them on his own terms.

Tomas had once been a policeman, and had been sickened by the amount of graft and corruption in the force. After his partner was shot by E.L.T. fanatics robbing a bank, he quit the police and became a gun-for-hire—so long as the guns were pointed at the E.L.T.

Carlos was bulky, easygoing and good-natured. He'd told Terry he had lost a son to a mine planted by rebel forces and had never forgiven them. He liked big guns and big-breasted women, not necessarily in that order.

Like ghostly wraiths they glided through the lush undergrowth, making no more noise than would prowling ocelots. They were seasoned professionals, as much at home in the dankest jungle as in the darkest alley.

Terry smelled the encampment long before he saw the faint flow of a fire. Smoke carried for miles, but the rebels didn't seem to care. Overconfidence, Terry suspected, with a dash of arrogance for extra measure. Three hundred yards out he gave the hand signal for his team to flatten and crawl. Two hundred yards out he signaled for dispersal. Dino and Tomas angled to the right, Terry and Rico to the left. Carlos crawled on straight ahead, alone.

By oh-two-hundred they were in position. Terry and Rico were in thick brush above a cluster of tents and shacks, Dino and Tomas were concealed within a stone's throw of the farmhouse, and Carlos had set up the M-60 on a ledge overlooking the entire camp.

Now all they could do was wait. Terry hunkered down, his back to a tree. It had been two years or better since he was last in the jungle, and he had forgotten the clammy sensation, the bestial snarls and shrieks, the rustling of vegetation. He tried to doze off, but he was asking the impossible. His nerves were stretched as taut as piano wire. Too much was riding on the outcome of the mission, not the least of which was his own peace of mind.

Rico had squatted beside a boulder and never moved once the rest of the night.

Terry maintained radio silence. They weren't to talk until the extraction began. To occupy himself, he thought about his son, about what Dino had said about branching off on his own, about a lot of things—except Alice Bowman.

Dawn took forever in coming. Rico stirred when a faint pink tinge framed the eastern horizon, then suddenly signaled an enemy was in sight.

Easing onto his elbows and knees, Terry crabbed over for a look. A sentry was posted thirty yards below their position. As he watched, another guerrilla came up a path from the encampment and the pair exchanged a few words. Then the first man gathered up his submachine gun and headed down. The night sentry, Terry figured, being relieved by the day sentry. He glanced at Rico and nodded.

The small Tecalan melted into the jungle.

Terry didn't take his eyes off the sentry, who made himself comfortable. He was waiting for it, but he still almost missed seeing Rico take the man down, because he blinked at the same instant Rico heaved up out of the weeds. Lightning-quick, Rico slipped a garotte over the rebel's neck and wrenched. The wire bit deep, shearing through flesh and severing the sentry's jugular. The man was dead before he had any inkling what had occurred.

Terry couldn't have done it more efficiently himself. He saw Rico quietly drag the body into the weeds. Rising in a combat crouch, he cat-footed down to join him. Voices from the tents and elsewhere indicated the rest of the rebels would soon be up and about. From the sound of things, there were a lot more guerrillas than he'd anticipated.

Word of the massive buildup of government troops near the pipeline should have reached the stronghold the day before. Terry had reckoned the camp would be all but deserted. But when he saw eight or nine officers sleepily file from the tents and spied scores of soldiers lying on the ground amid the trees, he knew he had miscalculated. Either word hadn't reached them or the rebel commanders felt there was no need to send reinforcements.

To attempt a rescue in the face of such formidable odds was certain suicide.

Then an older officer bellowed and a young guerrilla rushed over and snapped to attention. A brief exchange resulted in the younger man running to a large bell, like those customarily found in Tecalan churches. He commenced jerking on the rope and loud peals resonated off the adjoining slopes. Instantly the camp was astir as the rebels mustered to head out. They lined up in pairs, their weapons slung, bandoliers crisscrossing their chests, some with backpacks, some carrying supplies. At a wave from the officer they marched into the jungle and within a minute, the sounds of their passing had faded.

Terry activated his radio. "Uptown Bravo-One, this is Downtown Alpha-One. I counted eighty-four regulars leaving camp. Copy?"

"Affirmative, Alpha-One," Dino responded. "I make it about two dozen hostiles still on site."

Terry trained binoculars on the tree line above the farmhouse. He couldn't see them, but Dino and Tomas were there and would go after Calitri, the Italian banker, at the same time that he went after Peter Bowman.

The encampment quieted. Most of the remaining soldiers were eating breakfast. Out of the cookhouse came a muscular rebel in a fatigue cap, carrying a bowl of rice toward a stand of trees.

Terry had to shift position to see where the man was headed, and when he did, he smiled. "Bravo-One, this is Alpha-One. We have a solid visual on the wood shack. Solid confirm on the Kessler intel. We're looking at breakfast in bed for one—repeat one—hostage."

"Roger, Alpha-One. Be advised we have a solid visual on breakfast for one at the farmhouse. Delivery in progress."

Terry swung the binoculars toward the farmhouse and saw another rebel climbing toward it with another bowl of rice. Everything was coming together nicely. He signaled Rico, and they started toward the wood shack.

The muscular guerrilla had taken the bowl inside and emerged empty-handed. Now he was leaning against the shack.

None of the rebels, Terry noted, were particularly vigilant. That overconfidence factor again.

A bunch of men near the cookhouse had finished eating and one produced a soccer ball. Weapons and shirts were stashed on the sidelines as an impromptu game got underway.

Terry and Rico were almost in position. He marveled at how quietly the small Tecalan merc moved and saw a fierce glitter in Rico's dark eyes when Rico glanced down at the guerrillas. His hatred of the rebels was pure and plain.

They came to an ideal vantage point. Squatting, Terry said into his mike. "Alpha-One here. Time for curtain call."

"Delta-One is up and ready," Carlos replied.

"Roger, Delta-One," Terry said. "Bravo-One, let's go final on a headcount."

Dino's voice crackled in Terry's headset. "This is Uptown Bravo-One. We have a two-man detail on the farmhouse."

Terry swept his binoculars over the soldiers below. "Roger that. Okay, downtown we have, starting at the wood shack, one guy in a fatigue hat. We'll call that six o'clock. Moving up to nine o'clock we count five outside the barracks. Another fifteen playing football on the parade ground. That gives us twenty-one visible downtown, with two uptown at the farmhouse. Twenty-three confirmed." And there were probably a few more unaccounted for in the various tents and buildings.

"Acknowledged. Uptown Bravo-One is good to go," Dino said. "It's your call Alpha-One."

Terry took a deep breath. "Bravo-One, Delta-One, be advised Alpha-One is going hot. Repeat. Alpha-One is going hot." Replacing the binoculars, he signaled to Rico to cover him and slipped toward the shack.

The guy in the cap was puffing on a cigarette, watching the soccer game, the soldiers involved yelling and laughing, having a fun time.

No one else was anywhere near.

Ten yards out Terry slung the M-16 and drew out his boot knife. The double-edged blade glinted in the sun. He held it low to the ground so the gleam wouldn't give him away as he sank onto his belly and snaked toward the guard's back. He moved with consummate care, avoiding dry twigs and careful not to snag his uniform.

The guard abruptly snuffed out his cigarette, straightened, and stretched.

Terry had the impression the man was about to turn. Surging upright, he hurtled forward and clamped his left hand over the rebel's mouth while simultaneously slicing the razor edge of his knife across the man's throat. The steel bit inches deep, half-decapitating him, and the muscular guerrilla folded like a house of cards.

His knife dripping blood, Terry darted to the doorway and ducked inside. It took several seconds for his eyes to adjust to the murk. When they did, he involuntarily gave a start. Although he knew what to expect, knowing it in no way prepared him for the foul odor and the actual ghastly sight.

Peter Bowman was hunched over on the floor, hungrily cramming rice into his mouth with his fingers. Any semblance to the photographs Terry had seen was purely coincidental. Peter was a filthy wreck. Literally skin and bones, his arms and legs looked like brittle broomsticks, his unkempt hair plastered to his head. His clothing consisted of tattered pants. Festering sores dotted his feet and his thigh bore a crude bandage. He was as close to death's door as it was possible to be and still be alive.

"No, no," Peter said without looking up. *"He terminado."*

Terry realized he was afraid the guard had returned for the bowl before he was done eating. "Peter?" Terry said softly.

Peter jumped and spun, spilling some of the rice. "What? Who's that?" His eyes were wide, dilated.

"No, it's okay, it's okay," Terry assured him, crouching. "We have to be quiet. Nice and quiet now, okay?"

"How did you—? Where did you—?" Peter blurted, shaking like a leaf. Timidly, he reached out and touched Terry as if to prove to himself Terry were real.

Terry had witnessed the symptoms before. Bowman was on the verge of a breakdown. Another week or two and there wouldn't have been anyone to rescue. "Peter!" he said sharply. "We're here to get you out, okay? We're going to take you home. But I need for you to be very quiet. Do you understand what I'm saying?"

The reality was sinking in. Peter's face rippled, reflecting fear, astonishment, hope. "You're not fucking with me?"

"No, mate. I'm for real."

"Jesus," Peter exclaimed, his eyes watering. "I thought I had lost it."

"We have to hurry," Terry mentioned. "Can you walk?"

"Try and stop me," Peter responded and unsteadily rose.

Terry smiled, the grin freezing in place when his

earphone buzzed and Carlos urgently growled a warning.

"Alpha-One! Alpha-One! You have a bogey en route. Two o'clock."

A glance confirmed it. A heavyset guerrilla was strolling directly toward the shack.

Chapter 16

Terry Thorne motioned for Peter Bowman to be quiet. He leveled his M-16 but didn't want to use it unless he absolutely had to. The plan was to get in and out without engaging the locals. Silence and stealth were essential.

The heavyset guerrilla was smiling, as yet unaware that anything was wrong. "Rambo? *Buenos dias, compañero.*"

Terry glanced at the body of the muscled rebel he had killed and berated himself for not dragging it around the corner. Sloppiness, nothing but sheer sloppiness. When he was with the S.A.S. he'd never have made such an amateurish mistake.

A row of bushes blocked the oncoming rebel's view. Another two steps and he saw the shack and the body lying in a spreading scarlet ring. Shock registered, and he opened his mouth to shout.

Terry sighted down the M-16. Just as he was about to fire he saw Rico materialize out of the greenery. The small Tecalan held a glittering blade, which he plunged into the portly rebel three times with quicksilver rapidity. The man died on his feet, his cry dying in his pudgy throat. Rico began to pull him down into the undergrowth, but as he did the man's finger tightened on the trigger of the assault rifle he was carrying, and four rounds banged into the dirt.

Rico dragged the body out of sight, but the harm had been done.

Yells erupted from various points around the encampment. The soccer players stopped playing to turn and stare.

Terry's earphone sputtered to life, with Dino demanding, "Alpha-Downtown! What the hell was that? What's going on?"

A cook emerged from the cookhouse, a greasy apron around his waist, a shotgun clutched in both hands. He gazed to either side, then warily came toward the wood shack.

The soccer players were still staring, confused, uncertain.

"Alpha-One? Alpha-One?" Dino was growing frantic. "Give me a status report."

"This is Alpha-One," Terry replied. "We're blown. Repeat. We're blown."

"Son of a bitch," Dino fumed.

His eye to a gap between the planks, Terry saw the cook hesitate.

"Rambo? Hey! What the hell is going on up there?" the man hollered in Spanish. "What's up? Why the shots?"

Terry glanced at Peter. "All hell is about to bust loose. Stick by me, right? I'll get you out."

The cook advanced again. He spotted the body and jammed the shotgun's stock to his shoulder, aiming at the doorway. "Hey!" he yelled to the other rebels. "Over here! Something is wrong!"

That was when Carlos opened up, the M-60 thundering with the cadence of a chainsaw. With a cyclic rate of six hundred rounds per minute, it spewed lead fast and furious. The cook was riddled where he stood, chunks of flesh and gore bursting from his shattered form as he melted to the grass, a human sieve, leaking blood.

"We're loud! We're loud!" Terry shouted into his mike, and grabbed Peter's wrist. "This is it. Stay low." He stepped to the doorway, but halted when he heard automatic fire and Rico's voice blistered his ear.

"Alpha-One! You are not covered! Repeat, you are not covered! I am pinned down—" The rest of Rico's statement was lost in a chatter of weaponry.

Just bloody great! Terry thought and barreled out the doorway anyway. Above all else, he had to get Bowman out of there. But on his second step the ground in front of them was pockmarked by miniature dirt geysers. Pushing Peter back, Terry retreated into the shack and crouched. Across the way, screened by trees from Carlos, was the guerrilla who had taken rice up to the Italian at the farmhouse. Evidently he had been on his way down when all hell broke loose, and now he had the shack centered squarely in his sights.

"This isn't going the way you planned, is it?" Peter asked.

"You have a gift for understatement, mate," Terry muttered. Up on the hill more gunfire could be heard. Dino and Thomas, he assumed, making their bid to rescue Calitri. They'd have a harder time of it now with the farmhouse guards alerted.

Additional soldiers appeared, rushing from the tents and barracks. A few fired wildly into the jungle. The soccer players were scrambling for their weapons, all of them shouting at once, adding to the general confusion.

Carlos knew his job. Nine of the rebels went down, shot to pieces, and the rest dived for cover as the big M-60 raked the camp from one end to the other. An officer emerging from a tent was chopped in half in the act of drawing a sidearm. A guerrilla more foolhardy than the rest pinpointed Carlo's position and tried to rush up the slope, only to be met head-on by a withering leaden hailstorm.

"Alpha-Two! Where are you?" Terry asked.

"Still pinned down, Alpha-One," Rico responded. "Three of them have me in a cross fire. I am doing what I can."

Terry faced Peter. "We have to make a run for it. Break right the second we're outside, and I'll cover you."

Before either of them could move, scores of stinging wood slivers and sharp chips were blasted inward by a spray of autorounds. Terry recoiled as his face and chest were peppered. "Down! Get down!" he cried, pulling Peter beside him. More slugs tore through the planks, stitching them from top to bottom, the handiwork of the rebel gunner across the way.

"Delta-One," Terry barked. "We're clay pigeons here! Can you do anything about it?"

"Negative, Alpha-One," Carlos answered. "He's protected by trees. I've tried, but I can't take him out." He paused. "Hold on."

A line of rebels had risen from near the cookhouse and were streaking toward the shack. They had rightly divined Peter was the target of a rescue attempt and were determined to prevent his being taken. Carlos opened up with the M-60 again. Large-caliber bullets seared their torsos, their heads, and their limbs, and they sprawled across one another in a macabre dance of death.

The rebel who had the shack dead to rights continued to pour in blistering fire. The walls, the roof and the floor were being dissolved by the rain of rounds.

Terry twisted toward Peter. "Have you ever handled a pistol?" he shouted to be heard above the hammering slugs.

"A little," Peter said.

"Take this." Terry shoved his .45 ACP into Peter's hand. Pulling two grenades from his web belt, he explained, "These are flashbangs. They blind an enemy. One for you, one for me. Pull the pin, here." Terry touched one of the metal rings. "Then throw it. They go off on impact. Got it?"

"What are we doing?" Peter held the grenade as if he were afraid it would go off in his hand.

"I'm going out," Terry said, crawling forward. "We're being cut to ribbons here. If I don't make it, you're to get to the farmhouse on the hill. That's our extraction site."

Some of the soccer players were trying to get closer, but the M-60 was holding them at bay. Terry spotted a sniper with a rifle who had climbed onto the barracks and was fixing a bead on Carlos. Instantly, he brought his gun to his shoulder. He had the M-16s selector set to Semiauto, and his three-round burst chewed the man's face into so much raw meat.

"Delta, Delta," Terry bawled. "Alpha-One is going mobile. Moving on the count of three." He mentally made the count, then hurled himself into the open, toward the gunner screened by the trees. The man swiveled to take aim, gaping when Terry threw the flashbang in an overhand arc. It went off only a few feet from the gunner's face, a brilliant flash of blinding light, and he threw his hands over his eyes and screamed.

Almost in the same motion Terry brought the M-16 to bear. His next short burst knocked the gunner flat.

Two rebels were approaching from the left flank. Pivoting, Terry trained his weapon and felled them in midstride.

"Alpha-One! Alpha-One!" Dino bellowed. "We have our package. Are you clear? Come in, Alpha-One!

A heartbeat later Carlos advised them, "This is Delta! I'm reloading!"

Peter had followed Terry out and was blinking in the harsh glare of sunlight. "Come on!" Terry said, zigzagging toward the terraced hill.

From out of weeds not far from the cookhouse, four guerrillas appeared. They had snuck up without Carlos spotting them, and they caught Terry and Peter flat-footed. Terry leaped in front of Peter to shield him with his own body as the quartet prepared to fire. He might be able to get one or two, but the rest were bound to score.

But not if Rico had a say. He had disposed of the rebels pinning him down, and now he engaged the quartet, his SMG coring sternum after sternum. Precise. Thorough. Supremely deadly.

"Go!" Terry said, pushing Peter ahead of him. Peter was in pain and limping badly, but he ran for all he was worth as the air sizzled with scorching lead and the earth around them was repeatedly perforated by fired rounds.

"Bravo-Uptown, this is Delta!" Carlos yelled. "Downtown in full evac! Repeat. Downtown is pulling out!"

Or trying to, Terry thought. He fired on the fly, felling a rebel here, another there. Rico overtook them, laying down a suppressing fire of his own. Between their M-16s and Carlos's M-60 they had the majority of the remaining guerrillas pinned down.

"Roger, Delta," Dino acknowledged. "We are option blue. L.Z. Uptown is option blue."

That meant Dino and Tomas were ready for extraction. Terry gazed up the slope, wishing he could say the same. "Call in Big Bird!" he ordered.

"What about you, Alpha-One?" Dino asked.

"Call in Big Bird!" Terry repeated. Whipping an AN-M8 smoke grenade from his belt, he lobbed it ahead of them and dense white smoke swiftly coalesced into a spreading cloud. He plunged into it, Peter and Rico nearly stepping on his heels. "We're on our way!"

The firing temporarily tapered. In the unexpected lull Dino's voice rang crisp and clear over the helmet link. "Big Bird! Big Bird! This is Bravo-Uptown. We are option blue! We are good to go!"

Terry poured on the speed. They had to reach the extraction site in three minutes. The chopper pilot wouldn't wait, not with the landing zone so hot. Dino and Tomas were already there. Carlos was supposed to jam a stick into the M-60's trigger guard and make a break for it the moment he heard "option blue," but he was still firing away, jeopardizing his own life to protect theirs.

Pointing a finger at Rico, then at the ledge, Terry commanded, "Get him out of there!"

The small Tecalan dutifully veered off.

A trail hemmed by heavy undergrowth unfolded before them, winding from the valley floor to the farmhouse, the same trail used by the rebels. Terry flew up it, hauling Peter after him, and glanced back. Several guerrillas were in pursuit a hundred feet or more behind. Elsewhere, a pair of rebels were tugging at a green tarp to get at something underneath.

Carlos was *still* firing, dropping enemies all around.

Terry and Peter rounded a bend and Terry suddenly stopped. From his backpack he yanked an M18A1 and bent at the side of the trail to rig a trip wire.

"What's that?" Peter asked, huffing from his exertion. He was peaked and perspiring heavily. Fresh blood stained the bandage on his thigh.

"A claymore mine," Terry revealed.

Over the radio came Rico's voice. "Delta! This is Alpha-Two! Get out of there! I'll cover you!"

"I see you!" Carlos said. "Just another few seconds!"

Terry jogged upward, supporting Peter by the elbow. Voices alerted him rebels were almost to the bend where the claymore was set. Another second, and the morning was rent by the explosion and a chorus of shrieks.

"Look!" Peter shouted, pointing.

The Huey was streaking in low behind the farmhouse, its rotors shimmering in the sunlight. It alighted in a field behind the house, out of sight of the rebels below, as prearranged.

"Faster," Terry urged, hustling Peter along. They had two hundred yards to cover, almost all uphill. He glanced back just in time to see two guerrillas who had removed the tarp take hold of a rocket launcher. It resembled an old RPG2 and had a long pipelike body. They got set to fire, and in another second a rocket flashed from the front of the tube.

The ledge where Carlos was positioned burst skyward, an artificial volcano. Amid the downpour of dirt and debris, a second blast produced a roaring ball of flame.

The M-60 went quiet.

"Did they get him?" Peter asked.

Dino leaped on-line. "Downtown! Downtown! What's your status? What the hell just blew?"

The men with the rocket launcher were feeding another rocket into the tube. They rotated toward the hill, toward Terry and Peter, exposed on the footpath, but a flurry of rounds from Rico ended the threat they posed.

Behind Terry boots pounded. Whirling, he cored two rebels. He had to help Peter, who was lagging, and watch for enemies at the same time. From the direction of the farmhouse a door slammed, which surprised him. Dino and Tomas were supposed to have disposed of all hostiles on the premises. Had they missed some?

"Delta! Delta!" Dino was beside himself. "What the hell is going on? Someone answer me, damn it!"

Terry was going to reply but Rico beat him to it.

"This is Alpha-Two! Delta is down! I am bringing him."

"I'm coming!" Dino called.

In another thirty yards the path began to level off, a tangle of vegetation hemming both sides. Terry and Peter had to move in single file. Almost too late Terry glimpsed a shadowy figure crouched on the right. A guerrilla, knife in hand, sprang toward Peter, thrusting cold steel at Peter's neck.

Terry fired from the hip, the impact bowling the rebel over. Immediately another rebel rose on the left, armed with a rifle. Spinning, Terry fired again, his bullet penetrating the man's temple. A third time Terry pivoted, taking out a slab of beef who recklessly charged out of the bush brandishing a machete.

The trail took them past the farmhouse and on toward a small shed. Beyond was the field, and perched in the middle was the Huey, its bay doors beckoning wide. Terry saw Rico and Carlos approaching from off to the right, the smaller man supporting Carlos, who was peppered with shrapnel cuts and dirt. Dino was almost there, reaching out to help.

Peter staggered toward the chopper, on the borderline of collapse. "I'm about done in," he husked.

"Just a little further!" Terry was backpedaling, watching the jungle. "Come on, mate! You can do it!" A face appeared at a farmhouse window and he stroked the M-16, drilling holes in the glass. A few more steps brought him abreast of the shed.

"Grenade!" Peter suddenly yelled. "Look out!"

Terry heard it hit the ground near the shed. He threw himself in the opposite direction, but he was well within the blast radius. An invisible sledge hammer slammed into him, and he was tossed like a rag doll, end over end. The M-16 went flying from his grasp. Tumbling a dozen yards, he came to rest on his side, his ribs aching, his body battered, but apparently intact.

Tiny bits of debris were in Terry's eyes. They stung abominably, making his eyes water. He sat up, the world around him a blur. Momentarily defenseless, he blinked furiously and wiped a sleeve across his face. He still couldn't see clearly. But he had to get moving. Shoving to his feet, he ran toward the copter, past the smoking ruin of the shed.

To the left a ditch yawned. With no forewarning, out of it popped the rebel who must have thrown the grenade. Young, feral, radiating hatred, he raised an SMG and took deliberate aim.

Terry had nowhere to go, nowhere to seek cover.

"Juaco!"

The shout from Peter snapped the young guerrilla

around. He went to shoot, but Peter had thrown the other flashbang grenade and as it struck Juaco's chest, it detonated. Screeching hideously, Juaco was reduced to a human Roman candle. Yet he didn't go down. In a monstrous show of raw will he stumbled up out of the ditch and trained his weapon on Peter.

Over by the chopper, Tomas cut loose. Across the field Dino did likewise.

The young rebel collapsed, combustion and lead taking their toll. He screamed as he died, a scream of the damned, a scream of consummate anguish.

Terry swiped at his eyes again, but everything around him was distorted. He felt a spindly arm wrap around his waist.

Peter had come back for him. "Come on, buddy! You're holding everything up."

Smoke was rising from the encampment, and there were yells from far off. But no more gunfire pierced the morning as the two of them stumbled to the Huey and, with Tomas's help, clambered into the bay.

Seconds later it was Dino's and Rico's turns, the three of them levering Carlos inside.

"The eagle is good to go," Terry said into his mike, and the pilot lifted off. The Huey headed north, away from Canon Verde, looping eastward once they were out of rocket range.

"We did it!" Dino exclaimed, kneeling beside Calitri, who was slumped over in shock near the cockpit.

Rico and Tomas were bent over Carlos.

"Quit fussing over me," the lighthearted merc declared. "A few dozen nicks and scrapes aren't worth all this bother."

Terry unhooked his canteen, uncapped it, and upended it over his head. He was hot, his face dusty, sore, and flushed with fatigue. Pouring water into his eyes, he pressed his sleeve to his face to dry them. His vision cleared and he saw Peter Bowman staring at him in a mixture of gratitude and budding joy.

"Who *are* you?"

"Oh. Terry Thorne." Terry held out his hand. "Nice to meet you."

Peter bent nearer to be heard above the rotors and the hubbub of the others. "My wife! Alice! How is my wife?"

Terry pressed his sleeve to his face again in case his expression gave him away as he answered, "Alice is great. Just great. She's missed you. She'll be waiting for you when we get back."

"I can hardly wait," Peter Bowman said.

The drop-off point was Dino's warehouse.

From the air, Terry spied Alice and Sandro by the jeep. An ambulance was on hand. So were a bevy of Italians, Calitri's two sons just in from Rome and a cluster of Italian Embassy personnel.

The pilot lightly lowered the Huey to the tarmac. Dino hopped out first, helping the banker over the skids. The Italians came running, both sons crying. A doctor tried to examine Calitri amid all the hugging, finally gave up, and directed he be taken to the ambulance.

Terry hopped down and extended a hand to Peter, but Bowman was already sliding to the ground. Arms outflung, Peter hobbled toward the vision of loveliness running to meet him. They stopped a few steps shy of one another, Peter looking Alice up and down as if he couldn't believe how incredibly beautiful she was.

At that moment, Terry envied him more than he had ever envied anyone.

"I've missed you so much," Peter said, choked with emotion.

"I know. Me too." Alice was misty-eyed.

Nervous, awkward, Peter said, "I can't even—"

Alice placed a finger to his mouth. "Don't. Not now. Just hold me."

Terry's throat constricted as they melted into each other's arms. They clung together, comforting one another, a perfect fit. Tearing himself away, Terry jumped at finding Dino right next to him.

"Are you all right?" Dino quietly asked.

"Sure." It was the biggest, baldest lie of Terry's life, and they both knew it.

"Rico's getting the van. We can't hang."

"I know, I know." Terry moved toward the Bowmans. Sandro had hurried over and was assisting Peter toward the jeep. Alice started to go with them, then turned. Forcing a smile, Terry said, "We did it."

"You did it."

The Italians had the banker in the ambulance and were readying to depart. A van screeched around the helicopter and out sprang Rico and Tomas. Working swiftly, they began transferring Carlos from the bay to the vehicle.

"What's going on?" Alice asked. "Why is everyone in such a hurry?"

"You've got to get out of here."

"What?" Alice looked at him.

"We're all going to be very unpopular with certain people, powerful parties who will want to vent their anger any way they can."

"Oh." Alice was thrown. "I thought we'd at least have the chance to sit down together for a while."

"For what?" Terry said. "To get better acquainted? The three of us?" He saw her mouth compress into a thin line. "There's a six o'clock American flight to Dallas. You can just make it. Everything has been taken care of. Sandro has your passports in the jeep. Norma volunteered to pack your household belongings and ship them to you."

"You had this all worked out before hand?"

"A good soldier always plans ahead," Terry quipped. Alice didn't smile. "Terry—"

"His leg looks bad, but it can wait until Dallas."

"Terry, please—"

"This is important," Terry snapped. "No phone calls. No high-fives. No champagne. Go straight to the airport and get on the plane."

"Where are you going?"

"I don't know," Terry admitted. "Whatever's leaving first."

"This is just . . ." Alice glanced toward the jeep where Peter and Sandro were waiting, then gave him a tender look. "I was drowning. I was so lost. God, there's so much I want to say." She reached out, but caught herself. "Tell me you know how much you mean to me."

"We're even," Terry said, willing himself not to let his true feelings show.

"We'll never be even. I've given you nothing."

Now it was Terry who reached for her, but lowered his arm. "Alice, look. I had forgotten what it's like to want someone. I'd fallen into a rut, and I would never have made it out without you. Believe me, we're even."

"You deserve better than this." Alice's lower lip quivered. "It will break my heart more than anything if you don't know how much I mean that."

Terry nodded. He couldn't bring himself to say anything for fear he would break down. She wanted to say more, he could feel it. To forestall her, he gripped her wrist and walked her toward the jeep. Opening the passenger door, he stood aside so she could climb in beside Peter. "Get them on that flight," he directed Sandro.

The jeep's gears ground, and it rolled toward the road. Alice looked back one last time; then Peter enfolded her in his arms.

Drained, devastated, Terry watched her drive out of his life. He barely felt Dino nudge at his elbow. His friend was holding two cold beers.

"So here's the plan. The two of us, right? We start our own shop. I run New York. You run London. We meet once a month in the Caymans to visit our money. What do you say?"

Terry stared after the jeep. It rounded a corner, and she was gone.

"Strictly white glove," Dino said. "Lots of long lunches. No more front lines. No more Canon Verdes. We'll sell some policies. Do some consulting. Hell, man. Think of it." Dino laughed. "When Ian hears we're going into business, he'll have a heart attack."

Terry accepted a beer and popped the top. "You and me, huh?"

"What's wrong with that?"

"I don't know as I want you visiting my money."

Dino smiled and raised his beer in a toast. "Here's to the future."

Terry Thorne tapped his bottle against his friend's. "To the future!" he declared and meant it.

Editor's Note

The following excerpt is taken from Thomas Hargrove's book *Long March to Freedom* (Ballantine, 1995 and soon available through www.1stBooks.com), a harrowing account of the author's ordeal as a kidnapped hostage of FARC [*Fuerzas Armadas Revolucionarias de Colombia*], a militant communist guerrilla faction. During the eleven months of his captivity, Hargrove managed to keep an ongoing diary of his experiences by secretly scribbling on two checkbooks, as well as in a few children's notebooks the guerrillas allowed him to keep. Hargrove was able to conceal his notes and entries in his money belt and his clothing, thus avoiding discovery when his captors inspected his belongings.

For almost a year, Hargrove was forced to live in cramped, squalid conditions, facing the daily torture of malnutrition, despair, and the frustration of never knowing when he might—if ever—be released. The excerpts below cannot fully convey the torment and humiliation that Hargrove suffered both physically and mentally, or recount all of the events, such as the times the guerrillas were forced to evacuate their camp because of the proximity of the Colombian army—only to return to the same fetid bivouac they had left days before, or to one whose conditions were even worse. These fragments of Hargrove's diaries are only bits of a traumatic whole.

More importantly, the selections do not reflect the tremendous will, faith, and courage that Hargrove displayed while he was kidnapped. He forced his intellect to remain rational, making the best out of his surroundings by employing anything he could scavenge and hoard. Little things became luxuries—a few beans secreted aside for later, scraps of wood for a meager fire in his cell, a melted stub of a candle by which to write. Hargrove's slimmest hope of being released was dashed time and again in an endless cycle of monotony, hunger, and fear. Yet it is proof of his iron resolve and astonishing spirit that Thomas Hargrove endured the 334 days he spent in the ransom trade.

The selections below were edited for flow and relevant content, and thus ellipses are not used in areas where they normally would. Every effort has been used to retain the essence of the text. Elements in brackets are both from the original text and the editor, as are the endnotes.

♦　♦　♦

I knew that Colombia was notorious for kidnapping, averaging some 6,000 kidnaps per year. But my profession is international agriculture development—applying science to agriculture to improve the lives of the world's poorest farmers. My colleagues and I thought we were immune to kidnapping and other acts of terrorism.

In January 1992, I began work as head of CIAT's[1] communication program. The CIAT research center and main experiment farm are near Palmira, about a

50-minute drive from our home in Southern Cali. I was 10 minutes away from home the morning of 23 September 1994.

At an intersection, I had to decide which of two main routes to take to CIAT. One is a nerve-racking drive through the heavy traffic of suburban Cali. The other route takes a bit longer, but is through the beautiful Colombian countryside.

I turned right off the Pan-American Highway and took the scenic route to work. That was the last decision I'd make for almost a year . . .

Soldiers are waving cars and trucks off the road a couple hundred meters ahead, but that doesn't worry me. *Reténs,* roadblocks, manned by the military or police, are part of the daily life in Colombia, especially around Cali. I pass the front guard, wearing tiger-striped fatigues and covering incoming traffic with an M-16. Still standard stuff, except that the soldier's hair falls to his shoulders and is held back by a knotted olive bandana.

[Another] teenage soldier motions with his assault rifle to pull up behind a truck. A soldier runs by, holding a .38 revolver. I've never seen pistols drawn at a *retén* before. Another soldier appears wearing— oh my God—a ski mask, waving a .45 automatic at me. His message is clear. Get out of the car. I hand Ski Mask [my] ID cards with my right hand, clutching my billfold with my left. He takes both. "I work for *el Centro International de Argicultura Tropical,* or CIAT," I explain. Ski Mask speaks to a *guerrillero* with an AK-47. I catch only one word: *gringo.*

"Who is this group?" I ask.

"*Las FARC,*" the guard says matter-of-factly.

Oh God, I think. These guys routinely kidnap wealthy Colombians and foreigners with multinational corporations. That's one way they finance their operations. But CIAT makes no profit, sells nothing, exploits no natural resources. Our purpose is to improve the lives of the world's poorest farmers and of urban dwellers who depend on their production. When I meet someone with authority, I'll be let go.

Guerrillas begin to converge on our cluster of vehicles. One has a baby face and can't be more than 13. But he carries an AK-47 and two bandoliers of .30-caliber ammo for an M-60 machine gun. He motions me to sit flat on the pickup bed. We speed away from the *retén*.

Friday, 23 Sep., 1994

Drive up valley. Have not been really scared yet. At least, not terrified, and I never really thought I'd die. Survey my possessions, clothes I'm wearing. When guerrilla took briefcase, gave me my dollar and peso checkbooks. Also 35 business cards. A watch with broken band. One ballpoint.

Thank God I can at least write . . . for now.

I wonder if everyone assumes that I am safe, or at least, alive. CIAT policy on kidnapping doesn't particularly assure me: CIAT will not pay one peso of ransom for anyone.

We must be 700 meters above the valley floor. We climbed until we reached trees at the mountain crest. Now we're walking under a canopy of trees and vines. To avoid any chance of being spotted by air, I guess.

Saturday, 24 Sep., Day 2

I have been a *prisionero* almost exactly 24 hours now. The guerrillas are sitting around a fire in the mud hut. I accept a cup of sweetened coffee. My last real meal was Thursday night, 22 Sept. So in the last 36 hours I have eaten one cup of tea, one cup of yogurt, one chicken wing with some rice, one Coke, and this morning, one cup of coffee.

I've learned that Juaco is in command. Later, [he] brings me a plastic sack with a toothbrush, a tube of toothpaste, a roll of toilet paper, and a bar of soap. He also brings a cold roll. It's tasteless and chewy, but I'll eat at least half of it. I have to keep up my strength. I must do everything possible to maintain my health. Thank God I'm not prone to colds. Sleeping in the cold dampness, with rain splattering on the canvas cover above you, is a good way to get sick.

I have in no way been mistreated, threatened, harassed. This life is hard, but the guerrillas are making me as comfortable as they are. But it's not because FARC is so benevolent—it's because these are Colombian peasants, very humble people. I also realize that in situations like this, the captors often build you up so that they can later tear you down and break you.

How long will this last? What if FARC holds me for ransom and CIAT won't pay? I'd then be pretty useless to FARC. Would FARC turn me loose? Or would that be a bad example?

I have very little hope of being rescued. We're too remote, the mountains are too rugged. And this valley goes on and on, and on the other side of the mountain ridges, more valleys. More mountains.

Juaco said I could not talk to [my wife] Susan directly, but could write a message, which a guerrilla would read to her via phone. I wrote: "I am okay. I am living with FARC in the mountains. My health is good, and my spirits are high. I live almost exactly like the soldiers who guard me. They will release me when permission comes from FARC HQ. I asked FARC to send this message. I was not forced. As proof, I will add something personal, something FARC could not know. My brother's name is Raford. I love you, and will be with you soon. Tom."

Tuesday, 27 Sep., Day 5
We reached our destination at 1710h—eight hours' ride. Then we ascended into another valley, wading down a stream of icy rushing water, slipping, groping through the mud. We had to cross two flimsy bridges over rushing rivers below. The second bridge was like a 10-meter ladder, one meter wide, thrown over the icy river, rushing white among huge boulders. Rotten wooden slates crisscrossed two beams every few feet. A slip would throw us into almost certain death.

We waded through more mud, crossed more streams until, at 2030h, a dark empty hut appeared. Someone had provided the guerrillas with a pan of cold rice topped with chunks of salty beef. I wasn't hungry, but hadn't eaten for more than 12 hours. I have to keep up my strength.

Thursday, 29 Sep., Day 7
Last night was forever. It was freezing, and wet. The nights are the worst. If only I could just sleep through them. I'm getting in my tent cell at six P.M. I can't read. I can't even sit on the side of my bed because my feet would rest in the mud . . . with nothing to do but try to be comfortable and warm—and try to sleep and to fight off *those thoughts,* the destructive, dangerous thoughts that come with the cold and the dark.

Sunday, 2 Oct., Day 10
Ramiro brings me dinner on a plate. Rice, lentils, and I can't believe it. Sardines! Three big solid sardines. I've only had one piece of solid meat in 10 days. The extra protein makes me feel strong, good.

I guess I've been spending 18 hours a day in the tent. Makes no sense to go outside. I can only stand in the rain, my feet in the mud, or go into the [guerrillas'] hut, which is no warmer than my tent. The lack of movement in the tent bothers me a lot. I can't stand; far too low. I sit on the edge of my bunk because the floor is straw-covered mud, always wet. So I must sit up in the bunk or slide onto my back and lie down. My hips are sore from this.

Tuesday, 4 Oct., Day 12

Am getting sores on my shoulders and back. Probably caused by getting sunburned six days ago, plus the dampness, and not exposing my skin to air for six days. Plus the dirty clothes. I'm sitting on a rock overlooking the camp, writing. I've been airing the sores on my back and shoulders. Cirle approaches my rock and we talk awhile. "Don't worry, the *tren de mulas* arrives today," she says. "It will bring lotion for your *llagas,* and dry rubber boots, another shirt, and socks, underwear, everything you need."

"The *tren* was due yesterday, but didn't arrive," I say.

"But it's so far. Four days by foot to the nearest village. The route is uncertain. You can only travel by day."

Dinner is a greasy piece of fried cheese and a greasy piece of fried bread. I was about to turn in when a *guerrillero* rode up on horseback, leading a mule loaded with three sacks. The long-awaited mule train, or at least part of it, had arrived!

Apparently, a good liquor supply arrived. I go to bed, but a party has started in the hut. It's getting louder and louder. As the party noise increases, I hear other ominous sounds: rifle bolts being slid, ammo clips inserted. Someone cuts loose with an AK-47 on full automatic. An M-16 joined in, rock-and-roll. I hear drunken shouts, and someone shooting a .45 into the air. The way these guys handle weapons—even when sober—scares me. As I'm contemplating this, a *guerrillero* runs past my tent, spraying clumps of bushes on full automatic, hot, spent cartridges bouncing off the canvas.

Saturday, 8 Oct., Day 16.

Javier just told me not to climb the mountain slope behind the hut anymore; to stay right here next to camp. I told Javier to go fuck himself and walked away. I guess I'd better be careful; it's getting to me. This is Day 16 of being held by a group of 16-year-olds with third-grade educations. I'm back in my tent, angry. That's not going to improve the situation; I can't help it. I'm a prisoner who's committed no crime. Captured, like a slave, to sell. By an organization whose portrayed motives are to bring about human rights, end slavery of the countryside. What hypocritical bullshit. Be careful, Tom. Keep your mouth shut. Letting loose of your built-up anger, contempt, and frustration for a couple of minutes could really hurt you. Your job, Hargrove, is to survive. Anger and self-pity won't help you. Being smart will.

Tuesday, 11 Oct., Day 19

Juaco returned last night. The process has reached the stage I have anticipated and dreaded. Juaco has met with the *comandante* of the Cauca Front of FARC. I am to write a letter to Susan in Spanish asking that she pass my request for help to CIAT administration. That's all. Juaco stressed that the letter must be written very clearly and that I must not try to set a trap, pass secret information, etc. The letter is to go out tomorrow. I asked about my ransom. Juaco said he doesn't know what amount has been set. "I suspect that whatever is set will be too high," I told Juaco. "It's better to go ahead and kill me now."

Juaco looked shocked. "We're not going to kill you," he said.

Wednesday, 12 Oct., Day 20

Dinner is served. Rice topped with a type of potato salad and some cabbage and carrots. I eat all of the latter, every sliver. As Day 20 ends, I know that my release won't come soon. But I'll be okay through the long night that begins in a few minutes. Then tomorrow, I'll live through another tomorrow. Then tomorrow night. I don't know why prisoners have written of taking it one day at a time. It's not that way. It's one day. Then one night. And the night is as long as three of the days. But I'm learning how to handle it all.

Maybe I should describe the inside of my tent. It's 10 feet long six to seven feet wide. I can sit up in my bunk but can't stand anywhere. To my right is the mud wall of the hut with one candle in a niche. To my left is my little log table, 1½ feet high, on which three candle stubs burn. The canvas roof slopes then drops straight down to my left about 3½ feet from the bunk. An old rubber boot at the end of the bunk is a urinal. A cheap plastic belt came with my second trousers; I've made it into a clothesline along the wall that will hold some socks. It's cold and wet. I probably average 18 hours a day in here.

Sunday, 16 Oct., Day 24

If I only had a date, if I knew when this will be over and I'll be freed. But what if my freedom is two months from now? Or six months or one year? No, it's better not to know what happens next and live one day at a time. I know I'll survive today, and if so I'll make it through tonight. I'll worry about tomorrow tomorrow.

The rash on my feet has started again and there is no way to get medicine to treat it. But I'm lucky that the foot rash has been my worst sickness. I'm sure these kids don't realize that they're lucky, too. What would they do if the *prisionero* became sick up here? I'll bet it's two days' hard march to the nearest medical treatment. A person could so *easily* die up here. I don't know why we're not all sick. This camp is mud, littered with sardine cans. Potato peels and food scraps are thrown down the hill. Dishes are washed in cold water, and can never really be clean. Maybe the cold weather is healthy. The food scraps, for example, don't seem to rot. But my health is remarkably good. My psychological health, too, I think. Every few days I go off behind the hut alone and cry a few seconds, and feel better afterward. There's nothing wrong with that as long as the guerrillas don't see it. But I don't allow that to happen at night. Not locked, for what seems forever, in the cold and cramped wet darkness of a tent I can't escape.

1620h: Dinner is served. It's rice and beans, same as lunch, minus the sardine piece—and hot chocolate. I remember and pull out the piece of cheese [I had] stashed away. It tastes—and chews—like rubber.

The secret to survival here, it seems, is to strike a balance between not giving up hope and not hoping for too much.

Wednesday, 19 Oct., Day 27

I'm disturbed by the number of flies I saw near the spring this morning. The cause is obvious. The guerrillas [are] now dumping much more raw garbage there (it's where they wash dishes). We're going to have sickness here if this continues. Especially if the weather turns warmer. In fact, this entire camp is becoming a garbage heap with cans. Plastic, soap, dishes, papers strewn indiscriminately. The latrine situation is fairly healthy, though: a stream down the hill.

0300h: *Bam!* Another gunshot. Inside the hut again. Then half a dozen clips, 10 to 12 rounds each, fired into the darkness. I go back to sleep only to be awakened again at 0400h by 10 rounds, fired systematically on semiautomatic, into the darkness. Then more automatic weapons fire. I get up and leave the tent at around 0800h, half expecting to see a dead guerrilla or two from all the gunfire. Ramiro is outside. "What was all the shooting about last night?" I ask.

Ramiro looks embarrassed. "Nothing."

"Everyone was drunk and just shooting for fun?"

"No one was drunk." Ramiro can't lie worth a damn.

That's when Viejito emerges from the hut, clutching a brandy bottle in one hand, his Galil in the other. He aims at something along the hill to our east and fires a couple of rounds.

I try to go to sleep but I can't. The volume of gunfire picks up. The boys are shooting 9 or 10 rounds at a time on full automatic again. A burst of automatic fire, then I hear some shouts. A cow's lying on her back, feet kicking and thrashing her head wildly. It looks like one of the silly bastards has shot a cow. My first reaction is sheer joy. There'll be trouble over this. Someone is going to be in deep shit. My feeling of satisfaction is like revenge. And the meat! They'll have to butcher her, and that means we'll have some good red meat!

1440h: Am returning to the cow. Had been to the

hut to try and find a machete to butcher the cow. Walking across the meadow, three more shots rang out from the group around the cow. Who was it? Did Juaco shoot Viejito? Back in my tent, I can still hear the wailing. Ten minutes later, Melena slogs back to the hut, crying.

"Juaco," she says, *"see suicidio,"* and she mimics sticking a rifle muzzle under her chin, pulling the trigger, and the top of the head splattering into the air. She disappears into the hut. Leidi returns a few minutes later.

"Pack everything to march, Don Tomás!" she says. "We're leaving."

Friday, 21 Oct., Day 29
The [new] camp is called La Playa, and sits in a valley by the river with steep mountains on both sides. I'm in my cubicle determined to write all that happened yesterday. A guerrilla girl from camp enters my room and asks what I'm doing. "Studying Spanish," I reply. She picks up my notebook and starts reading. She studied the first page, then rushes out the door with my notebook. I'm confused and irritated and follow. She has gathered two of the other guerrillas around her and is showing them the draft of my letter—in Spanish—to Susan. She's talking fast and pointing to the word "CIAT," and the reason's obvious. She's found proof that I'm CIA. I start again with the explanation; then I remember the 30 business cards in my pack. I give her a card, point out to the guerrilla and her friends the name of my institution.

Saturday, 22 Oct., Day 30
We're going back up the mountain to the Valley of Death, where the clouds and rain are perpetual and

the terrain is swamp. How crazy is FARC, anyway? The team sent to guard me went berserk up there. Discipline was lost; the commander committed suicide.

Inside the hut, they've fixed one wall like a studio, with a blanket for background and lit by a naked lightbulb. Javier, Gustavo, Viejito, and Melena put on masks and bring out their Galils and AK-47s. Marli is focusing the camera, checking the light.

Look, Hargrove, you knew this might come and you have no choice. You have to make this video, so do it with as much dignity as possible. Whatever happens, don't lose your pride, don't break in front of these ignorant children.

All is ready. The guerrillas put on their masks, brandish their weapons, and pose around me. "*Hola,* Susan." I give the date, and say that my health is fine—and will stay fine. I recite my special message to the [directors] of CIAT, but I say the entire name, not the acronym.

I hope it does more good than harm.

Friday, 28 Oct., Day 36

[Being kidnapped is] like being taken, suddenly, and nailed in a box—or a coffin. You're left there in silence and darkness while the rest of the world goes on. You can only assume and pray you'll be released. You're in a state of inertia, but your mind continues to function. And you wish, so much, that it wouldn't. And then there's that dark fear that they'll never open the box, that you'll go silently insane in the box and then . . . slip away forever.

Tuesday, 1 Nov., Day 40

My back hurts a lot because of this jacket. It's so short and tight, and the bottom elastic band rides around my navel, constantly pulling and forcing my shoulders into a semislump. But I must wear it always, because, first, it's so cold and I have nothing else. More important, I have to carry these diaries inside the jacket. I can't risk leaving them in the tent. If the guerrillas saw all this writing, they'd be confused. It would also hurt my chances for release.

Wednesday, 9 Nov., Day 48
Almost seven weeks of captivity now, and I'm looking at a harsh reality. If I were to be released anytime soon, I'd been freed days or weeks ago. I don't know what CIAT is doing, but it's not enough. You'd better quit fooling yourself, Hargrove, and put yourself into a mental state to prepare for a long wait. But how long? Six months? A year? FARC has me for only one reason: ransom. My life, and my health and comforts, will probably be less valuable as time, with no ransom, goes on. I'll continue to live until that decision is taken out of my hands.

Thursday, 10 Nov., Day 49
0915h: I feared last night could turn dangerous, and I was right. Around 2015h, a burst of five rounds fired full automatic from the door. Commotion in the hut, then a short burst from the woods. Viejito is evidently stalking and blasting shadows in the woods. I'm lying in darkness [and] I can't see what's going on [from] the floor by my bunk.

I hear drunken, or stoned, cursing, then that cold sound of a rifle bolt and more voices pleading with Moño. He's apparently pulled his Galil out and chambered a round and is threatening the others. More pleading and the sound of steel against steel as more

257

bolts are pulled. There's a scuffle, more cursing, crying.

1015h: It was a dangerous night, all right. A combination of drugs, anger, and automatic weapons. Those guys were drinking brandy, but alcohol isn't the chemical that fueled the craziness. It was *basuco*[2], I'm sure.

Saturday, 12 Nov., Day 51

I must sleep on my right hip, so I wake up each morning staring at the same scene: the dried black mud of the hut wall, crisscrossed with reinforcing pieces of bamboo. The bamboo is sun-bleached white and looks like human bones. Sets a mood for the day. . . .

I woke this morning, looking at the bones and thinking how I hate these vermin, and wondering how I'll survive this cold and lonely day, the start of my eighth weekend.

I doubt that any of the FARC have any idea of the contempt in which I hold them. I stay apart, avoid conversation other than communicating the essentials, because conversation can be very dangerous. Stop it, Hargrove, the day is just beginning. Don't infect your mind purposely. Someday you might not be able to suppress that infection; the sick yellow pus will explode in stinking bursts that could mean your death.

Looking at myself. I'm so dirty. As filthy as this camp. I need to wash clothes and myself, but it's impossible with this cold, wet wind. There's standing water outside the door of the hut. It's covered with a film of scum and grease and garbage thrown directly into it. Even most animals know to keep their living area clean. I'm afraid of myself; my anger and contempt are so close to the surface when I see or hear one of the FARC. But I must stay away from them, talk only when essential. Spare myself what I might do to myself. Protect yourself, Hargrove. And protect your diary.

Saturday, 19 Nov., Day 58

0700h: Heard an announcement of my kidnapping this morning at 0630h this morning. Couldn't get it all, but Moño had Radio Notícias on, and I heard "CIAT, el Centro, etc." Then something about scientists, worldwide, then my name—definitely—the word *secuestro* [kidnapped]. Something about hoping for release for the *communicador*. I rushed into the hut. What I want to know is what the news angle was. That I'm kidnapped isn't news, not after two months and one day. And my kidnapping was on the news the night of 23 Sept. I've decided that lots of news publicity would be best for me because it would apply pressure on three fronts: 1) FARC—I'm the first scientist working for agricultural development to be kidnapped, and that could make FARC look bad. 2) Colombian government—this should be embarrassing, especially if CGIAR[3] is described and the news includes that Colombia joined CGIAR this year. Could help pressure the government to do something. Prisoner exchange, for example. 3) CIAT and CGIAR—the first kidnapping in the system will look bad—especially for attracting donor funds to CIAT and for recruitment.

0750h: I've been thinking about my release for almost two hours. About the four-day ride, and when and where I'll be released and what I'll do then, will I fly to Cali, take a taxi to CIAT, or to home? Will Susan know I'm coming? Thanksgiving dinner? Just after eight A.M. Moño told me—and I know I can't believe Moño, but this seems so specific—that the Colombian government is negotiating my release with FARC, and that negotiations are almost complete.

That the government is being "pressured" by rich countries to get my release. He stressed that my release was imminent. Could he lie so specifically? If this is just something to satisfy me, it's the cruelest blow yet. Probably is, you've been told shit like this before. Don't build yourself up for the worst. You'll be here for Christmas, and FARC is even ordering new clothes for you.

Sunday, 20 Nov., Day 59

Ramiro opened the tent. "A letter for you," Ramiro said, handing me a blue envelope. A *letter? For me?* How? Who? I stood outside, and opened the letter in near darkness. The note was handwritten, on a sheet torn from a ring notebook. At the bottom of the page was signed *"Atentamente"* [sincerely], *El Comandante*. It was a response to my letter to the commander of the Cauca branch of FARC. The second thing I noticed was the date—18th Nov., two days before. So it's not four days to FARC headquarters after all. The note was mainly an acknowledgment of receipt of my letter, but included, "I read your note, with great care. I was especially interested in what you said about CIAT's activities in Colombia. . . . Your family is fine although very worried about your situation. We agree with your family and you in hoping that you will leave soon, and in good health. I close hoping that your conduct is good. We will treat you accordingly." I at least know now that I'm not forgotten.

12:15h: Lunch: rice and boiled potatoes. Isolation from affection must affect one. I've had no exposure to friendship—giving, receiving, sharing—of any kind for more than two months. A strange dog wandered in this morning. She obviously has beagle blood, black and tan, about 1½ feet high, long floppy ears. Intelligent and affectionate. I called and she came to me. I scratched her ears, under her chin, and she jumped up and started licking my face. Suddenly, without realizing it, I started crying and couldn't stop. It was the first, the only act of kindness, of friendship since my kidnapping.

Tuesday, 22 Nov., Day 61

An hour earlier, the final shades of darkness were covering the Valley of Death. I heard the arrival of a packhorse. I retired to my tent. As usual, at around six P.M. I was trying to coax a flame from the wet wood while waiting for a guerrilla to secure my tent from outside for my 12-hour night. I pulled on my rubber boots and went outside to join the excitement. In the team hut, the guerrillas were digging excitedly into two large burlap sacks.

"Regalos para Don Tomás," Moño shouts. *Presents.* A new roll of toilet paper and two new shirts and trousers. I can hardly believe my luck. But I don't show much emotion. First, I wouldn't need the new clothes if these bastards hadn't kidnapped me. Second, their arrival—as the guerrillas are assuring me that my release is imminent—seems ominous. Does the investment in new clothes mean they now plan to hold me here longer?

I take my plastic bag of new clothes, returning to my tent. Javier enters [the tent] first and he's holding something. "Sit here!" Javier says, pointing at the others. Ramiro and Viejito are giggling nervously. Something's wrong Then Javier holds up the metal object, letting it drop. It's a chain. He holds my left foot and starts wrapping the chain around my ankles.

"What are you doing?" I demanded indignantly as

Javier jerks at the chain, tightening it. He's never liked me, and obviously loves this opportunity.

"We're chaining you."

"Why?"

"Orders."

"You son of a bitch," I say in English.

"Speak in Spanish," Javier says, working the padlock through chain links and shutting it. "Don't worry, Tomás, tomorrow we'll free you," says a female voice. It's Leidi. Free me? Maybe this is preparation for my appearance at some sort of release ceremony. If [I] can take this, I can take anything, if it gets me out of here.

"Wait, you're saying I'll be free tomorrow? Leave the valley?"

"No, no," Leidi laughed. "We'll take the chains off tomorrow morning and leave them off until night."

"Are you mad, Don Tomás?" Ramiro says, giggling.

Javier slipped the other [side of the chain] through a link in the mud wall and someone pulled tight, locked the chain around my ankle with a huge, heavy chain of steel, and everyone laughed at the chained *gringo*.

"I hope you sleep well, Don Tomás," Javier says.

Thursday, 24 Nov., Day 63

Thanksgiving in chains. Thanksgiving dinner was *carve*—the artificial meat—cooked with green beans, carrots, and rice. And a special treat: a piece of new onion. As usual, I took more than I needed, and began the process of hoarding again. Tomorrow, I'll try and steal the whole onion. But stealing has been hard lately because it's so cold, and raining all day, so the guerrillas have all stayed inside the hut around the fire.

Friday, 25 Nov., Day 64

Lunch today: rice and beans. Dinner: the same. I made the news again today. Radio Palmira announced that a video of Dr. Thomas R. Hargrove, kidnapped on 23 Sept., had arrived at CIAT—proof that I was still alive on 22 Oct., when it was made. My God, it took 33 days for the video to get there? Ended with "CIAT is funded by 25 nations." It's good that the "extra" information—what they [FARC] need to know about CIAT—is included.

Tuesday, 29 Nov., Day 68

Wednesday, 21 Dec. That can be my target day. I'm glad each day is over because it's then one day closer—but closer to what? Twenty-one Dec. seems logical because if FARC releases me gratis as a gesture of goodwill, it will be for Christmas. If I'm released before then, it will be for ransom, I fear. Twenty-one Dec. is only three weeks and two days away—23 days. I've already been here 67 days—so I can last that long. What happens if I make survival until then my goal, then 21 Dec. comes, then Christmas—and I'm still here?

Wednesday, 30 Nov., Day 69

Talked with Moño. He says it's doubtful I'll be released before Christmas. My God, after what I wrote just a few hours ago! "Talks with the government aren't going well, and there's more fighting," he said. "Also the government insists on militarization of the mountains." FARC wants "free zones." Putting it all together—and the chains—is it possible that the game for me has changed? That it's no longer just ransom, but I've become a pawn in the politics? If so, I'll probably never be freed.

Maybe I should forget about a Christmas release. FARC knows that CIAT wants me out before Christmas, so may put up a much tougher bargain. I talked with Moño a little about the morality of this, but that's useless. It always comes down to, "I'm only following orders."

Friday, 2 Dec., Day 71
1130h: Talked with Moño. He says I may be released in five to six days and will spend Christmas with my family. I know not to believe him, but when he says that, I always build false hope. I can't help it, it's natural.

1750h: Something strange seems to be happening. A new guy—a tall stranger—arrived. It's getting dark and cold, yet no one is building a fire. Gustavo said they told him not to make a fire and that I should go lie down in my tent. Everyone is talking in low voices.

Saturday, 4 Dec., Day 72
Tall Stranger came to my tent around 0830h and handed me a letter, my second letter from the commander of FARC/Cauca. I started reading, and almost fell off my bunk. The second paragraph read: "We have information that you are a full colonel in the army, a hero of the Vietnam War, an expert in counter-guerrilla warfare, a communications expert, and a member of the U.S. Academy of History." I'd have a tough time fabricating more ludicrous—and more dangerous—charges. The commander then asked that I respond in writing to those charges.

Monday, 5 Dec., Day 74
A terrible chilling thought shot through me suddenly in the cold as I awoke from bad dreams at dawn.

264

Beatings, even torture, may follow as my situation worsens steadily. FARC obviously takes the new accusations—that I'm a full colonel, counterguerrilla warfare expert, etc.—seriously. That's why I'm locked in this dark room.[4] And I can't really disprove anything from here. Will FARC try to make me tell want they think I know? Rough play would not be beyond them. Imagine being tortured to divulge information that you don't have. The accusations really leave me alone and helpless. I'm now probably beyond any help that CIAT could give. Also the Colombian government and the U.S. government, since I'm not even what they charge me with. Hargrove—you're alone. You're totally alone and to survive, at least with your sanity, will be tough.

What about my sanity? I think I'm okay, but I can't be sure. Like this morning. I was let out of the room to brush my teeth and empty my urine bottle. Was outside in early morning sunshine for four or five minutes. Then was shut back in the room. That was so bad I wished honestly that I'd never been let out. No breakfast this morning, after no dinner last night. Is FARC trying to purposely starve me? To weaken me? To destroy my will? My last meal was a piece of fried beef intestine and some rice at 1500h yesterday.

Wednesday, 7 Dec., Day 76
Leidi brought "lunch"—eight pieces of hard candy, each the size of a thumbnail. I asked for lunch. Said no lunch—economizing. Did not offer breakfast either. No doubt, they're starving me.

Wednesday, 14 Dec., Day 83
I just had a shock. I don't know how to take this. I had one of the bags of hominy, plus the plastic jar I

filled this A.M. I looked in the bamboo leaves that compose my mattress. Couldn't find the bag. Then I opened the jar. EMPTY, and has been washed clean—so someone searched my things while I was gone. And took the food I had [hid] away. The notebook pages were still where I left them.

Monday, 26 Dec., Day 95

Moño handed me a newspaper. What is this about? Is he about to announce my release, and they're all here to watch? I should know better. These brutes always come in groups when there's special humiliation in store. "We're here to take your photograph," Moño said, and I saw a Poloroid camera that the guerrilla had in the plastic sack. No use trying to fight this one. As we left my cell, I realized I was wearing my blue short-sleeved shirt. Today was the warmest day of the kidnapping. If the folks back in Cali see that, they will think that I'm in the lowlands—not the mountains. [I] managed to put on my red long-sleeved shirt over the blue one—oh, so casually—as we changed rooms. No one noticed. "Sit down and hold up the paper," Moño said. I did, so the headlines could be read clearly. They took photos and let me see them. I look awful.

They said the photos would be delivered to my family in Cali. Whatever comes of the army charges this means I'm still in the ransom game.

Lunch: rice and beans. Dinner: a watery potato soup, cold.

Monday, 2 Jan., Day 102

I feel sick and weak. Last night I ate half of the steak and *arepa* saved from New Year's Eve. It was 24 hours old but the best steak I ever had. I saved back half for another banquet tonight—a piece half the size of my palm. Got real sick later, had diarrhea and vomiting all night. The food was too rich for my system. Or had it spoiled? Do I throw away what's left, heaven forbid? Survive, figure it all out later.

Wednesday, 4 Jan., Day 104

Happy Birthday, Tom G! I thought about you a lot last night. I can make it through today, and that's one day closer to freedom. Or death, which is also freedom. But I'm not ready for that step yet. Am still sick, especially at night. It's now almost two weeks. "I need medicine," I told Moño. He gave me another packet of *sal de frutus* (Alka Seltzer). "This is the best medicine."

It scares me to think about getting really seriously sick. He wouldn't know enough to get me to medical treatment even if it were available. I now have to hold my trousers up with one hand while I walk, despite the extra notch in my belt.

Tuesday, 10 Jan., Day 110

It's been one-third of a year now—in three days. I seldom have an appetite and I'm not as hungry as before. Maybe my body has adjusted to a survival level. Eating is no pleasure; it's an obligation to keep myself alive.

Wednesday, 1 Feb., Day 132

Do I write too much negative, too much gloom? Probably, but what else can I write? Maybe I should list some things I'm happy I have here: I have the canvas strap I found; without it I couldn't keep my trousers up. My new bottle of *ají*. The pan I found and cleaned; with it I can wash my hands and face. My new notebook and pen. My health, which seems okay right now. Candles.

I'm no longer routinely chained through the day. The *equipo,* or backpack, that Julio gave me—I use it to carry everything of value, like my plastic bottle of reserve beans. The plastic bag I found yesterday. My precious diaries. My special belt and two checkbooks. My 370-ml brandy bottle lets me drink water with meals. And I have six blankets now—enough to stay warm except when it's really cold, like most nights now.

Tuesday, 7 Feb., Day 138

The chances that FARC will release me seems incredibly, dismally remote. And FARC could decide to execute me at any time. The thought of dying isn't what scares and depresses me so—but the thought of living on and on like this is pure anguish. Every morning I think I can't make it through today. Not another day of nothing, of emptiness and aching loneliness. But I *do* make it. If death is to come, I'd prefer to face it now rather than continue this existence. All I really know is what Moño has told me—and that can be very selective. If my family making international news of my kidnapping is such a big deal and it began three months ago, why do I hear about it only now?

Friday, 10 Feb., Day 141

Dinner: rice, spoon of pasta, piece of beef, but almost no meat. Gristle like leather. Moño has first guard. The price of your release, he said, is that your family agreed to pay the ransom. But the money was paid two weeks ago to a group in the Colombian army that claimed to represent or be in contact with FARC. It was a trick. This problem has delayed the negotiations, but I'm sure you'll be released soon.

"So with all this you think I'll be free fairly soon—that it won't take a year like I've planned?"

"No, but your situation is *muy delicado,*" Moño said as I entered my cell for the night.

Sunday, 19 Feb., Day 150

Lunch was a nice piece of beef, *arepa,* rice and lentils. But Moño brought out a little table he had made for me to eat my meals on. Wow. In conversation he said, "You're going to be released soon. Keep your faith."

"When? In a month? A week? Two days?"

He shrugged. "I don't know, but soon." Treatment really seems to be changing. Maybe I *will* go home.

Sunday, 12 Mar., Day 171

My freedom finally arrived, sort of. Moño told me orders to release [me came] from Marulanda himself. But I'm not going home, not yet. Fighting and soldiers surround us, so we're trapped until army pulls out.

Saturday, 22 Apr., Day 212

I asked Moño last night if there's any news about the plans to free me. His answer was awful: "We're analyzing the situation, Tomás. The problem is the army won't leave; they're on all the routes." If anyone does anything nice, I think they're getting me ready for freedom. I've thought that a thousand times in the 211 days they've held me. But that day never comes.

Saturday, 6 May, Day 226

Viejito and two other guerrillas arrived by surprise. One is a VIP and represents the *comandante.*

Moño brought me a legal-sized sheet of paper and

said I must write a letter to Susan in Spanish. Said that Susan does not believe I'm still alive, and I need to convince her.

I talked with [the civilian VIP] twice. "Yes, [ransom] will be paid," he said, "but I don't know how much. All arrangements have been made, and your family and FARC are in agreement. All that is lacking is this letter—it's proof that you're still alive."

Thursday, 25 May, Day 245

I'm starting the agonizing process again—of waiting, hoping, praying for my release. The previous five times have ended with hard crashes and vows not to be so foolish in the future. In addition to my letter of yesterday, they made me prepare three other items. All are proof that I'm still alive. First we made a Poloroid photo; I had to remove my boots and pose barefoot, to hide the fact that we're in the cold mountains, I guess. Next, a cassette recording in Spanish. Third, I had to copy a passage from the 23 May edition of *El País*. I can't believe the paper can reach here so rapidly. Civilization must be closer than I thought.

Monday, 26 Jun., Day 277

I'm to be released between 4 and 11 July, Moño says. "That's the *plazo* [deadline]," set for the final payment of the ransom. I must have strength.

Monday, 17 Jul., Day 298

Just learned from a guerrilla that Colombian army has set a base at Santo Domingo, which is entrance to get to this area. "Then we're trapped?" I asked.

"Yes, without an exit."

"Then we'll be here a long time more?"

"Sí."

*   *   *

"Le toca de salir," I heard, and glanced at my watch. It was 6:30 A.M. on 21 August.

"What did you say?" I asked. The answer was the same: "It's your time to leave."

"Leave . . . to where?"

"To your family, in Cali."

"When?" I was suspicious, afraid to believe it.

"This morning, after breakfast."

"Is this a joke?"

"No. In two days, you'll reach an area where you can hire a car to take you home. This is to cover expenses." The *guerrillero* handed me a banknote for 10,000 Colombian pesos—about 12 US dollars.

I folded my last diary entry, stuffed it into the packed money belt, and tried to sleep. I felt sure that I was finally going home.

---

[1]*El Centro International de Agricultural Tropical,* an agricultural research and development center sponsored by about 40 international organizations, tasked with developing improved varieties and strains of staple crops.

[2]*Basuco*, meaning "bazooka" in English, is a derivative of the cocaine-production process, a relatively cheap byproduct smoked among the poor in South America.

[3]Consultative Group on International Agricultural Research.

[4]The previous day, the guerrillas broke camp and marched 5 hours to another FARC camp in the mountains. Hargrove was immediately placed in a tiny room, and guarded around the clock.

Editor's Endnote

Indeed, Hargrove finally did go home. After folding
his diaries into his clothing and saying good-bye to
his captors, he began a two-day march through the
mountains with five of the FARC guerrillas, hiding
from Colombian Air Force spotter planes overhead.
At night, they made camp in the cold rain, eating what
few supplies they carried along with them. After walking through mountains for almost two days, the guerrillas, fearful of encountering the Colombian army,
released Hargrove. Six hours later, Hargrove came to
the hut of an Indian potato farmer, who gave him a
ride on his motorbike to the town of Tacueyo. From
there, he managed to get a lift to Santander, and on
to Cali. Fifty pounds lighter, his hair turned orange
from malnutrition, Thomas Hargrove walked into his
house unannounced, into the surprised—and ecstatic—
arms of his wife and two sons.

For the past eleven months, Hargrove's wife Susan,
his sons, and his friends, counseled by professional
security advisors, had been negotiating down FARC's
original demand of $6 million through radio contacts.
When negotiations soured, the family had to endure
weeks of silence. Then even after they made a pay-

ment far less than the $6 million originally demanded (but still a substantial amount), FARC did not release Hargrove, and demanded a second ransom payment.

In his absence, Tom's friend and professional colleague, Bill Smith, initiated a support message board called The Friends of Tom, which grew to over 575 members. On the fourth day after his return home, Tom flew back to Texas. His family, who stayed in Colombia to close the house, joined him two weeks later.